Trail of Destruction

LINDA JOHNSON

Cover design by Donna Casey

ISBN: 978-0-9961823-4-8

DEDICATION

To my mother, who taught me that with hard work and perseverance,
I could accomplish anything
.

PROLOGUE

The evening twilight cast eerie shadows over the park as the boys huddled between two bushes. It was early spring in Lake Forest, a suburb of Chicago, and although there was a chill in the air, neither boy felt it. Brad leaned toward Terry, his voice hushed. "He should be here any minute now."

"Are you sure he walks home this way?"

"Positive. Are you ready?"

"Totally, man. I'm psyched."

Brad peeked around the bush. "No sign of him yet." He paused. "We've got to get this done today or tomorrow. The scout for Duke's track team is going to be at our meet on Saturday and I need them watching *me*, not Rivera. They've got one more full-ride scholarship to offer and I want it."

"Why's it so important to you? Your dad could swing tuition, couldn't he?"

"Of course, but I deserve that scholarship. I've been busting my butt on this team for four years. Then Rivera transfers in this year and suddenly he's the star."

"He shouldn't even be allowed to live here. I can't believe they let illegal aliens go to our school. I mean this is Lake Forest, not Wheeling."

Brad shifted his weight, peering down the path again. "He better get here soon." He turned to his friend. "So what about you? Are you still set on the army?"

"Yeah. I want to go overseas and kill me some towel-heads."

Brad laughed. "I have to admit the idea's appealing. But, God, could you imagine my dad's reaction if I chose the army over college? He'd have a fit."

"College is where you belong anyway. You've got it all mapped out. College, law school, a couple years in your dad's law firm, and then politics. I'm counting on my best friend being president someday so we can rule the world. With you in office, we'd finally get rid of all these assholes that don't belong in our country. Ship 'em all back to where they came from."

"Then stick with me, because it's going to happen. I'm not going to let anything get in my way. Just like now – I'm not going to let Rivera take away my scholarship." Brad peered around the bush again. "Speaking of… here he comes. Pull down your ski mask." He tugged his own mask down and held his finger to his mouth.

The boys waited in silence until they heard footsteps approaching where they were crouched, hidden from view. The noise grew louder until their quarry was right next to them. Brad held his arm against Terry, forcing him to wait a couple more seconds. Then he leapt up. "Now!"

As they rushed to their feet, their target turned around, his eyes like saucers, his mouth open with shock. "What the hell?"

Terry flew at the boy and tackled him to the ground. He began to pummel the boy's face with his gloved fists, his arms moving in manic frenzy. "Get the hell out of our school, you wetback. Go back to your own country."

Brad could hear the thwack as each punch landed, followed by sharp cries of pain, until the boy lay still and silent. He reached down and grabbed Terry's arm. "That's enough. We don't want to kill him."

Terry rocked back and landed one more punch before getting to his feet. Standing over the boy, he kicked him in the gut. "Beaner trash."

Brad yanked his ski mask off, knowing the boy was unconscious and couldn't identify him. "Go get me the bat."

He watched as Terry went over to the bushes and retrieved the weapon. He smiled as his friend handed it to him. "One more thing to make sure this piece of garbage doesn't stink up our track team any longer." He raised the bat over his head and with all his strength swung it straight down on the boy's knee. A loud crack echoed through the still evening and his face broke into a huge grin. "Now we're done here."

* * *

The next morning when Brad came down to breakfast, his mom was at the stove making bacon and eggs; his dad and brother were at the table, hunched over the newspaper.

"Good morning," Brad said, going over to kiss him mom on the cheek

"Hi, honey. I was just going to wake you. How did you sleep?"

"Great, thanks." Brad flashed his patented golden boy smile. God, his parents were so clueless. As long as he followed "The Rules" -- get straight As, earn a varsity letter, and take the prettiest girl to prom -- he could do no wrong.

Ryan looked up, his eyes wide. "You've got to read this, bro. A kid in your class got beaten up yesterday on his way home from school. In fact, he was coming from track practice. Juan Rivera, do you know him?"

"Yeah, he's on the varsity team with me. What happened?"

"A couple of kids jumped him in Lake View Park. Beat him up pretty bad. Broke his leg." Ryan shook his head. "It's really sick. Paper says it was a hate crime. While they were whaling on him, they were telling him to go back to Mexico."

"It's terrible," his dad chimed in. "Obviously, I'm opposed to illegal aliens. Anyone who wants to come to our country should follow the legal procedures to do so, like Maria did," he said, referring to their Mexican housekeeper. "But still, that doesn't give anyone the right to beat some poor kid up."

Brad felt his stomach clench as he looked at his father. He had found out his dad was banging said housekeeper after he came home from school early one day and walked in on them. He had made a quick exit before they saw him, but the memory was burned into his skull. "You're right, it's horrible. I can't imagine anyone doing that. So, is the kid going to be all right?"

"Yeah, at least physically," Ryan said, "but can you imagine how he must feel? I'm going to see if I can interview him for the school paper. It's important to get his story out there for the other students to read – a firsthand view of racial intolerance."

"You're right," Brad said. "That's a good idea." *God, his brother and his causes,* he thought. *What a loser. Like Don Quixote flailing away at his windmills.* "I wonder what his family's going to do."

"There's a quote in the paper from his mom that they're probably going to move out of Lake Forest. Go somewhere where there are more Latino families."

Brad manufactured his most earnest look. "That's probably the right thing to do, don't you think? Maybe they'll even decide to go back to Mexico. Not have to worry about something like this happening again."

.

PART ONE

CHAPTER 1

Brad listened as his best friend and campaign manager's deep voice rang out. "And now it is my great honor to present to you... the... next... governor of Illinois... Brad Newcomb!" Taking in the words that he had waited months to hear, Brad felt electricity course through his body. He watched as Terry first flung his right arm out in a grand gesture and then folded his left hand across his waist, making a deep bow as though introducing royalty. And that's exactly what Brad felt like as he strode across the stage. As the anointed governor, he was now the king of the state. This was the last critical step to hurl him into position to run for president, and then he would truly be the king of the world.

Brad strode across the stage knowing that his lean, athletic frame would catch the eyes of the women in the audience. He was well aware of how his looks and charisma had helped him win this and previous elections. He knew his charcoal black hair and piercing blue eyes gave him a commanding look that men respected and women fawned over.

When he reached the center of the stage, he shook Terry's hand and then engulfed his friend in a big bear hug. Terry let go first, stepping back and looking directly into his friend's eye. They both knew how important this election was as the stepping stone to launch him into the national arena. Only the two of them knew Brad's plans -- governor first, president next. Brad nodded to his friend before moving to the podium. He lifted his arms, flashing the V for victory sign as the crowd erupted. There was nothing like this feeling – having an entire room of people bowing at his feet as if he was the winning quarterback at the Super Bowl.

Brad leaned into the microphone and began to speak, but he was drowned out by the raucous cheers of his supporters. Stepping back, a wide grin spread across his face as he took in the scene. There were hundreds of people packed into the hotel ballroom, yelling out his name and waving "Newcomb for Governor" placards. As he looked out into the sea of faces, his eyes were like magnets locking onto the most attractive women in the audience. As he made eye contact, he could see them melt under his gaze. God, he thought, it was so easy to manipulate people into believing he was who they wanted him to be.

Brad turned to look at his wife and children who had followed him onto the stage. Carolyn stood with one arm around each of their children, a bright smile on her face, looking completely at ease in the glare of the spotlight. He expected no less from her – she was a natural in front of an audience. He knew when he married her that she would make the perfect political wife. As she saw him turn to her, she stepped forward and reached out for him. When they kissed, there was another surge of cheering from the crowd.

As Carolyn stepped back, Brad looked at his children. He felt a twinge of irritation as he noted his son's discomfort. At thirteen, Tyler looked like a poster child for adolescent anguish. Trying desperately to look cool, his deer-in-the-headlight gaze and flushed face screamed, "Get me out of here!" In contrast, fifteen-year-old Emily seemed as relaxed as her mother in the limelight. Brad watched as Emily squeezed her younger brother's hand and then leaned over to whisper to him. Whatever she said had the desired effect, and Brad saw a genuine smile light up his son's face, replacing the forced one that had been pasted on seconds before. Brad was going to need Tyler to toughen up now that he was governor. Unfortunately, his son seemed to take after his weak uncle more than his strong father.

Turning back to the crowd, Brad grasped the edges of the podium and leaned into the microphone. "Thank you! Thank you all!" As the crowd quieted, Brad continued, his voice exuberant. "It is my great privilege to have been chosen as your next governor. I couldn't have done it without everyone in this room. It is because of your hard work and efforts that I am standing here in front of you!" The crowd exploded in another tidal wave of applause and Brad stepped back, basking in the attention, allowing the adulation of the room to wash over him.

As he stood reveling in the glow, he thought about the path he had taken to get here. There were his glory days in high school where his athleticism made him a track and field star and his brains made him the school valedictorian. After high school, he had cruised through Duke University, first getting his undergraduate and then his law degree. After graduation, he had worked at his father's law firm for a few years before entering politics. He had been elected as an alderman, then lieutenant governor, and now governor. He had yet to lose an election. Every time he was in front of an audience, Brad knew his magnetism would take hold and carry the crowd away on whatever magical carpet he was sailing. From an early age, he knew he was above all others -- destined for greatness.

Looking out into a mix of familiar, vaguely recognizable and totally unknown faces, Brad spotted his parents with his brother, Ryan, and his sister-in-law, Michelle. They were clustered tightly together in a spot at the side of the room. As he met his brother's eyes, he saw Ryan make a fist pump in the air and mouth, "Way to go!"

For an instant, Brad flashed back to a scene from his teenage years. He was sitting at a table with his parents and brother at a track and field banquet. As his name was called out as the winner of some trophy or another, he remembered that Ryan had flashed him a grin and gave him a celebratory high five. His brother was three years younger and had always seemed perfectly content to take a back seat to his starring role.

Brad pointed at his brother in acknowledgement before turning back to resume his acceptance speech. As he looked out over the audience, now listening in rapt attention, he knew they were putty in his hands.

* * *

Ryan watched with genuine admiration as his brother worked his magic on the crowd. Brad looked like a movie star up there. Ryan knew that even though he had inherited the same basic features as his brother, his was the forgettable look of the leading man's best buddy. And while Brad capitalized on his looks and flourished in the public eye, Ryan fiercely guarded his privacy, sharing his life with only his wife and a small circle of loyal friends.

As Brad continued his speech, Ryan turned to look at his parents. His father's face was lit up like that of an eight-year-old who had just hit his first homerun. His mother stood smiling with her eyes closed, her hands clasped in front of her as though in prayer. Just seeing them made Ryan smile, knowing this was one of the happiest days of their lives.

Ryan looked over his shoulder at his wife, who was standing a few steps behind him. He shook his head and laughed as he saw her hunched over her Blackberry, her thumbs rapidly texting away. He took a step back and gently elbowed her. Michelle's head flew up, her long auburn hair swinging around her face in wild disarray, her warm brown eyes widened – busted! She shrugged her shoulders and they both grinned.

"Spreading the word about Brad's win, right?" Ryan teased his wife.

"Right. That's exactly what I was doing." Michelle smiled sarcastically before her face grew serious. "Really, I just had to make a quick check on a client who went into rehab this afternoon. I'll put it away now." Ryan's wife was a social worker who worked with recovering drug users and alcoholics, and no matter where she was or what she was doing, Ryan knew that a part of her mind was always preoccupied with her clients. Brad's speech was ending and as the crowd began to applaud, Ryan watched as Michelle slipped her Blackberry into her pocket before his parents turned around.

"What a speech!" his dad crowed. "Can you believe that's our son up there, Martha?"

"Isn't it wonderful, John?" his mother exclaimed as she hugged her husband. She turned to Ryan and embraced him. "Your brother – the governor!"

"There was never a doubt," Ryan said. "Brad's never lost anything he's gone after."

"Just think," his father said. "Our family name will be in the history books forever. I can just see the *Chicago Tribune* headline tomorrow – 'Newcomb Wins Election in Landslide!'"

"Well, it's not like you don't see your family name in the *Trib* now," Michelle reminded her father-in-law. "Ryan's by-line is in there every day."

John gave a dismissive wave. "It's not exactly the same thing. There's a world of difference between writing the news and making the news."

Martha reached out and squeezed her husband's arm gently. "Now, John. We're proud of *both* our sons' accomplishments." She smiled at Ryan. "Not everyone's cut out for public office. That's just what makes Brad's achievement today even more special. I know you're as proud of your brother as we are, right honey?"

"Of course I am, Mom," Ryan assured her. He felt Michelle take his hand and he turned to look at her.

"Let's go get some fresh air," she said.

"Sounds good." Ryan turned back to his parents. "We'll be right back."

Putting his arm around her shoulder, Ryan led his wife through the throngs of supporters. When they got to the exit door, he pushed it open and stepped back for Michelle to pass through. Following her, he spotted an empty bench in the hotel lobby and pointed to it. "Let's grab a seat."

"You know I love your parents," Michelle began when they were seated. "But sometimes your dad..." She shook her head, biting her lip.

"Oh, he's just happy for Brad. You know it's always been like this."

"Yeah, but just because you don't want to be governor..." Michelle shook her head. "You're a respected journalist at the *Chicago Tribune*. Your dad acts like you're a janitor over there."

"Lighten up, honey. He's not that bad. You know Brad's always been the favorite son. He's the first born. He's been a superstar his whole life." Ryan shrugged. "Besides, it took all the pressure off me growing up. Compared to him, I got off easy."

"I just wish they'd appreciate you a little more."

Ryan could see the frustration in his wife's eyes. "That's what you're here for. To be my number-one fan. Brad can have all his groupies -- I've got you."

"Always." Michelle took her husband's hands in her own. "I love you, sweetheart."

Ryan leaned down and kissed his wife. "And aren't you glad I've never had any political aspirations?"

"Really glad. That's not a life I'd want for either of us."

"Me, neither." Ryan looked around as the crowd began to spill into the lobby, everyone jazzed up by Brad's win as though they were the ones getting elected. "This whole scene is definitely not my thing. Brad and Carolyn were born for this -- they're going to make a great governor and first lady."

"As long as your brother keeps his nose clean. You know this position has a history of corrupting its officeholders."

Ryan frowned. "Are you kidding? Mr. Straight Arrow?"

Michelle raised an eyebrow. "You and your family have blinders on when it comes to your brother. He's not the saint you think he is."

CHAPTER 2

Six Years Later

Ryan put his arm around his wife's shoulder as they meandered up the long walk to Brad and Carolyn's stately Georgian home in Mettawa, a tiny Chicago suburb next to Lake Forest, where the population of horses exceeded that of its human residents. Although the official governor's mansion was located downstate in Springfield, Ryan knew that his brother rarely stayed there, preferring to use his Mettawa house as his home base. He conducted most of his official duties out of the governor's office in Chicago's James R. Thompson building.

As he approached the front door, Ryan couldn't help but feel a twinge of jealousy. The imposing house, really more of a mansion, was a far cry from his and Michelle's modest Chicago townhouse. It could be straight out of *Architectural Digest.*

Ryan rang the bell and almost immediately the door was opened by one of Brad's bodyguards, who recognized him and stepped aside. Before they could enter, his niece appeared, a wide smile on her face.

"Emily!" Ryan exclaimed. "What are you doing home from school?"

Emily gave her uncle a big hug. "Dad called last week and asked if I could come home for the weekend. Tyler's here too."

Ryan took in his niece's perfectly pressed shirt and slacks – no jeans and sweatshirt for her. She was a junior at Duke, having followed in her parent's footsteps to their alma mater, and she was already eyeing law school. She had a sweet but serious air about her, and had been a grown-up by the age of four.

"So it's a full family powwow, huh?" Ryan said. "I wonder what the occasion is."

Emily shrugged. "Beats me. Nobody's told me anything. But it sure is nice to get some home-cooked meals, so I'm not going to complain."

"Are your grandparents here yet?" Ryan asked.

"Yeah, they got here about fifteen minutes ago. They're in the living room with Dad. Mom's still out at the stable. Dad told me to go find her and let her know everyone's here. You know how she loses track of time when she's with her horses."

Ryan watched as Emily stepped off the porch and began to make her way to the stable, about a hundred yards back from the house. From here, the barn looked like it could be a guest house. Carolyn had worked with the architect to design a structure that mimicked the details of the main house, incorporating the same brick and even the same shutters framing the paddock windows. In addition to the stable, the facility included a large outdoor arena as well as a small indoor ring that allowed Carolyn to ride throughout the harsh Chicago winters. Today was an unseasonably warm, sunny March afternoon, so no doubt his sister-in-law was outdoors taking advantage of the beautiful weather.

In no great hurry to join the rest of the family, Ryan stood on the porch, holding his wife's hand, until Emily disappeared into the stable. "We'd better head inside before Brad sends a search party out for us too," Ryan said.

A few minutes later, he and Michelle stepped into the formal living room where his parents and brother were gathered, drinking cocktails and chatting animatedly.

"There you are," Brad said, standing up to welcome his brother and sister-in-law. "We thought you got lost."

Ryan shot Michelle an "I told you so" glance before stepping forward to greet his family. When he was settled into a loveseat, beer in hand, Ryan turned to his brother. "So what's the big occasion? Something must be up for you to have dragged your kids home from college."

Brad shrugged. "It's been a few months since we all got together. Maybe I just thought it was time for a family dinner."

Ryan raised a suspicious eyebrow. "You do remember what I do for a living, right?"

Brad laughed. "I can't believe I'm being interrogated by my own brother."

"Hey, you invited me. I'm just following the clues."

Brad held his hands up in mock surrender. "All right, you've caught me. I've got some news, but you'll have to wait until dinner when we're all together. I may have managed to get everyone over here, but somehow they've all disappeared on me. Tyler's up in his room with his nose in his books and Carolyn's down at the stable. It's not enough for *me* to want everyone in the same room. Apparently, it's going to take food to lure them all together."

"I guess I'll put my notes away till then." Ryan pantomimed stuffing an imaginary notebook into his breast pocket. Then he leaned forward, his eyes locking on Brad's. "Unless this is really big news. Should I go get my tape recorder?"

Brad shook his head. "We're off the record today. You're here strictly as my brother, not a journalist."

"Okay, big brother. Whatever you say." Ryan held up his empty glass. "You can pour me another beer to help dull my natural curiosity."

"Did I hear Brad's pouring drinks? Count me in, dear," Carolyn said, as she glided into the room, shadowed by her daughter. She greeted her in-laws with genuine warmth before turning to Brad, her hand outstretched to take the martini he had prepared.

Brad started to hand it to her and then teasingly pulled it back. "You get this on one condition. You take it upstairs with you to the shower." He glanced at his watch. "Dinner's in an hour, and you need to replace that eau de manure you're wearing with something a little more fragrant before we sit down to eat."

Carolyn laughed. "It's a deal. You know I'm immune to the horse odor myself, but I did notice the rest of you wrinkling your noses." She took the glass from Brad and with her other hand gave his arm an affectionate squeeze. "I won't be long. Good thing I'm such a natural beauty, right?"

"You *are* a natural beauty, my love," Brad said. "But it still takes you forever to get ready."

"I promise I'll be down in time."

Ryan watched her go, thinking that Brad's words were not just those of a loving husband. Thanks to good genes and healthy living, at fifty-two Carolyn seemed to get more beautiful with each passing year. Other than having to touch up a few gray hairs, she was a natural blonde with striking green eyes and a face that could have found its way into the fashion magazines if she had desired. Instead, she'd had a successful career in advertising, working at a couple of the major agencies in Chicago before retiring to raise her children. She'd taken up riding to fill her days when they had started school, and now that they were in college, she devoted even more time to her horses. What had started as a hobby had become a passion, and she was a strong contender in the highly competitive "A" rated hunter jumper circuit. Ryan thought that Brad had made the perfect choice for a political wife. Not only was she beautiful, she came from old North Carolina tobacco money and owned a hefty trust fund that had been put to good use in Brad's campaigns.

After Carolyn left the room, Emily bounded over to the sofa and nestled herself between her doting grandparents. Ryan listened as his parents peppered her with questions about her college life, while she happily regaled them with stories of her adventures. With his parents preoccupied with Emily, Brad slid his chair closer to Ryan and Michelle, and the three were soon engrossed in conversation about the always lively world of Chicago politics. When one of the wait staff announced that dinner was served, Ryan was surprised at how quickly the hour had flown by.

As the two brothers stood to make their way to the dining room, Ryan put his arm around Brad's shoulder. "Okay, bro, we're all gathering for dinner just like you wanted. Time to let us in on the big secret." Ryan had a pretty good guess as to what his brother was planning to reveal. A beautiful home, a rich and gorgeous wife, and Governor of Illinois would be plenty for most men, but Ryan knew his brother wanted even more.

CHAPTER 3

Michelle lagged behind the others as they walked to the dining room. She always dreaded get-togethers with her husband's family, and today she felt an even higher level of anxiety than usual. She tried to shake off the mood as she sat down.

When the family was gathered, Brad looked around the dining room table. "Good thing we had a son and a daughter so we could pull off this boy-girl seating arrangement at our family dinners. Emily Post would be so happy."

"Leave it to you and Carolyn to have the perfect family unit," Ryan said.

"There's plenty of room to add a couple more to the table in case you and Michelle decide to have kids," Brad said. "You could always adopt, you know."

Michelle heard the hint of superiority in Brad's voice. Brad knew that she and Ryan had tried to have kids, but couldn't. She opened her mouth, a cutting reply on her lips, but her husband jumped in first.

"I think that train left the station a long time ago," Ryan said. "At this point, I think we have to wait for Tyler or Emily to add to the Newcomb clan." He eyed his niece and nephew. "Any budding romances at school?"

Michelle watched Tyler's face flush beet red as he shook his head and sank lower into his chair. Her nephew was a freshman at Stanford in computer science, and going away to college had done nothing to take away his shyness.

Ryan turned to his niece. "How about you, Emily?"

She flashed a coy smile. "Lots of dates, but no one serious yet. After all, I *am* concentrating on my studies."

"Good answer with the folks writing the tuition checks sitting in the room," Ryan said. "I'll have to get the real scoop when they're not around."

The light banter continued throughout the salad and main courses. When dessert and coffee were served, Brad cleared his throat. "As my ever-so-sharp brother has already deduced, I do in fact have some news to share."

Pausing until he had everyone's undivided attention, he dropped his bombshell. "I've decided to run for president."

A moment of silence filled the room before John stood up from his chair, beaming. He came around the table and engulfed Brad in a hug. "I'm so proud of you, son. You're going to make an outstanding president."

Brad chuckled. "Thanks, Dad. I appreciate your confidence."

"I'm just calling it the way I see it. The Republicans have been in office for eight years, and the country's restless for change. Besides the fact that Bob Ellington, who will no doubt get the nomination out of party loyalty, has about as much charisma as a boiled potato."

Everyone at the table laughed, envisioning the likable, but boring vice-president.

"Which means the Democrats have a great shot to take over the White House again," John continued. "Except that the current crop of candidates hasn't mustered up any excitement. You have a great opportunity to jump in there. Based on your past campaign successes, the voters are going to love you."

"Your father's right," Martha said. "We've seen how the voters have responded to you here in Illinois. There's no reason to think the rest of the country is not going to follow suit."

Michelle had to agree on that point. She knew better than anyone how Brad could manipulate people to do his bidding, although she was the only one in the room who would call it manipulation.

"Have you thought about your platform yet?" Ryan asked.

"I've got people working on position papers, but the overriding theme will be something along the lines of 'moving forward.' Like Dad said, the country is ready for some new blood, fresh ideas. If there's a strong Democrat in the running, I think the party will win. And I hope I can be that candidate."

Brad's voice grew with excitement as he warmed to the subject. "I see taking a two-pronged approach. I'll play up my background and experience as governor to win over the middle-aged and older voters. I've accomplished a lot over the last six years in getting the state budget balanced while shifting funds into more educational programs and health services. I don't think there's a state running more efficiently than Illinois right now. And then there's my record on crime reduction. Ever since I hounded the House and Senate into passing some stronger gun-control laws, we've seen a significant drop in crime. I think the American public is ready to see the same measures we've taken here implemented on a national level. People are getting tired of being held hostage by the NRA."

As she listened to her brother-in-law, Michelle had to admit that, in spite of her personal feelings toward him, he was qualified to be president. He had been an outstanding governor and he had the brains, the ambition, and the ego to take the next step.

"How do you think you stack up next to your current competition?" Ryan asked.

"There's only one other governor in the race now -- Collier from Alabama. The size of Illinois and my record here blows him out of the water."

"Other than maybe getting the southern vote, I agree," John said. "He's pretty weak."

"Obviously, where I'm vulnerable is my lack of foreign policy experience," Brad continued. "Both senators in the race have that over me. But, knock on wood, everything's been pretty quiet on that front. We're not engaged in any wars, and the terrorist threat level is down. As long as that stays the case, I think America will be more concerned with domestic policy issues."

"You mentioned a two-pronged approach," Ryan said. "What's the other half of your strategy?"

"I'll be the youngest contender in the field, and I'll use that to try to get the young voters behind me. None of the other candidates have put together a strong internet campaign. There's a big opportunity for me to dominate that venue."

"Cool!" Emily exclaimed. "Can Tyler and I help?"

"I was hoping you'd ask. How about if I put you both on my campaign staff during the summer?" Brad pointed at Tyler. "I was thinking my son, the computer geek, could handle the nuts and bolts of the website."

"Excellent," Tyler said.

Brad pointed to Emily. "And my articulate daughter could write a daily blog from the campaign trail."

"That would be sweet," Emily said.

"Any other volunteers?" Brad asked, looking around the table.

Michelle dropped her head, avoiding eye contact, waiting for someone else to respond. It didn't take long for her father-in-law to step in.

"You know how successful I was in raising funds for your governor's race," John said. "I'd be more than happy to start knocking on doors again. That's the benefit of retirement. I have plenty of time on my hands."

"And you know how much I've enjoyed working on your past campaigns," Martha chimed in. "I can't wait to get started on this one." She turned to Carolyn. "You've been quiet. What do *you* think of your husband's plans?"

Michelle regarded her sister-in-law with curiosity, wondering how she would respond. She knew Carolyn valued her privacy much more than her husband did.

"Well, I've had a little more time than you to get used to the idea," Carolyn said. "I have to admit that I was a little overwhelmed at first. I'm pretty happy with our life as it is." Carolyn reached over and took her husband's hand. "But I'm definitely on board now. I think Brad is exactly the kind of man this country needs as president. His experience running the state is only half the story. As far as I'm concerned, it's his character and integrity that sets him apart. With all the dirt that seems to surround so many of our politicians these days, I think Brad is the moral compass this country is looking for."

Hearing those words, Michelle felt a shudder go through her body. If Carolyn only knew, she thought.

Brad reached over to squeeze his wife's hand. "Thanks, love." He turned to Ryan. "So how about you? Can you fit in some time to help your big brother?"

"I promise I'll do whatever I can," Ryan said. "I think my weekend golf game can take a back seat until the election's over."

"Thanks, bro." He looked at Michelle. "And how about you, Michelle? I'd love to get your thoughts on mental health issues. I know that's a cause that's near and dear to you and has been all but ignored on the national level."

Michelle cringed. Those were almost the exact same words he had used twenty years ago when he had shown up at her apartment one evening. She and Ryan had been dating for a couple of years, but had hit a rough patch and were taking a break. Brad had asked to see her, pretending that he was interested in her opinions as it related to a new mental health facility that was opening in his ward. Instead he had used the opportunity to seduce her into a one-night stand that she could never forget or forgive herself for. She had not told Ryan even after they had reconciled and married, and the secret continued to haunt her.

As she weighed her response, she was aware of Brad's eyes boring into hers. Even though she knew it would be devastating to him if the truth ever came out, between his political career and the fact that he and Carolyn had been married at the time, she still felt as though sometimes he enjoyed tormenting her in a twisted cat and mouse game. Just like he was doing now, he would ask a question or make a statement that to anyone else sounded totally innocent, but would have a hidden meaning for her that would bring back memories of that awful night.

"I'm not even going to pretend I have any spare time to help with the election," she finally said. "My client load right now is more than I can handle. But I'd be happy to offer my input as it relates to your health platform. I'll write something up and send you an email." *Anything to avoid a one-on-one meeting,* she thought.

CHAPTER 4

It was eight o'clock sharp when Brad stepped into his office in the Thompson Center in downtown Chicago. As soon as he sat down, he reached for his phone to summon his best friend and chief-of-staff, Terry Brinson. His eyes wandered around his office, taking in the well-appointed room. When he had been elected six years ago, Carolyn had redecorated the space from floor to ceiling. She had chosen a soft butter yellow for the walls, a handsome Oriental rug for the floor, and rich mahogany office furniture. Ironically, she had actually used photos from the White House oval office to guide her selections. A shiver of excitement passed through Brad as he thought about making a move to the real deal.

He was lost in thought when Terry arrived at his door. "Good morning, Governor."

Brad smiled at the formality. He and Terry had been best friends through all of grade school and high school. Both had been outstanding students, as well as team mates on the high school track and field team. They had then chosen different paths for college and their initial careers. Where Brad had gone to Duke and then worked in his father's law firm, Terry had gone to West Point and into the military. In spite of the separation, thanks to email, phone calls, and Terry's military leaves, during which he had spent as much time with Brad's family as his own, they remained close. When Brad had decided to run for the lieutenant governor's office, he had convinced his friend to leave the military and become his campaign manager. The timing was perfect in that Terry had just completed a second tour of duty in Special Forces, and he was feeling more than a little burned out. He had jumped at the chance to help his friend. Together they had first swept that election and then, a few years later, the gubernatorial election as easily as they used to decimate their track and field opponents.

In spite of the fact that they were as tight as brothers, Terry always addressed Brad as Governor or Sir when they were at work. Brad had tried to shake his friend of the habit, but Terry's military training was too well instilled in him. Now Brad realized it was good practice for when his friend might need to call him Mr. President.

Brad waited for Terry to settle into the chair across the desk from him. "So how was your weekend?"

"Good. I came in on Saturday and finished reviewing the report from the Department of Transportation. I have the Executive Summary right here for you."

"Did you at least manage to take Sunday off?"

Terry smiled. "I did, actually. I went for a morning run along the lake and then spent the rest of the day holed up in my apartment reading newspapers and watching sports. I'm ready for action again."

"That's good, because I'm going to need you running at full strength after we make the announcement."

"So we're on schedule for today?"

Brad nodded, a wide grin spreading across his face. "We are. I told my family yesterday."

"How did that go?"

"Great. They're all behind me. I even have Emily and Tyler psyched. They're going to run my internet campaign."

"They'll be perfect. They'll know exactly how to appeal to the young voters." Terry began to drum his fingers on his arm chair, already beginning to plot out campaign strategies. "So what about Ryan? Are we going to get some press coverage from your brother?"

Brad shrugged. "Not likely. He keeps his family and career as separated as church and state. In all these years, he's never written a word about me."

"I know. Isn't that a little strange? The fact that his own brother is in such a high- profile office, and he's never written anything about you?"

Brad held up his hands. "I'm not going to push it. That's between him and his editors. The other writers at the *Tribune* have treated me pretty fairly over the years anyway. It's not like I need my little brother's endorsement."

"So what about me? Are you still sure you want me to be your campaign manager? A presidential campaign is in a whole different league than what we've done before."

"I'm positive. We'll bring some people onto the campaign staff who have experience in presidential elections, but I still want you to be the one in charge. It's important to me to have someone at my right hand whom I trust completely. You've always told it to me straight, and that's what I'm going to need. I don't want someone who just tells me what they think I want to hear."

Terry looked down at the daily briefing sheet that he provided each day. It was filled with the governor's appointments, as well as Terry's notes to help prepare Brad for each of the meetings. "What about my responsibilities here, sir?"

"I'll promote Ken Andrews to acting chief-of-staff so that you can devote yourself full-time to the campaign." Brad leaned forward in his chair, his eyes locking on Terry's. "So what do you think? Are you still on board?"

Terry nodded, his chin set with determination. "Absolutely. I can't wait until you're elected president and start fixing all the crap that's wrong with the country."

Brad listened as his friend vented about immigration policy, gays in the military, and his other hot buttons, all of which Brad had minimal interest in. He let Terry think that they agreed on the issues, because he needed his friend to give him one hundred percent effort if he was going to get elected. Brad knew Terry had no political aspirations himself; he was totally willing to stay in Brad's shadow. Terry was the one person in the world whom Brad could count on to give him his full support and do anything that he asked him to do. He would take a bullet for Brad if it came to it.

When Terry finally finished his diatribe, Brad jumped in. "So you'll set up the press conference for this afternoon?"

Terry launched himself from his seat. "I'll get right on it, Governor."

Brad leaned back in his chair and watched his friend bound out of the office. He knew Terry was as excited as he was about making the leap onto the national stage. *If my popularity in Illinois translates to the rest of the country,* he thought, *this election will be a piece of cake.*

CHAPTER 5

Not waiting for his driver to do the honors, Brad opened the car door and jumped out onto the driveway in front of his house. "Pick me up at the usual time tomorrow morning," he called out over his shoulder. He raced up his front walk, his bodyguard scrambling to keep up with him. Brad yanked open the front door, which was unlocked as usual. His home was on a five-acre lot, which was fenced with a wrought iron security gate at the entrance that kept unwanted visitors out. As he stepped into the foyer, one of the staff was waiting to greet him. After handing over his coat and briefcase, he asked where his wife was. Before taking off to find her, Brad nodded to his bodyguard, a signal for the man to have a seat in the foyer. He would remain there for the night, guarding the front entrance, unless Brad summoned him.

A couple of minutes later, he stepped into the library, where he found Carolyn sitting on the sofa, surrounded by her beloved dogs, Daisy, Annabelle, and Coco. She had one of her corgis on her lap and the other two positioned like bookends on either side of her. They swiveled their heads in unison as he walked into the room, four sets of eyes boring into his. The dogs wagged their tails in greeting, but made no attempt to get up from their comfortable spots.

He walked over to the sofa and leaned down to give Carolyn a kiss, before taking turns patting each dog's head. "I'm going to fix myself a drink. Do you want one?"

"No, I'm fine," Carolyn said, nodding toward a glass of water on the cocktail table. "I'm still trying to rehydrate after my afternoon ride. Dexter was being lazy, and I really had to get after him. I was sweating up a storm when I finished, but at least we ended on a good note."

"Do you have a show this weekend?" Brad asked as he opened a cabinet, revealing a mini bar.

"Yes, I'll be at Ledges again. There are three shows left this season." Ledges was a winter series of indoor horse shows that ran from December through April each year. The facility was located about two hours northwest of Chicago in Roscoe, Illinois, and it was the only game in town for riders who wanted to compete during the winter months but didn't want to travel to the Florida shows. There were two "A" rated shows each month, and unless Carolyn was on her deathbed, she and her horse would be there competing. There was a champion and reserve champion awarded at the end of the series based on each rider-and-horse-team's point accumulation. "I'm in second place right now, but I've got a chance to move into first if we do well this weekend."

"I'll drink to your good luck then," Brad said, lifting his gin and tonic in a toast before taking a sip. He walked to an armchair across from Carolyn and set his drink on the end table next to it. Before sitting down, he loosened his tie and draped his suit coat over the back of the chair. "So did you see my announcement?"

Carolyn nodded. "Yes. I made sure I was here to watch the evening news. I recorded all the shows for you."

Brad leaned forward eagerly. "How do you think it went?"

"I thought you were great. Your prepared statement was right on point. You covered the issues that are most important to you. And you handled the Q and A well. You were articulate, polished -- basically, I thought you looked very presidential." Carolyn smiled. "But I may be a little biased."

Brad laughed. "I should hope so. But I'm glad to hear I have my wife's vote, at least."

"Count on it. So would you like to watch the news now or after dinner?"

Brad looked at his watch. They usually ate an early dinner, shortly after he arrived home. "Do we have time? If you don't mind, I'd rather not wait."

"I guessed as much, so I arranged for a late dinner." Carolyn picked up the remote and aimed it at the TV. They started with the local news and then worked their way through the networks, analyzing each segment as they watched.

When the last one had been aired and discussed, Brad leapt from his chair and began pacing around the room. The corgis jumped off the sofa and started to follow at his heels, tumbling into each other whenever he made a quick turn. "I think that went as well as it could have gone. Of course, the real test will be in a couple of weeks, after the press has time to do some digging."

"What could they find that would hurt you?"

Brad shrugged. "You know when I balanced the state budget, I had to make some cuts. People lost their jobs. There are bound to be some disgruntled ex-government workers out there who want to complain about the job I've done."

Carolyn shook her head. "I don't think they'll generate much sympathy. You did what you needed to in order to get the state back on track. Most of what you eliminated was deadweight. Not to mention what you did in cleaning up the bidding process for construction projects. You got rid of all those under-the-table deals, and now jobs are getting done on time and under budget."

Brad nodded. "I know I made the right decisions. I'm just saying that I've made some people unhappy, and I'm sure my detractors will jump at the chance to bad mouth me."

"I guess that comes with the territory. I wouldn't worry about it, though. Based on your approval ratings, you've got a lot more friends than enemies out there."

"Except for the NRA contingent. I can't count any friends among that group. Once I pushed through the new gun control laws, I burned those bridges but good."

"You can't expect to get everyone's vote. But the drop in violent crime since you spearheaded that effort speaks to how effective it was."

Brad smiled and sank back down into his chair. "I know you're right. I'm just trying to be prepared. And I am really proud of the gun control laws we passed. Even though that's a state issue, as president, I would push hard for all the states to follow our lead. In fact, I've decided that gun control is going to be one of my primary talking points in the campaign. I think people are tired of escalating gang violence and crime rates. I don't think anyone other than the rabid NRA members really believe that citizens have a constitutional right to own assault weapons."

Now that Brad had stopped pacing, the corgis jumped back onto the loveseat beside Carolyn. She nuzzled each one playfully until they settled down. "I think having gun control as one of your talking points is a great idea. I know how passionate you are about it, and that's going to come across to the voters. So what comes next, now that you've announced?"

"Our top priority is raising money. Terry's putting together a slew of fund-raising events. Dinners, cocktail parties. Mostly in the Midwest initially so that I can take advantage of the connections I've got. Then, once we've got some money in the bank, we'll start expanding our coverage. We'll need to hit all the major metro areas and, of course, all the states with early primaries."

Brad watched as Carolyn bit her lip and began to rub Daisy's back. "I know it's going to be hard for you to leave the dogs and horses to come with me. Most of the appearances I can make on my own, but there are going to be times when I'm going to want you with me."

Carolyn nodded. "I know, Brad. I promised I'd support you, and I will."

Brad walked over to Carolyn and leaned down, scooping Coco up and depositing her in the corner of the loveseat so that he could sit next to his wife. He took her hand. "You're one of my best assets, you know. You're beautiful, intelligent, funny. People love you."

"Then I'll be there. Whenever you need me." Carolyn squeezed his hand. "Why don't you go change while I check on dinner?"

"Sounds good." Brad leaned over to kiss her before he got up to leave. He knew she wasn't excited about campaigning or the prospect of being the president's wife, which is why he hadn't shared his plans with her earlier. But that didn't bother him, because he also knew that she'd do whatever he asked. Manipulating his wife to do what he wanted was just part of the game.

CHAPTER 6

Ryan was watching a Chicago Bulls game when he heard the garage door go up. He switched off the TV and walked quickly into the kitchen, opening the door for his wife. He leaned down to kiss her as she stepped through the doorway. "Hi, honey. How was your day?"

Michelle dropped her briefcase onto the floor and put her arms around her husband. "Awful." She leaned against Ryan, her head buried in his chest. "One of my clients OD'd last night."

Ryan rubbed Michelle's back. "I'm sorry, hon."

Most of Michelle's clients were able to keep their drug and alcohol addictions at bay, due in large part to her counseling. However, it came with the territory that on a fairly regular basis someone would fall off the wagon. And very infrequently, but heart-breaking each time it happened, one of her clients would lose his life to an overdose. Ryan didn't bother with empty platitudes about her doing everything she could. They had been down this road enough times that he knew she just needed him to hold her.

After a few minutes, Michelle stepped back. There were tears in her eyes, but she smiled up at her husband. "Thanks. I needed that."

"Did you have dinner yet?" Ryan asked.

Michelle shook her head. "No, but I'm not really hungry."

"Then why don't you go get comfortable and join me in the den for some mindless television? I was just watching the Bulls get annihilated by the Miami Heat."

Michelle picked up her briefcase and began walking toward their bedroom. "I'm not sure watching the Bulls lose will do much to improve my mood. Could we find a sit com to watch?"

"I'm sure there's something I can find," Ryan said, heading for the den.

He had an old episode of *The King of Queens* running when Michelle joined him. "Is this all right?" he asked. "I think we've seen it before."

Michelle smiled as she padded over in her sweatpants and fuzzy slippers and plopped down on the sofa next to him. "Only about six times. But it's perfect."

"How about a foot rub?" Ryan asked, patting his lap.

"Even more perfect." Michelle arranged a pillow for her head and lay back, lifting her feet onto Ryan's lap.

They watched the rest of the episode in silence, not even talking during the commercials. Ryan knew his wife needed time to veg out before she could rehash her day. When the show was over, he picked up the remote to search through the guide.

Michelle lifted her head. "You want to just turn it off?"

"Sure." Ryan powered off the TV and turned to his wife, knowing she was ready to talk.

Michelle spent the next half hour telling him about her day and her client. Occasionally Ryan would interject, but mostly he kept quiet, letting her get everything off her chest.

When she was finished and he knew she was ready to put the trauma of the day behind her, Ryan filled her in on his day at the newspaper and the story he was working on. "I'm getting close to wrapping up my series on the Cook County School Board. When it comes out, there should be a pretty big shake-up. Now I just have to find my next tale of corruption. Good thing we live in Chicago – I never seem to run out of mayhem."

"And more Pulitzers for you."

"Can't have too many of those. So did you hear that Brad announced today?" Ryan asked, changing subjects.

Michelle shook her head. "No, I was listening to a CD in the car, so I didn't hear the news. I guess he didn't waste any time going public, considering he just told us his plans yesterday. So what was the reaction at the *Tribune*?"

"Great. With him being from Illinois, it gives us a leg up on the non-local media. We'll probably get some of our stories on him picked up by other papers."

"I didn't actually mean how it would affect the paper's bottom line. I was curious whether your counterparts thought he'd make a good president."

Ryan shook his head, smiling. "Sorry. I guess I'm starting to sound like the publisher. All we hear about these days is how the newspaper industry is dying, and we have to come up with ideas to keep us afloat."

He paused, considering her question. "I'd say the response from the reporters on the political beat was pretty positive. On the whole, they're a pretty cynical group, but Brad has managed to stay on their good side from the beginning."

"So do you think your editor will try to get you to write a piece on your brother?"

Ryan laughed. "He can try, but it's not going to happen. You know I love Brad, and I respect the work he's done in office. But I lived in his shadow as a kid, and I don't want to go back there. It's not even that my childhood was all that bad. In fact, there were a lot of advantages to not being the golden boy in the family. I never had the same pressures that he had growing up."

Michelle raised her eyebrow. "Or the adoration."

"Yeah, Mom and Dad kind of went overboard when it came to him, but it was hard not to get caught up in Brad's limelight. It still is. That's why the voters keep electing him." Ryan shrugged. "So far, the *Trib* hasn't made my relationship with Brad an issue. I've never covered politics before, and just because my brother's running for president doesn't make me any more qualified to start now. As long as I can keep doing what I've been doing, Brad's campaign won't affect me at all."

CHAPTER 7

Henry Worthington, the publisher of the *Chicago Tribune*, stood by his enormous picture window at the front of the Tribune Tower, gazing down at Michigan Avenue. He watched as a bus pulled up and a group of morning commuters began to disembark. He was too high up to see their expressions, but he could tell a lot from watching the way they moved. There were some who had jumped up from their seats and started racing for the exit, even before the bus had stopped. Most of those were carrying Starbucks cups, their caffeine jolt obviously doing its job. Others sat waiting for the crowd to disperse before pushing themselves up from their seats and wearily making their way down the aisle.

The buses were one way to get from the train stations located in the heart of the Loop to North Michigan Avenue. Henry occasionally commuted that way himself on days when he didn't want to deal with the traffic coming in from the suburbs. The good old days of having a chauffeured limo take him everywhere had ended when his newspaper, like every other one in the country, had started bleeding revenues as more people turned to the internet for their news. With a sigh, Henry turned from the window and made his way to his desk. He reached for his phone and dialed the extension for the paper's political editor.

"Marty Glascow here," the voice bellowed.

"Good morning, Marty. Would you come see me please?"

"Sure thing, Henry. I'll be right there."

A few minutes later, the editor bounded into his boss's office. Henry could swear the temperature in the room rose by a couple of degrees, the man exuded so much energy. With a few quick strides, Marty covered the length of the office and took a seat in the guest chair, throwing his leg over the arm rest.

"Busy day in the trenches with Newcomb announcing yesterday," Marty said in lieu of a greeting.

Henry nodded. "That's exactly why I called you in here. The story's going to be big, and I want to make sure we capitalize on it. I want to throw an idea out at you."

Marty moved his leg off the arm rest and hunched forward in the chair. "I'm all ears."

"How about if we pull Ryan Newcomb off the general assignment desk and have him cover his brother's campaign full-time. I'm envisioning an in-depth, behind-the-scenes series of articles covering every detail of the campaign. I'd want him to use his family ties to negotiate full and exclusive access. Wherever Brad Newcomb goes, Ryan is right there with him."

Marty reached out and grabbed a Waterford crystal paperweight off Henry's desk, not noticing his boss wince as he began to casually toss it from one hand to the other. "You know I've wanted Ryan assigned to my desk ever since his brother became governor, but you've always told me that wasn't an option. What gives now?"

"I'm not sure it is an option. When we hired Ryan, he told us he had no interest in politics, and when his brother was elected alderman, he made it a point to reiterate his position. And he's done an excellent job for us, so I never wanted to push the issue. But this is different. A presidential campaign is a national story. We can market his involvement as an award-winning journalist who just so happens to be the candidate's brother and has unlimited access to all the inner workings of the campaign. And then I want to try to syndicate his articles to newspapers across the country. We've got a clear leg up here, and I want to exploit it."

"Don't you think we'll get some resistance in terms of objectivity?"

Henry shook his head. "We're not trying to pull a fast one. We're not hiding the relationship between the Newcombs. We're capitalizing on it. We can even highlight it in the title. We can call it 'A brother's point-of-view' or something like that. For that matter, we can even run the articles on the op-ed page."

"And you think other newspapers will pick up our stories?"

"It depends. Ryan has to be able to provide information that no other reporter has access to. And Brad Newcomb has to become a front-runner in the race, which I happen to think he will. That guy's got more charisma than Tom Cruise."

To Henry's relief, Marty reached forward and set the paperweight back on his boss's desk before leaning back in his chair. "All right, so when do we tell Ryan?"

Henry shook his head. "Well, first thing, we don't tell, we ask. And I want *you* to do that. You need to sell him on this idea. Push the fact that we think we can syndicate his articles. Give him a national presence. You know -- the whole big fish, big pond pitch."

Marty nodded, his fingers drumming a beat on the arm rest. "Don't worry. I'll get him to do it."

Henry raised his hands. "Let me make myself clear. I want you to do everything you can to convince Ryan this would be a great opportunity for him. But bottom line, if he doesn't want to do it, we back off. He's too valuable for us to risk alienating him. There are a hundred other papers out there that would kill to have him on their staff, so I don't want to do anything to risk losing him. Besides, if he's not enthusiastic about the idea, it's going to show. What makes Ryan so good is the passion he brings to every story he writes. If that's not there, there's no point to my suggestion."

Marty leapt from his chair. "Understood. I'll make this assignment sound so good, Ryan'll be begging me for it."

CHAPTER 8

Ryan's fingers were flying across his keyboard when his phone rang. His concentration was so intense that he literally jumped at the sound. He stopped typing, his fingers hovering over the keyboard as he contemplated not answering. With a sigh, he reached over and yanked the handset to his face. When the caller identified himself, Ryan cringed. *I should have let it go to voice mail,* he thought.

"I want to talk to you about a great opportunity," Marty said. "How about if I buy you some lunch?"

Ryan closed his eyes. It did not take being an investigative reporter to figure out why the paper's political editor wanted to buy him lunch the day after Brad announced his candidacy. "I'm pretty busy today, Marty. Can we just do this here?"

"Sure, no problem. We'll do lunch another time. What time could we meet?"

Ryan glanced at his watch. "How about eleven?"

"Works for me. Let's meet in the conference room on my floor."

"All right. I'll see you then."

Ryan replaced the headset and turned back to his story, but he found that his train of thought had been broken. He grabbed his favorite mug and headed to the coffee maker. Returning to his desk, he took a few sips before grimacing. *What kind of god-awful swill is this?* he thought. He went back to the coffee maker, thinking that maybe someone had forgotten to make a fresh pot this morning. He opened the cabinet and reached inside to pull out a new filter bag. Unbelievable -- someone had substituted a generic for the usual gourmet brand. He shook his head in disgust before throwing the filter bag back into the cabinet and slamming the door. Things at the newspaper must be worse than he thought if they couldn't even afford decent coffee anymore.

Back at his desk, Ryan tried to pick up the threads of his story, but his mind kept going to his upcoming meeting with the political editor.

He knew Marty was going to ask him to write a story about Brad. Ryan had made it clear in the past that he didn't want to cover his brother, but he could understand the newspaper trying to get him to change his mind. Brad's decision to run for president was a big deal, but it didn't change the way Ryan felt. He was going to have to make it clear to Marty that his mind was made up, and the newspaper was going to have to live with his decision.

At a few minutes before eleven, Ryan got up from his desk and made his way to the conference room. He arrived early, but wasn't surprised to see Marty already waiting for him.

Marty's voice boomed out a welcome. "Hey, buddy! Good to see you. Thanks for meeting with me on short notice."

"No problem," Ryan said as he pulled a chair out and sat.

"So, pretty big news about your brother, huh? You think he's going to be our next president?"

Ryan shrugged. "You'd know better than I would. What do you think?"

Marty smiled. "I think your brother could sell Florida swampland to the natives. He's got quite a gift when it comes to campaigning. The only thing holding him back right now is that he's not all that well known outside of the Midwest. But plenty of other governors running for president have dealt with that before. It's just a matter of raising the funds and hitting the road. And when he does that, I think his campaign's going to take off like wild fire. He's got a great success story and a silver tongue to tell it with."

Ryan nodded. "I hope you're right. I think Brad would make a great president, and I hope that when the time comes, the paper will endorse him."

"I think there's a pretty good chance of that, but a lot can happen over the course of a campaign." Marty leaned forward, his eyes smoldering with enthusiasm. "There's nothing more exciting than following a campaign from start to finish. Think about Obama. He went from near obscurity to rock star status in a few months. Your brother has that same kind of charisma. He's the kind of candidate that people are going to get excited about."

Ryan squirmed in his seat, knowing the pitch was coming.

"And that's where you come in, Ryan. Not only do we see your brother being a success on the national stage, we see *you* there as well. You're an excellent journalist, and you have the awards and the loyal following to prove it. But like your brother, your reputation is limited. The *Tribune's* readers know you and love you, but now we think it's time the rest of the country got to know who Ryan Newcomb is. And your brother's foray into the presidential campaign gives you the perfect launching pad."

Ryan leaned back in his chair, forcing a polite smile. Too bad for Marty that the ball he was pitching was going to end up a strike and not the homerun he was hoping for.

"Here's how we see it playing out," Marty continued. "You work out a deal with your brother for full and complete access to his campaign. I mean everything. He sneezes, and you know about it. In return, you write a series of articles from an insider's point-of-view. We want really in-depth stuff on him, not just what he's feeding the rest of the media. In exchange, we'll promise to give him more coverage than he'd get as a typical candidate. And it won't stop there. Not only will your pieces run in the *Tribune*, we think we'll be able to syndicate them. Which means that not only will your brother get the national exposure that he needs, but you will too. Just think about your byline appearing in newspapers around the country."

"What about questions of objectivity? Surely no one's going to expect me to remain unbiased while I'm writing about my own brother."

"We're not going to hide your relationship to Brad; we're going to exploit it. We'll bill this as an award-winning journalist's in-depth look at his brother's presidential run. You've got the reputation and credibility that you can pull this off without it coming off as a puff piece. I know you, Ryan. Brother or not, I know I can count on you to tell your story straight. The fact is that there are going to be days when your brother shines and other days when he falls flat on his face. I'm going to expect you to cover the missteps right along with the highlights. And that's what's going to give the series its credibility. When you write about the bad days on the campaign trail, I want the readers to feel a brother's anguish. And when you write about the good days, I want the readers to feel your pride."

"But if I put that kind of emotionalism into it, don't I lose my credibility?"

Marty exploded. "Absolutely not. Think about George Will's articles. He's a diehard Republican and every sentence he writes exudes his philosophy. He doesn't hide his party affiliation. He revels in it.

And that's what his readers expect. And the newspapers that publish him don't make any apologies."

"But that's why most newspapers publish his articles on their op-ed pages. His work is more opinion than news."

"So what? So your pieces run on the op-ed pages. Who cares? They're still syndicated around the country, and you and your brother both get famous."

Ryan pushed his chair back from the table, putting more space between him and Marty. "I don't know. Politics just isn't my thing."

Marty pounded his fist on the table. "God, Ryan. This isn't just about politics. It's about a guy making the leap from a small pond to a big pond. Or in this case, more like a big pond into the ocean. And it's about a brother being right there as the whole thing unfolds. We think this story could be huge."

Ryan sat quietly for a minute, considering Marty's pitch. "You really think you could syndicate it?"

"Absolutely. Newspapers all over are in the same boat as we are. More than ever, we're relying on articles originally published in other papers to fill our own. The amount of money we pay out to buy outside articles is nothing compared to what we'd have to pay in salary and benefits to add more staff. And every newspaper out there is doing the same thing so, just like us, they're hungry for good stories to publish. And I think the series I'm proposing you write will be a slam-dunk."

Ryan got up and began pacing around the room. "I admit that the offer's tempting. I mean, how could it not be? Every writer wants to be syndicated and get a bigger audience. But I just don't know that this is the way I want to do it – riding on my brother's coattails."

Marty's next words came out as soft as a whisper and stopped Ryan dead in his tracks. "You may not have a choice here, buddy. This idea's coming from the top. And Worthington would have my head if he knew I told you this. But he let me know that if you don't agree to it, you're on a short list of staff we may have to cut."

"*What?* You've got to be kidding!" Ryan felt as though he had just been knifed in his gut. "You said it yourself before. What about the awards I've won? My loyal readers?"

"All of that only goes so far, Ryan. You know what the newspaper industry is like right now. We're all treading water like crazy to stay afloat. The days are gone when a writer could pick and choose his stories. These days, if you want a job, you take the assignments we give you."

Marty stood and walked over to Ryan, his nose mere inches from the other man's face. "Listen, Ryan. I'm just trying to be straight with you. I don't want to see the newspaper fire you. I think you're too good to lose, but that's not my decision. But it doesn't have to come to that. You write this series for us, and not only do you keep your job, you take a percentage of the syndication fees. It's a win-win situation. And even if this series isn't your ideal assignment, it gets you out there. And your next series can be something totally different. Something *you* choose. Once you have a national following, you can write your own ticket."

Marty grabbed Ryan's arm. "Don't be short-sighted. This is a phenomenal opportunity for you."

Ryan stepped back, loosening Marty's grip. "All right, just let me think about it."

"Great. I know you'll make the right decision."

"It sounds like I might not really have a choice here."

Marty shrugged. "You have a choice, Ryan. You just may not like your options. But if it was me, and I was choosing between losing my job and writing a series that was going to get me syndicated, well, I don't think it would be that hard a decision to make."

Ryan laughed sarcastically. "Right, when you put it like that. But it's not that simple for me." He turned for the door. "I'll give you my answer tomorrow."

CHAPTER 9

When Ryan got home that evening, he walked into the kitchen to find Michelle stirring a pot of homemade tomato sauce. As he leaned in to kiss her, he could smell the garlic and oregano rising up from the simmering pot. "Mmm. That smells great, hon. What can I do to help?"

"You can toss the salad. I've got everything out already." With the spoon she was holding, she pointed to the kitchen counter where the romaine, parmesan cheese, croutons, and Caesar salad dressing were laid out. "Other than that, we're all set. The garlic bread's in the oven, and I'll throw the pasta in to cook now that you're here."

"So how did I score a home-cooked meal in the middle of the week instead of our usual take-out?" Ryan asked, as he started tossing the salad ingredients.

"My last client appointment got cancelled, so I made a detour to the grocery store on the way home. After you called me from work, I thought you might need some comfort food tonight."

Ryan turned away from the salad and walked back to the stove. He wrapped his arms around Michelle's waist and buried his head in her shoulder. "Thanks. This is exactly what I need tonight."

The couple hugged for a few minutes before breaking apart and resuming their dinner preparations, a comfortable silence between them. When their meal was ready, they sat down at the kitchen table, and Ryan began to fill his wife in on the details of his conversation with Marty.

"I really don't want to do this. First of all, I'm just not interested in this story. The idea of following a politician around on a campaign trail leaves me cold. I can't imagine spending the day watching someone run around sucking up to everyone he meets. Not to mention having to listen to the same tired speeches over and over."

Ryan reached forward and tore a piece of garlic bread off the steaming loaf. "I mean maybe it would be interesting for a few days, but not for the length of time they're talking about. They want me to do this for the duration of Brad's campaign. The first primary is nine months away. And then, if he makes it that far, we're talking another ten months before the general election. That's a hell of a long time commitment."

"Would they let you work on other stories while you were assigned to this one?"

"We didn't talk about it, but they'd have to. I'd go crazy working on just one story for so long, especially one I don't even want to write in the first place." Ryan shook his head. "And then there's the whole issue of trying to juggle objectivity with writing about my own brother. I'd want to present an honest look at the campaign, but how could I write something negative that could jeopardize Brad's chances at getting elected. Every word I wrote, I'd be thinking about its effect on him."

"You could be in a pretty difficult position if you discovered some information about your brother that could hurt him." Michelle put her fork down and reached across the table to squeeze her husband's hand. "But it's not just the story, is it?"

Ryan sighed. "No, it's the whole idea of being in Brad's shadow again. It was one thing as a kid. Back then, it was just the way things were. And like I've told you before, there were benefits to having all the attention focused on Brad. My parents were not all that crazy about my decision to go into journalism, but as long as Brad was headed for law school, there wasn't much push-back. They paid my college tuition, showed up at graduation to shake my hand, and that was that. Until I landed the job at the *Trib*, I don't think Dad even read any of my stories. Now that they're delivered to him on his doorstep each morning, they're kind of hard to ignore." He paused. "Although I still think he probably just skims them after he's pored over every word written about Brad."

"I hate to say it, but I think you're right," Michelle said. "The last time we saw your dad, I brought up a story you had published that morning. He looked at me with this blank stare and made some excuse about not having had time to read the paper that day. I think I was more embarrassed than he was."

"Well, I guess this series would be one way to get Dad to read my work. Hell, he'd probably have the stories framed. Put them up on the wall next to all the photos he has of Brad shaking hands with the rich and famous."

Michelle laughed. "Oh, God, that wall. What are there? Twenty pictures of Brad, and two of us?"

Ryan joined in laughing. "Yeah, and one of the two is us at Brad's wedding."

Their laughter died, as Ryan took a bite of pasta. He swallowed and set down his fork. "You know that picture of us at Brad's wedding is kind of a metaphor for this story. Yes, I'd have a role, but basically it would be all about Brad. And as much as I love the guy and want him to win this election, I really don't want to spend close to two years of *my* life living *his* life."

Michelle poked at her salad. "But if you don't do it…" The words hung in the air between them.

Ryan met his wife's eyes. "I might be out on the street."

"Do you really think they'd let you go?"

Ryan took a long drink of water before answering. "In this environment, I guess the answer is yes. That's what Marty told me anyway."

"I wish I could tell you just walk, but we can't exactly make it on my salary alone, can we?"

"Not if we want to keep paying the mortgage."

Michelle jabbed at her pasta in frustration. "I'm sorry, honey. I know my job doesn't pay well."

Ryan reached across the table and took his wife's hand. "There's nothing to apologize for. What you're doing is important. You save lives. You make society better. How many people can say that about their careers?"

"You're right. Just call me St. Michelle." She smiled as she squeezed Ryan's hand, before releasing it. "But seriously, what are our options?"

"Your one and only option is to keep doing what you love to do, regardless of the salary."

"And what about you?"

"My options are pretty limited too. There isn't another paper in Chicago that's in the same league as the *Trib*. The *Sun-Times* has contacted me before, but I'm just not interested in working there. And I don't think either of us wants to move to a different city, right?"

Michelle shook her head vehemently. "Chicago's our home. I don't want to move away from our friends and family."

"Me neither. Which leaves me with one option. I do the series they want, and I keep my job."

"I hate the idea of you doing something that's going to make you unhappy. Following Brad around for two years would make me miserable too."

Ryan looked at his wife and wondered for the millionth time why she had such a strong aversion to his brother. He assumed it was because she was such a down-to-earth person and didn't tolerate the typical bullshit that goes along with being a politician and trying to appeal to as many people as possible. He could ask her about it, but she would just deflect the question like she always did. "You've never exactly been a big fan of my brother, have you?"

Michelle shrugged. "I just haven't fallen under the spell everyone else around him seems to be under, including your whole family and most of the state." She pointed her fork at Ryan. "You realize that if you write this story, you might just find out some things about Brad that you don't want to know."

"You really think there's some deep, dark secret he's hiding?"

"I just think that with that ego of his, he's probably not lived a monk's life."

"You mean you think he's sleeping around?"

"It's not exactly unheard of among politicians."

Ryan shook his head. "No way. I know he flirts a lot, but that's all just a game. You know he adores Carolyn. He'd never cheat on her. His style may rub you the wrong way, but you can't argue with his success."

Michelle put her fork down and raised her hands up in mock surrender. "I give up. Your brother's perfect, and I'm the only person in the world who doesn't know it."

"Well, perfect or not, I don't want to do this story. I'm going to talk to Brad about it tomorrow. If I'm lucky, maybe he'll kill the idea for me."

CHAPTER 10

"I love it!" Brad exclaimed, looking across his desk at his younger brother. "I want my campaign to be totally transparent. Too many politicians try to spin every move they make. I want voters to see the real me. I have nothing to hide, and I want the voters to know that."

"Are you sure?" Ryan asked. "If we do this thing, I'm going to have to report what I see – the good, the bad, and the ugly. Are you sure you want that level of transparency?"

Brad leapt up from his seat and circled his desk, plopping down in a chair next to Ryan. He scooted in close to his brother until their knees practically touched. "In someone else's hands, I'd be concerned. I'd never trust a reporter I didn't know and who might have some hidden agenda. But in your hands, I have no qualms. I know that you'd be totally fair and honest in your reporting."

Ryan looked puzzled. "But don't you want to put a little distance between you and the voters? Don't you want them to see you in the best possible light?"

Brad shook his head. "I'm not afraid of revealing a few flaws, if that's what it takes for the voters to feel like they're seeing the real me. I think the pros far outweigh the cons. This would give me a real leg up. For one thing, it would set me apart from the other candidates. No one else would dare let a reporter shadow them everywhere on a campaign."

"But you're only doing it because I'm your brother. Don't you think the readers will think I'm biased?"

"Of course you're biased." Brad laughed, giving Ryan's shoulder a playful shove. "You damn well better be biased."

Ryan smiled. "Don't worry. I am. I want you to be president. But the point is that I might not be the right person for this job. If the readers don't think I'm credible, what's the point?"

"You're *exactly* the right person. First of all, because I wouldn't allow anyone else to do it. And secondly, because you *are* credible. And that'll come through in your writing. You're not going to put a nice coat of varnish over everything. You'll write it the way you see it, and if that includes some bad with the good, that will only prove to the readers that you're giving it to them straight."

Brad held his brother captive in his gaze. He had no doubt that he could manipulate Ryan into writing exactly what he wanted him to write. His brother's articles would give him a huge leg up against his competition. "I think this is a fantastic idea, Ryan. You and me, twenty-four/seven on the campaign trail." He pounded his fists on the arm rests. "Let's do this thing!"

* * *

When Ryan left Brad's office to tell the *Tribune* he would do the story, Brad called Terry into his office to fill him in.

"No way, Governor. As your campaign manager, I'm telling you this is a terrible idea!"

Terry leaned forward in his chair. "It's just too dangerous to give someone in the press full access to our campaign. The whole point in dealing with the media is to control what we tell them. We don't want anyone, including your brother, to have full access to you. Let's take an example. What if we're discussing one of the other candidates? We need to speak openly without worrying about what we say showing up in the paper. And what about our campaign strategies? Same thing. We can't reveal our every move to our opponents."

Brad held up his hands. "You're right. You bring up some good points. Why don't you make a list of whatever you think needs to remain confidential, and we'll run it by the *Trib*? If they're reasonable about this, they'll know there are things we can't have published. And if they agree to that and still think there's enough of a story here, then I want to do it."

"How often would the articles run?" Terry asked.

"Ryan said that the *Trib* is willing to make this a daily column, plus they'll try to syndicate it. You know our biggest problem right now is lack of recognition outside of the Midwest. If they're successful in syndicating the articles, they would go a long way in getting my name out there in parts of the country where I'm relatively unknown."

Terry shook his head. "I don't know, Gov. I see the advantage of extra publicity, but…"

Brad jumped in. "Exactly! And you know what they say. There's no such thing as bad publicity."

Terry shook his finger at his boss. "You're not that naïve. You know as well as I do that that might be true for celebrities, but not for politicians."

"But there's not going to be bad publicity. Not with my brother writing the story. He's not going to write anything that would damage my chance at the presidency."

"I wouldn't bet on that. He's a reporter, and it's his job to dig up dirt." Terry paused, his face reddening. "I hate to bring this up, but you know you have some skeletons in your closet."

Brad waved his hand dismissively. "I assume you're referring to a few indiscretions. First of all, they were only one-night stands. No phone calls, no emails, no ongoing relationships. No record of anything. Even if one of those women surfaced, it would be her word against mine. And secondly, I swear there will be no more of those. I want the presidency too badly to risk it for some meaningless sex. I swear, I will be a total Boy Scout from this point forward."

CHAPTER 11

Carrying her plastic tray filled with a salad and iced tea, Amy Hewlett threaded her way through the food court searching for an empty table. She smiled to herself, acknowledging how most of the men stopped chewing as she passed, their eyes glazing over like love-struck teenagers. She was petite, barely five foot two, if she stretched herself tall. She was thin, with just the right curves in all the right places. Her bottle-blond hair hung straight down just past her shoulders, framing her heart-shaped face. Her eyes were cornflower blue and wide-set, giving her a look of perpetual innocence. Although she had turned thirty-eight on her last birthday, when she went into a liquor store, she was carded more times than not.

Finding an open table, she set her tray down and looked over toward the Burger King. She waved at her friend Tina, who was carrying her own tray laden with a Whopper, fries, and a Coke. Amy would have happily traded meals with her friend, but one look at Tina's plump frame reminded her why she couldn't. She watched as her friend approached the table, not generating more than a quick glance from any of the men she passed. Amy couldn't resist a self-satisfied smile as she poured the low fat dressing over her salad.

Tina's tray landed with a thud, her body following suit. "I'm starving! I don't know how you survive on that rabbit food."

Amy shrugged. "I had a big breakfast," she said, thinking back to her bowl of Special K and Equal.

Tina raised her eyebrows, and both women smiled, acknowledging the little white lie. Both of them were well aware of their own circumstances. Tina was happily married to a man who loved food as much as she did. Amy, on the other hand, was divorced and on the hunt. With her biological clock ticking louder and louder, she couldn't afford any extra pounds.

"So how was your morning?" Tina asked.

"The usual. The dragon lady came in snarling this morning. It was all I could do to paste a smile on my face. I don't remember being such a bitch to everyone when I was going through my divorce."

Tina laughed. "Trust me. You weren't, or we wouldn't still be friends. God, how long ago was that anyway?"

"Five years." Amy sighed. "And I'm still looking for Mr. Right. If anyone had told me then that I'd still be searching, I might have overlooked Bob's flaws."

"As I recall, flaw number one was that he changed his mind about having kids. And I know you well enough to know that's still a deal breaker for you."

Amy nodded. "It is. I'm still holding out hope for that white picket fence and house full of kids."

"You and I both know you've had plenty of chances to get married again." Tina glanced around the room. "And judging by the number of guys who keep trying to catch your eye, I think you pretty much just need to snap your fingers."

As though testing her friend's theory, Amy raised her head and surveyed the food court. Picking out the most attractive men in the room, she smiled and let her gaze linger for a moment on each of the chosen ones. Then she dropped her eyes and picked up her iced tea. She flicked the straw with her tongue before taking a long sip. When she looked up again and saw the men's mouths hanging open, she gave Tina a quick wink.

"They may all be ready for a quick roll in the hay, but the question is whether any of them are marriage material. And sadly, based on five years of dating, the answer is probably not." Amy shrugged. "What can I say? I'm looking for the perfect man, and I'm not willing to settle for anything less."

"And I can tell you based on fourteen years of marriage, there is no such thing." Tina paused and raised her eyebrows suggestively. "With one possible exception, of course."

"Governor Dreamy!" the two women said in unison before dissolving into a wave of schoolgirl giggles. They were both diehard *Grey's Anatomy* fans and at some point had realized that their governor bore more than a passing resemblance to their favorite character, Dr. McDreamy.

"So speaking of, what do you think of him running for president?" Tina asked.

"I think he'll get the vote of every woman who's got a pulse," Amy answered.

"Including you, of course."

"He may get more than just my vote. I'm thinking about joining his campaign staff." Amy speared a forkful of lettuce before continuing. "I hear he's interviewing for a personal assistant, and I think I'm going to apply. There's no one who would work as hard as I would."

"You're just hoping for some late night meetings," Tina teased.

Amy shook her head. "I know he's happily married, and you've seen the first lady. She's gorgeous. Anyway, I'd never have an affair." She sighed, thinking that it seemed like all the good men were taken. "Not even with Governor Dreamy."

CHAPTER 12

Amy marched into the governor's outer office, flashing a big smile at Brad's secretary. "Hi. I'm Amy Hewlett. I have a three-thirty appointment with the governor."

The secretary looked down at an appointment calendar, checking off Amy's name. "Have a seat, and I'll let him know you're here."

Amy sat down in one of the waiting area chairs and picked up a magazine. She thumbed through it, hoping for an article to catch her eye, but she was too keyed up to focus on anything other than her impending interview. As the minutes ticked by, she glanced at her watch. She was surprised to see that only ten minutes had passed. It had seemed twice as long.

When she heard the secretary's intercom buzz, Amy looked up anxiously. She watched as the woman spoke into her phone and then turned to Amy, smiling as she said the magic words: "You can go in now."

Amy jumped from her seat, throwing her shoulders back and tugging at her suit jacket. Opening the governor's office door, she took a deep breath before stepping into the room. Her eyes met Brad's and they both smiled. "Hello, Governor. I'm Amy Hewlett."

Brad rose from his chair and stepped around his desk, his arm extended. "It's a pleasure to meet you, Amy."

As they shook hands, Amy felt a jolt of electricity. *Hold it together,* she cautioned herself, feeling like a schoolgirl.

Brad gestured to the chair in front of his desk. "Have a seat. Would you like some coffee?"

"No thanks, I'm fine," Amy said, thinking the last thing she needed was caffeine to fuel her already jangled nerves.

Brad settled into his desk chair and picked up Amy's resume. "I've had a chance to review this, and you seem very well qualified. So what makes you interested in this position?"

"I've really admired the work you've done as governor, sir, and I believe you'd make a wonderful president." Amy smiled, her eyes earnest. "I would be honored to help you achieve that goal. If you hire me, I can promise you that I'll be the most enthusiastic, hard-working person on your campaign staff."

Brad chuckled, leaning back into his chair. "That's a pretty big promise. You do realize that personal assistant is a code word for gopher. You're going to be handling all the exciting tasks like fetching coffee and taking my suits to the dry cleaners. It might be hard to muster any enthusiasm when you're trying to get a ketchup stain off my suit coat before I head into my next meeting."

Amy smiled, blushing. "I didn't mean to sound so naïve. I know that for some people, those tasks might seem menial. But the way I look at it, my job would be to make things run as smoothly as possible so you can concentrate on the big issues." She raised her eyebrows. "And, by the way, I happen to be a killer when it comes to club soda and ketchup stains."

Brad held up his hands. "I believe you. And if you can bring the same positive attitude to this position that you're showing me today, that's exactly what I need. I know from past experience that campaigns can get pretty grueling. It's vital that I surround myself with people who are really committed."

Brad spent the next several minutes talking about some of his plans for the campaign and the issues that were most important to him. As she listened, Amy grew more excited about the possibility of joining his staff.

"One of the things I need to point out is that we'll be doing a lot of traveling. How do you feel about living out of a suitcase?" Brad asked.

"That's not a problem for me. I love to travel, and I don't have any home commitments. I'm not married, no steady boyfriends." Amy smiled. "I don't even have a dog."

As they continued to talk, Amy could feel herself relaxing. They were interrupted when Brad's intercom buzzed. He held up a finger and grabbed his phone. When he hung up, he smiled at Amy. "Our time's up, I'm afraid. I've really enjoyed talking with you, but my next appointment is here."

They both stood, and Brad came around his desk. He shook Amy's hand and walked with her to the door. "We'll be in touch soon."

"Thank you, Governor. It was a real honor to meet you."

* * *

Brad closed the door behind Amy and walked back to his desk. He picked up his phone and called his chief-of-staff. "I think I found my personal assistant." He picked up Amy's resume and gave Terry her name and current position. "I want you to run a background check for me, and if she vets, I'll need you to work out her transfer with her boss."

"I'm hoping you're going to tell me that she's a nice grandmotherly type, gray-haired and fifty pounds overweight," Terry joked.

Brad laughed. "Sorry to disappoint you. As it happens, she's a knockout. But you have nothing to worry about. I've coated all my pants' zippers with Teflon. Like I told you before, there's no way I'm doing anything to risk this campaign."

When he hung up the phone, Brad allowed himself a momentary fantasy of being in bed with Amy. She was one of the sexiest women he had ever met, and he'd had a hard-on for the entire length of the interview. It was a good thing he wanted to be president so badly, because keeping his vow of extra-marital celibacy wasn't going to be easy.

CHAPTER 13

Over the next week, Brad concentrated on putting state matters in order so he could focus on his presidential campaign. Today was the day that Ryan would start his series of articles, and his door was open when he heard his brother arrive. "Come on in, Ryan," he called out. "I just got off the phone with my lieutenant governor. Starting tomorrow, I'll be turning over my day-to-day responsibilities to him."

Ryan stepped through the doorway and made his way to one of the guest chairs in front of Brad's desk. "Did I get my days mixed up? I thought you wanted me to start today, but I can I come back tomorrow."

"No, no. I did tell you to come in today. My schedule's a mix between state business and campaign issues. That means I'll have to kick you out a few times, but I want you to be here for all the campaign meetings. I want to make sure you're a part of this from the ground floor up."

Brad's intercom buzzed and he picked up his phone to talk to his secretary. A couple of minutes later, Amy stepped into the office carrying a stack of papers.

"Come on in," Brad said. "Those papers I asked you to bring up are for Ryan here."

Brad watched as she handed the papers to Ryan. "I'd like you to meet my brother, Ryan Newcomb. Ryan, this is Amy Hewlett. She's just joined my campaign staff as my personal assistant."

"Pleased to meet you, Ryan," Amy said as they shook hands. "I'm a big fan of yours. I think you're an excellent writer."

"Thank you," Ryan said. "It's always nice to meet one of my readers. So what made you decide to join Brad's campaign staff?"

Amy blushed. "Well, I guess I'm a big fan of his as well. I think he's been doing a wonderful job as governor and I know he'll make a great president. I feel honored to be working with him."

"I see you've brainwashed another one, bro," Ryan said, winking at Amy.

"That's right," Brad said. "Now I just have to brainwash the rest of the country. One down and three hundred million to go."

The three chatted for a few minutes, until Amy excused herself. After she left, Brad pointed to the stack of papers Ryan was holding. "You'll want to review those. You should have my schedule for today. I'd like you to attend any meetings that are related to the campaign. I also had Amy make you copies of our travel itinerary for the next few weeks. As you can see, we'll be heading to New Hampshire next week. Then we'll be bouncing around the country for a while. Hitting the states with early primaries. We've also set up some fundraising events in cities where I've got key contacts."

"Key contacts meaning…"

Brad smiled. "People willing to write me checks and convince their friends to do the same."

Ryan nodded and began to review the material Amy had given him. After a few minutes, he looked up. "Looks like we'll be living out of suitcases for a while."

"We don't really have a choice. My biggest problem right now is lack of name recognition outside the Midwest." Brad paused. "But look at the bright side. It'll be fun traveling around the country."

Ryan raised one eyebrow, giving his brother his best *you've got to be kidding* look. "Right. Hanging out in airport waiting rooms and staying at cheesy hotels. Bring on those continental breakfasts."

Brad laughed. "Granted, my campaign donors would probably not want to see us staying at the Four Seasons, but we'll try not to book any dives. I'll make sure Carolyn has final say on our lodgings."

"Is she going to be on the road with us?"

Brad shrugged. "As much as possible, I hope. She's a great campaign asset. Although I think she's as excited about traveling as you are. She'd much rather be home with her dogs and horses. But she's a trouper. She'll do her part. How about Michelle? How is she going to feel with you spending all this time on the road?"

"Not real thrilled. But, unlike Carolyn, she doesn't have the choice of coming along. She wouldn't want to leave her clients for any length of time. Besides, we need *both* our salaries to pay the bills."

Brad's eyebrows shot up. "I'm surprised. I thought you were doing okay at the *Trib*."

"Better than most of my counterparts, but I still had to take a pay cut recently. The newspaper business is like a terminal cancer patient. We're dying a slow, painful death."

Brad drummed his fingers on his desk, his mind whirring. After a few minutes, he stood up and circled his desk, sitting in the guest chair next to his brother. He leaned in close. "If I get elected, I'd love to have you join my staff – maybe something in communications."

It was Ryan's turn to look surprised. "Thanks, bro. That really means a lot to me. But if newspapers are a sinking ship, I'm the captain who goes down with them. And if and when that happens, I'll pursue magazines or the internet. There'll still be opportunities for me."

"With your reputation, I know there will be. This isn't a handout. If I get elected, I want to surround myself with people I can really trust. And, besides Carolyn, the two people I trust most in this world are you and Terry."

Brad stood up and began to pace around his office. "If there's one thing I've learned as governor, it's that when you're in a position like this, everyone around you tells you what they think you want to hear. And if it's like this now, I can't even imagine the brown-nosing that goes along with being president."

He stopped, his eyes locking on his brother's. "I know you'll always be straight with me, Ryan. You know, keep me grounded."

Ryan laughed. "You want me to keep you grounded? So my job will be to let you know if you're turning into a jerk, huh?"

"Something like that."

"And what's the job title? President's buddyguard?"

Brad smiled. "I'm sure we could come up with something a little more official sounding."

Ryan held up his hands. "Really, Brad, I appreciate the offer. But I don't think life in the White House fishbowl is for me."

"You never know. Why don't we just leave the door open for now? When the time comes, maybe you'll change your mind."

PART TWO:
THE COUNTDOWN TO THE ELECTION

CHAPTER 14

July: Sixteen Months to Go

Brad sat in the center back seat of the black SUV, bookended by Terry and Amy, as the car sped down the streets of Charlotte. The candidate allowed himself a brief but appreciative glance out the tinted windows at the city's stunning architecture. "It's beautiful here. Everything looks brand new."

"Most of the buildings you're looking at have been built in the last twenty or thirty years, and many in the last ten," Ryan said, turning to face the others from the front passenger seat. "Developers have pretty much wiped out old downtown Charlotte and made it a showcase for modern architecture." He had made it a point to research every city they visited as background for his articles.

Terry handed Brad a note card with the call letters of the radio station and the name of the morning DJ he would be meeting with in a few minutes. This would be his third interview of the day. The first two had been at TV stations on their morning news programs, since face time was paramount. They would hit four radio stations during morning drive time and then swing by a senior center as their last stop before lunch.

The TV and radio interviews ran the gamut of topics, although Brad made sure to bring up gun control and crime reduction, which he was using as his signature causes. When he got to the senior center, he would switch gears and focus his talking points on promising to find a way to keep Medicare viable and capital gains taxes low. Although he would still talk about gun control, knowing that crime issues were a hot button with the seniors. After a few months on the campaign trail, he was becoming an expert on spinning his platform to appeal to whatever audience he was addressing.

The SUV pulled to a quick stop in front of the high-rise housing the radio station. Brad leapt from the car, his long legs like scissors eating up the sidewalk as he raced to the entrance. Terry and Amy followed in his footsteps -- Terry matching his boss stride for stride, Amy struggling to keep up with the two men in her high heels. When Brad paused so she could catch up, he smiled at her. "We need to buy you a pair of running shoes."

"Thanks, but no thanks. I hate that look. When women wear a nice dress and then spoil it with gym shoes. The only time you're going to see *me* wearing gym shoes is in a gym, so you'll just have to get used to waiting for me."

"Luckily for you, you're worth the wait," Brad teased her. "Besides, I agree with your fashion sense. And you've definitely got the legs for those high heels."

Moving aside so that Amy could go through the door first, Brad stole a quick glance at Terry and saw his friend's disapproval. "Lighten up, Terry," he whispered. "Just because I'm keeping my marriage vows doesn't mean I can't flirt a little. I even made sure my shadow wasn't in earshot." He nodded toward Ryan, who was still in the car, planning to listen to the radio interview from there.

Terry opened his mouth as if to say something, but then clamped it back shut. Without any further discussion, the two men followed Amy into the lobby.

* * *

The day passed in a blur of activity. After the media interviews and his speech at the senior center, Brad had a lunch meeting at the uptown city library where he met with adults learning to read and their mentors. With this group, he geared his talk around the importance of education and literacy programs, detailing how he had made those issues key components in his state budget.

Then it was on to a factory in one of the outlying towns. His prepared speech focused on the economy and steps he would take to ensure that American manufacturers would continue to remain competitive in an increasingly global marketplace. After his speech, the factory employees fired hardball questions at him, a result he had come to expect. He had found blue collar workers to be the most direct and confrontational of the groups he met with, but he appreciated their honesty and forthrightness. And based on the number of people who made it a point to come up to him and shake his hand after the Q and A session, he knew he had won over the tough group.

On their way back to the city, Brad had his driver pull off into a shopping center where he had spotted a Starbucks. Rather than sending Amy in alone for the coffee, Brad joined her and spent half an hour introducing himself and asking the people he met to share their concerns about the state of the country. These casual one-on-one encounters were his favorite part of campaigning. He would ask a general question and then give people a chance to vent. Nodding supportively while they were talking, the candidate would whip out a small notebook he kept in his breast pocket and jot down their thoughts and ideas. He could tell people lapped this up, as though their input would find its way into his presidential agenda rather than into his hotel waste basket at the end of the day.

After the unplanned stop at the coffee shop, Brad and Amy returned to the car. Making up for lost time, the driver sped back to the hotel, where Brad had an interview scheduled with one of the political reporters for the *Charlotte Observer*. When the meeting began, the candidate introduced his brother and asked if Ryan could sit in with them. Brad expressed his appreciation that the paper was publishing most of Ryan's articles.

"I'm really striving to make my campaign as transparent as possible, just like my presidency will be," Brad said. "I believe that having Ryan along to document my activities has helped to spread my vision to a greater audience than I could reach personally. And in that spirit, I would encourage you to ask me anything you want. Unlike some of the other candidates, you won't find me ducking any questions."

At the conclusion of the interview, Brad escorted the reporter from the living area of his suite to the exit. When the door was closed, he turned to Ryan. "That went well, don't you think?"

Ryan nodded. "You brainwashed another one," he replied, using a line that had become an inside joke between the brothers.

Brad walked to the desk and picked up his itinerary, glancing at his watch. "We have about an hour and a half before we need to leave for this evening's fundraising dinner. I'm going to check in with the lieutenant governor and make a few other calls. Why don't we plan to meet back here at six thirty?"

"Works for me," Ryan said. "It'll give me time to get some writing in."

When his brother left, Brad called Terry. He asked him to come by at six so they would have a half hour to spend together before they had to leave for dinner. They would go over the guest list, with Brad attempting to memorize the names and relevant personal information of his supporters.

"I called the airport, and Carolyn's flight is on time," Terry said. "I sent the driver to pick her up. She should be here any minute."

"Great. Hopefully, this time she remembered to pack her evening dress in her carry-on." They both laughed, remembering her last trip when they had received a frantic call from her at the airport telling them her luggage was lost. They had sent Amy out shopping for an evening dress with just enough time for Carolyn to get to the hotel, change into it and not be late for the dinner.

"For someone with as good taste as Amy has shopping for herself, she sure picked out an ugly dress for your wife," Terry said.

"Yeah, she said she wanted to get something conservative, but I think she went a little overboard. Carolyn looked more like a nun than a First Lady."

Hearing the hotel door opening, Brad looked up. "And speak of the devil, here she is. And it looks like she's got all her luggage."

Brad hung up with Terry and went to greet his wife. "I'm glad you're here. I've missed you."

"I missed you too," Carolyn said, stepping into his arms.

* * *

When the couple came back to their suite after dinner, Brad loosened his tie and flopped onto the bed. "That was a great day, but I'm exhausted."

"You're like the Energizer Bunny," Carolyn said. "You'll sleep a few hours and wake up ready to do it all over again tomorrow."

"You're right. I'm made for this. And you are too. You were the perfect First Lady this evening, as always. I know you'd rather be at home, but it means a lot to have you by my side."

CHAPTER 15

When the hotel phone rang with a five o'clock wake-up call, Carolyn groaned, ducking her head under her pillow. She listened to Brad thank the hotel employee and then felt the bed shake as he got up to face the day. They would spend one more day in Charlotte before heading to Atlanta. Carolyn's first appointment was a luncheon with the local chapter of the Democratic League of Women Voters. Grateful to be able to sleep in after their late night out, Carolyn was sound asleep again within a few minutes.

She woke at eight and ordered breakfast from room service. A half hour later, her tray arrived with lukewarm scrambled eggs and a bowl of mushy fruit. She picked at the food, although she was relieved that at least the coffee was piping hot. One of the rules on the campaign trail was that they didn't send food back to the kitchen, no matter how awful it was. They didn't want to get a reputation for being difficult. Besides, they needed every vote they could get, cooks and waiters included.

Carolyn finished breakfast while reading the newspaper and watching the morning news shows. She put on her workout clothes to head to the hotel fitness center, thinking that she would much rather be back at home getting on her horse instead of a treadmill. An hour later, she was back in her room, getting dressed for the day. When it was time to leave for the luncheon, she heard a knock on her hotel room door and opened it to let Amy in. Normally Carolyn had her own personal assistant travel with her, but the young woman was home sick, so Amy was taking her place.

"Good morning, Mrs. Newcomb. That's a beautiful suit you have on."

"Thanks, Amy. No need for you to do any shopping for me on this trip. My luggage arrived intact."

"Oh, I didn't mind at all last time. I've never had a job where I get paid to go shopping. It's not a bad gig at all."

Carolyn smiled. "I guess. I'm not much of a shopper myself. I usually try to get most of what I need from catalogs."

"Not me. I love the thrill of the hunt."

The women continued to chat amiably as they made their way down to one of the hotel ballrooms where the luncheon was scheduled. When they arrived, Carolyn gave Amy her purse for safe-keeping while she began to circulate through the room, shaking hands with as many of the league members as she could. About a half hour after they arrived, the league president made an announcement asking the women to find their tables. When she saw that most of the group was seated, she introduced Carolyn as their guest of honor.

Carolyn took the microphone from the president and waited for the applause to die down before beginning her speech, one of hundreds she had given over the years. Before retiring to raise her children, she had worked in the advertising field as an account executive, and she had given many presentations during her career. She had found that a little humor at the beginning always lightened up the room, even with the most hard-nosed clients. She used this same tactic in her campaign speeches, usually finding something local to comment about. The other trick she had learned was to keep her speeches short.

Twenty minutes later, Carolyn sat down to a round of appreciative applause. As she looked around the room, she could tell that she had made a good impression. She acknowledged to herself that campaigning came as naturally to her as it did to her husband. The only difference was that he thrived on it, whereas she barely tolerated it.

She managed to choke down the dry chicken breast, cold rice pilaf and overcooked broccoli as she listened to the league president run through the other items on her meeting agenda. After the gathering was adjourned, Carolyn remained behind, making herself accessible to the many members who stayed to talk with her. When the last of the stragglers left the ballroom, she checked her watch and signaled to Amy.

"That took longer than I thought it would," Carolyn said. "Is there still time for me to join up with my husband?"

"No, ma'am. When it looked like we were going to run late, I called Terry. He suggested that we head upstairs and get packed so that we're ready to leave when they get back to the hotel. They're close to wrapping up their day as well."

"I guess I got off easy today then," Carolyn said, as she began walking to the ballroom exit. "All I have left is a dinner scheduled this evening in Atlanta, right?"

"Yes. You and the governor will be having a private dinner with the mayor, his wife and a few other couples. I've got the names upstairs. Should I bring them to your room?"

"No, thanks. I can look at them on the airplane."

The women crossed through the hotel lobby to the elevator bank and Amy hit the call button. They watched as the elevator doors opened and a corgi leaped out, dragging her owner behind her.

Oh, she's beautiful," Carolyn said. "I have three of my own corgis at home. Can I say hello?"

"Of course. She adores people."

Carolyn dropped to her knees and the little dog jumped into her arms, smothering her with kisses. "This is just what I needed. I hate being away from my dogs."

"That's why I never travel without mine."

They talked for a while, swapping stories about their pets. When the woman and her dog left, Amy punched the call button again.

"Sorry to keep you waiting, Amy. You could have gone up without me."

"That's all right, ma'am."

"I guess you can see where my heart is. I know that I have to be here with my husband, but I'd much rather be home with my dogs and horses."

"I understand completely, even though I'm not much of a homebody myself. I really love the travelling and all the excitement of the campaign."

Carolyn smiled, touching Amy's arm. "My husband's lucky to have you on his staff. I'm glad to know that he's in such good hands when I'm not here."

CHAPTER 16

Amy stood in front of her hotel window looking out at the Atlanta skyline. Night had fallen, and she watched as some lightning flashed in the distance. She hated thunderstorms and hoped that what she was seeing was not going to come any closer.

Brad and Carolyn were at dinner with the mayor, so unless she got a phone call from them, she was off the clock for the evening. Feeling a little lonely, she decided to call her best friend back in Chicago. She sat down at the hotel room desk and pulled out her cell phone.

"Hi, Tina, it's me."

"Hey, Amy. It's great to hear your voice. I miss you. Lunch isn't the same without you here. I don't have anyone else I trust enough to complain to about work."

Amy listened as her friend filled her in on all the latest gossip.

"So how are things on your end?" Tina asked. "Life in the fast lane and all."

"That's an understatement. It's not just regular fast; it's speed of sound fast. Every morning I have to check the itinerary just to double check where I am."

"So where are you anyway?"

Amy spun her chair around so she could look out the window again. "Atlanta for a few days. The governor and his wife are having dinner with the mayor, so I have the night off. Usually when he doesn't have a dinner scheduled, we have strategy meetings in the evenings."

"That makes for a long day."

"You're telling me. But I love it. I'm so excited to be a part of this. I've never been happier in my life. This job is a dream come true."

"That's a big change from when you were working here."

Amy laughed. "I know. I used to dread getting out of bed every morning. Now I'm up before the alarm goes off. Instead of just going through the motions, now every day is different. It's just so exciting to be in the middle of something this big.

"Must be nice to feel that way."

"It is. I mean, if the governor gets elected, I'll have been a part of history. When I think about that, it just blows my mind."

"So is Governor Dreamy as great in person as he seems?"

"Even better," Amy gushed, warming to the subject. "He's so smart, and he's got such a great vision. He's really serious about making a change and leading this country in a new and better direction. He's going to make a wonderful president."

"I've been keeping an eye on the polls, and it looks like he just might pull it off."

"I know Brad's going to win. He's so well qualified and personable. The longer we campaign, the more supporters he's going to win over. Our numbers are just going to keep going up."

"So it's Brad now, huh? Are you on a first name basis?"

Amy could hear the teasing in her friend's voice. "Yes, although when we're out in public, I call him governor. But, in private, he's very laid back with his staff. From the beginning, he told us all to call him Brad." Amy paused. "Unlike his wife."

There was a moment of silence.

"So what's the deal there?" Tina asked. "What's she like?"

Amy hesitated, wondering if she was sharing too much, but then jumped in, not able to stop herself. "Kind of standoffish, although she puts up a great front in public. I mean, she's beautiful and articulate and everyone fawns all over her. But the minute the cameras are turned off, she just kind of retreats into her own little world."

"Really? I never would have guessed it from watching her on TV."

"I'm telling you, it's all just an act. I can give you an example. Today I went with her to this luncheon. She worked the room like a pro and gave a great speech. Everybody loved her. Then as soon as we were out of there, we run into this woman and her corgi. When I saw Mrs. Newcomb interact with the dog, I realized it was her first genuine moment of the day. She even admitted to me that she'd rather be with her animals than her husband!"

"You're kidding. She really said that?"

"I swear. I couldn't believe it myself. To be married to Brad and love her dogs more than him. She obviously doesn't deserve him."

"And are you telling me that you do?" Tina asked.

Amy was genuinely shocked. "Tina! How could you even ask me that? I've told you that I'd never have an affair with a married man."

"But, if he wasn't married…"

"Well, of course I'd be interested. Who wouldn't be? He's perfect. I've never met anyone like him. But he *is* married, so there's no point in even thinking about it."

CHAPTER 17

Two floors down from Amy, Ryan was sitting at his hotel desk working on his story. He struggled as he tried to come up with a fresh spin on the day's events. He had to admit to himself that he had enjoyed the first few weeks on the trail. But now that they were three months into it, other than the change of location, it seemed like every day was a monotonous repeat of the one before.

He was amazed that Brad could garner such enthusiasm every time he spoke, even when he was basically telling the same story over and over. *Maybe it's different when you're selling yourself,* he thought. *God knows, Brad certainly believes in himself and he's making others believe too.*

His brother's popularity numbers had continued to climb in every poll to the point that he was now one of two front runners. The first primary was about six months away and if his momentum continued, Brad could very well be the Democratic candidate for the President of the United States.

Ryan was genuinely excited for his brother. He knew how much Brad wanted to win this election, and he deserved it too. Watching his brother, Ryan knew that he was passionate about leading the country. And his ideas were sound. Most of the Democratic candidates had similar platforms, but Brad had made gun control and crime reduction his signature causes. He had championed strong gun control legislation in Illinois, and crime had plummeted. Even though it was a state issue, Brad felt that, as the nation's leader, he could push the states into following the same course.

And his ideas were catching on. Maybe it was because for the first time there was a clear example linking gun control to dramatically lower crime rates. Maybe it was that gang activity was spreading outside of the inner cities and gaining a stronghold in the suburbs and rural areas. Maybe it was that people were tired of being afraid to send their children to school, knowing that another Columbine could happen any day. Whatever the reason, for the first time in history, it seemed like the country was ready to pass gun control laws with teeth. And people admired Brad for taking such a strong stance. He was gaining a reputation for being a man with character – someone who would stand up for what he believed in regardless of the consequences.

Of course, as expected, there had been a huge backlash. The other Democratic candidates and the Republicans were both painting Brad as the candidate, who, if elected, would start chipping away at everyone's individual rights. And the NRA was frothing at the mouth. They had already started running ads attacking Brad.

On the positive side, Ryan thought that the various responses illustrated just how serious a contender his brother was. His opponents were genuinely worried that Brad would get elected. On the negative side, Ryan was stunned by how vicious some of the attacks were. He had seen the hate letters and witnessed the emotional protests. He used to think the term *gun fanatics* was just a label the liberals slapped on those people, until he saw firsthand the unadulterated hatred in the eyes of some of the protesters.

He had already written a number of articles about both his brother's ideas about gun control and the response he was getting, both for and against. Although he had tried to maintain a journalistic objectivity in his reporting, he was surprised to receive hate mail himself. Even though he had never stated his own support of Brad's ideas, people assumed that since he and Brad were brothers, he agreed with the candidate. It was a little disconcerting to be so closely associated with his brother again, just like when they were kids.

Ryan finished his article – this time he didn't touch on the gun control issue – and hit the send button to his editor. He picked up his phone to call his wife. As he listened to Michelle talk about her day, he was grateful to get a respite from the campaign talk he was surrounded with twenty-four/seven.

"So how about you?" Michelle asked. "How was your day?"

"The usual. I finished my story, so I thought I'd take a run and then watch some TV. I sure wish you were here."

"Me, too. Actually I wish you were home."

"Even better. I was thinking I'd talk to my editor about a vacation. I could really use a week or so away from here. I'm getting pretty burned out."

"That would be wonderful. Would you want to go somewhere or just come home?"

Ryan thought for a moment before answering. "I know that you could probably use a trip, but to be honest, I'd love to just be at home. But whatever you want to do is fine with me. I just want to be with you."

"Why don't you find out how much time off you could get? Say it was a week. Then maybe we could do a getaway weekend and spend the rest of the week at home."

"Sounds great. I'll call Marty tomorrow."

"Okay, I'll talk to you then. I love you."

"I love you too, honey."

Ryan hung up the phone and looked out the window. The storms in the distance had moved even farther away. He put on his gym shoes, anxious to leave his hotel room. He was beginning to feel like a caged animal. A run would give him a momentary escape, but as he had told Michelle, he needed more than that.

CHAPTER 18

Terry had his laptop open, making detailed notes covering every minute of Brad's day. Meticulously, he entered every contact that the candidate had made – names, addresses, phone numbers, and emails. Terry would pass these names onto Brad's son, Tyler, who would follow up with email requests for campaign donations. Tyler and his sister, Emily, had joined the campaign staff for the summer when they had finished their school year. Terry thought Tyler had done a great job designing his father's website. They were generating more and more hits every day, and the donations were streaming in.

Emily was writing a daily blog covering the campaign trail, which had caught on with the younger crowd. Between Ryan's newspaper articles reaching the older population and Emily's blog hitting the young, the campaign was reaching a wide breadth of potential voters. And that was on top of the mainstream media exposure they were getting. As Brad had surged ahead in the polls, he and the other Democratic frontrunner were getting the lion's share of coverage on the TV and radio stations and in the newspapers and magazines.

And the more coverage Brad received, the more in demand he was. At the beginning of the campaign, Terry was calling in every favor they had to schedule meetings and fundraisers. Now his phone was ringing off the hook with requests for Brad to make appearances around the country. Everyone wanted a chance to bend the ear of the man who just might get elected to the highest office in the land.

When Terry was through recapping the day's events, he switched gears to focus on tomorrow's agenda. First he sent email reminders to everyone Brad was scheduled to meet with; then he followed up with voice mail messages. When he was finished with those, he repeated the same process for meetings scheduled three days ahead.

It was close to midnight when Terry was finished. Exhausted from the day's activities, he stood up on wobbly legs and stumbled over to his hotel window. Pressing his hands against the window frame for support, he looked out over the city. Most of the buildings' windows were dark, and there were only a few cars on the streets.

Terry's mind wandered back to when he had been Brad's chief of staff in the governor's office. He had thought he had been busy then, but that was nothing compared to how he felt now where the days had become one big blur.

Brad had suggested adding more people to the campaign staff, specifically to take some of the pressure off him, but Terry had refused. He didn't want to relinquish any of the control he had. He viewed himself as the mastermind behind Brad's campaign, and he wanted his own fingerprint on everything the candidate touched.

When Brad had first discussed his desire to run for president with him, Terry had been more convinced than anyone else on earth that his friend could be elected. Now that they were a few months into the campaign, Terry was even more certain that Brad was destined to be president. It had become an obsession, and no matter how high Brad might climb in the polls, Terry wasn't going to take his foot off the accelerator until the last vote was counted. Getting Brad elected was Terry's whole life now, and nothing was going to stand in their way.

CHAPTER 19

February: Nine Months to Go

Brad stepped out of the heated SUV and into the brutal Wisconsin air. It was the middle of February, and the air temperature was six degrees below zero. He was wearing a wool suit and overcoat, but no hat or gloves. After all, impressions were everything. He didn't want his face hidden from the cameras or gloves on when he was shaking hands with his supporters.

Within a minute or two, he was sure his face was beet red and he could feel his eyes watering. He surreptitiously swiped the tears away. He certainly didn't want to look like he was crying in tomorrow's newspapers. He looked up to locate the building's entrance -- about fifty feet away. His legs moved woodenly toward the warmth as his outstretched arm shook hand after hand. Forty feet to go. Thirty feet to go. Almost there. What were these crazy people doing, standing out in the cold anyway? he wondered. They must be used to it, and they were certainly dressed for it. Bulky down coats, ski caps, thick gloves that made their fingers look like pork sausages, and almost all wore the bright green and mustard yellow colors of the Green Bay Packers.

They were at the Knights of Columbus hall in downtown Green Bay. This was where Terry had decided they should ride out the evening while they waited for the results of the primary. *We'll be in the heart of the heartland,* Terry had told him. *Right in the middle of mom, dad, apple pie and the American flag.* He got the apple pie right, along with cheese, beer, more cheese and beer, and people who looked like walking heart attacks waiting to happen.

With the Secret Service helping to clear a path, Brad made it to the doorway and staggered into the vestibule. Peeling off his coat, he handed it to Amy, squeezing her hand. "Find a place to hang that, and then bring me a glass of warm water. My throat is raw."

"Right away," Amy said eagerly, her eyes searching for a coat rack.

Brad turned to where he could hear a crowd gathered. With a few quick strides, he stood in the doorway of the meeting room. Pausing for effect, he allowed time for his supporters to notice him, and he was rewarded with a burst of applause.

"Hello, Wisconsin!" Brad yelled, pumping his fist into the air. "Are we going to win this primary?"

"Damn straight!" someone shouted, and the room erupted with cheers and whistles.

Brad motioned for Carolyn to join him, and then he lifted his arms like a Baptist preacher addressing his congregation. "Carolyn and I just want to thank you all for your hard work over the last several months. As we gather here this evening waiting for the results to come in, I know that I've had the hardest working group of people right here in Wisconsin behind me every step of the way."

The crowd cheered. Brad lowered his arms and stood patiently, waiting for the right time to jump in again. "As you know, it all started with the Iowa caucuses, where we won big. Then on to New Hampshire, where we finished a strong second. And since then, we've finished in first or second place in every primary and racked up more wins than any other candidate. And we're going to continue that winning streak here in the great state of Wisconsin."

Brad waited, allowing his audience to cheer for their home state. "But this isn't a time to get complacent. We've still got a long road ahead of us, and Super Tuesday is just a couple of weeks away. But all that matters right now, this very minute, is that we bring it home right here in Wisconsin."

As the crowd began to chant his name, Brad stood, basking in the limelight. After a few minutes, he lifted his arms once more. "Thank you all."

The candidate kissed his wife on the cheek and then they separated, both circulating among the supporters. Like a heat-seeking missile, Brad zeroed in on the prettiest woman in the room. He cupped her hand in both of his, his eyes looking deeply into hers as she introduced herself. "It's nice to meet you, Melissa. Thank you so much for being here."

"It's an honor to meet you. I'm such a big fan."

When Brad released her hand, he slipped the piece of paper she had passed to him into his pocket. He knew he would find her name and phone number scribbled on it. By the time he finished going around the room, his pocket would be jammed full of hopeful notes. Unfortunately, when he got to his hotel room, he would have to dump them all into his wastebasket. *What a waste of some prime ass,* he thought.

The evening wore on with Brad making a point to meet and greet every single supporter in the room. There were a few TV sets scattered around, all tuned to CNN. Several times his conversations were interrupted as the news anchor announced the latest primary results. At around midnight, enough of the votes had been calculated to name a winner. "And with forty-two percent of the vote in Wisconsin, Brad Newcomb has claimed another primary victory," the anchor intoned.

As the room exploded with cheers, Brad raised his hands over his head, his fingers in the victory sign. Looking around, he spotted Carolyn making her way toward Ryan, Terry and Amy, who were clustered in a tight group. He began to snake his way across the room to join them, as ecstatic supporters reached out to him, patting him on the back and pumping his arm like a slot machine.

When he reached his wife and staff, Brad hugged each of them. "Before we leave, I want to say good night to our biggest contributors. Carolyn, why don't you join me?" He turned to his assistant. "Amy, we'll need about twenty minutes to wrap things up here. Can you let the Secret Service know we'll be ready to leave then?"

Brad and Carolyn made their final circuit around the room before heading out into the vestibule. Helping his wife with her coat, Brad whispered in her ear. "We did it again, Mrs. Newcomb. Shall we go back to the hotel room and celebrate?"

Carolyn nodded as she smiled up at her husband. The couple walked out the front door and started toward the SUV.

"I can't believe there are still people hanging around in this cold," Brad whispered to his wife, looking at the small group of people clustered outside. As he stepped forward, his arm outstretched to shake more hands, he saw a glint of steel as a man pulled a handgun out from under his jacket. Instinctively Brad jumped back, his hands raised to cover his face. A primordial scream escaped his lips as a shot rang out.

CHAPTER 20

People talk about their lives flashing before their eyes, but for Brad, everything just went blank. He was at the bottom of a dark cave, with no light, no sound, no smell -- just nothingness. And then suddenly, he was in the middle of confusion, commotion, craziness. He was pushed to the ground with a body covering his and a voice yelling in his ear, "Stay down! Stay down!"

He heard the sounds of a struggle, bodies being thrown to the ground, grunts of exertion. "Grab him! Cuff him! Get the gun!"

He heard screams, first loud and then fading, and pounding on the pavement as the crowd ran for cover.

He heard Carolyn calling out to him, her voice laced with hysteria. "Brad, are you all right? Brad, say something!"

And then he felt a drop and something sticky oozing down his face. In a panic, he began to struggle. His hand came up, frantically wiping at his face. Looking down, he saw the vibrant red and started screaming, "Help me! I've been shot!"

Mustering all his strength, he rolled out from under the body pinning him down. Then he looked at the agent who lay next to him, and he realized where the blood was coming from. The man lay still, his eyes closed, his face white, a dark stain spreading out from his shoulder and trickling onto the pavement.

Crablike, Brad scrambled back from the unconscious man before being yanked to his feet by another agent. Like a ragdoll, he was tossed into the back of the SUV. The driver stomped on the gas pedal and the candidate was thrown back into the seat cushions.

"Get me out of here!" Brad yelled.

"I will, sir, just hang on," the driver said, as the car accelerated. "Don't worry about your family. The other agents will take care of them."

Brad sank down into the car seat, his head rolling back, his eyes closing. Now the flashbacks came. Not of his life, but of the scene he had just escaped from. "Jesus," he muttered.

His eyes popped open and he leaned forward, grabbing onto the front seat. "That agent -- he took a bullet for me."

"He did his job, sir. When we get you back to the hotel, I'll radio the agents at the scene. I'll find out if…" The driver paused. "I'll check on him, sir. I'll let you know."

Brad leaned back, cradling his head in his arms. He didn't move or speak until the car pulled in front of the hotel. The driver opened his door and walked him briskly through the lobby, into the elevator, and down the hall to his suite. With the door closed and locked behind them, the driver reached for his radio.

Brad poured himself a stiff drink and sank into the sofa. He gulped the whiskey down and then sat cradling the empty glass like an injured bird.

He heard the driver speaking in hushed tones and then the man came and stood over him. "Your family and staff are all fine, sir. They're in a car on their way here now."

The candidate looked up. "And the agent?"

"He was alive when the ambulance picked him up. He's on his way to the hospital now. They'll call us with a report as soon as they know anything."

Brad nodded. "Let me know as soon as you hear from them."

"Can I get you another drink?"

"No, I'm fine." Brad handed him the empty glass. "You can take this."

A few minutes later, the door opened and the candidate leapt to his feet. His wife burst through the doorway and Brad ran to her. They held each other tight as Carolyn sobbed, her face burrowed into her husband's chest.

Brad lifted his head and saw a circle of eyes boring into him. Ryan's face was white, his front teeth biting down onto his lower lip. Amy stood next to him, her arms wrapped tightly around her trembling body as tears streamed down her face. Terry was the only one whose face was a mask, although his hands, clenched into fists, told another story.

Brad felt Carolyn push herself back from him and he looked down into her eyes. Her hands reached up and cradled his face.

"I was so scared," she said. "I heard you say you were shot."

The candidate shook his head. "No, I'm fine. I saw the blood and for a minute I thought it was mine."

"Thank God you're all right. I don't know what I would have done..."

Brad took her hands in his and kissed them. "I'm right here."

"Oh, honey. What have we gotten ourselves into? Is this really worth it?"

CHAPTER 21

Brad stood in front of the hotel ballroom ready to begin his press conference. It was ten o'clock the morning after the assassination attempt, and there wasn't an empty seat in the room. He could feel the electricity in the air, and he was going to milk it for all it was worth.

"Good morning. As you know, an attempt was made on my life yesterday night. In an act of true courage, Tom O'Brien, a Secret Service agent, threw himself in front of me and intercepted the bullet. He was shot in the shoulder and underwent surgery last night. The reports I have this morning are that the operation went well and the doctors expect him to make a full recovery.

"I will never be able to fully express my gratitude for what this brave young man did. My family and I are forever in his debt. I ask that you all join me in praying for Tom O'Brien and his wife and three children."

Brad lowered his head in prayer for a few minutes before continuing. "The man who shot at me last night was apprehended at the scene by the quick actions of another Secret Service agent who prefers to remain anonymous. I am equally indebted to this agent for his role in saving my life and that of several other innocent bystanders who were with me.

"The name of the man who attempted to kill me is John McBride. I will not be politically correct and refer to him as the 'alleged' perpetrator." Brad used his fingers to connote quotation marks. "John McBride pointed a gun in my face and fired at me, and I can tell you that there is nothing alleged about that. I have no doubt that his intention was to kill me. And I have no doubt that it was to silence me in my crusade for responsible gun control. In their initial interviews with Mr. McBride, the FBI confirms that this was his stated agenda. In addition, a search of his house was conducted last night. Several guns were found, including many that would be illegal to own under the laws I signed into effect in Illinois and will try to enact throughout this country if elected president.

"I have had several people ask me whether this attempted assassination on my life will make me drop out of the presidential race. The answer is unequivocally no. Others have asked whether this will make me back off from my stand on gun control. And again, my answer is absolutely not. In fact, this man's actions have only made me more determined that we as a country need to put an end to the violence. The violence that is a direct result of our current lack of effective gun control.

"I want everyone in this country to know that I will not allow the actions of this man to deter me from what I know is right. I will continue to fight for effective gun control. And I will continue to fight for your vote so that I can work to pass those gun control laws. If I am elected president, I promise you that I will make it my mission to make every law-abiding citizen in this country feel safer. Safer when you are taking a walk through your neighborhood, safer when a stranger comes to your door, safer when you send your children to school, safer in your bed at night. The time has come for all Americans to unite in this cause, and with your votes, I would like to be the one to lead the way."

Brad looked out into the ballroom and nodded. "Thank you all for being here this morning, and I would now like to open the platform up to your questions."

There was a flurry of raised hands as the reporters shouted out for the candidate's attention. It was over an hour before Brad finished, but he stayed until every last question had been answered. After the press left, Brad pulled Ryan, Amy, and Terry into a private conference room.

"I've been reviewing your schedule," Terry said. "I can make a few phone calls and cancel --"

"We're not cancelling anything," Brad interrupted. "I meant everything I said in there. The last thing we need to do is to make any changes to my schedule or platform that could be interpreted as motivated by fear." He looked at his staff, meeting their eyes one by one. "Now I understand if any of you need to take a few days off, maybe go home."

Terry jumped in first. "I'm with you. I'm not going anywhere. I'll tell you one thing though. If the Secret Service hadn't caught that bastard, I would have personally chased him down and choked the life out of him with my own bare hands."

Brad reached forward and put his hand on Terry's shoulder. "Thanks, Terry. Let's not let anyone else hear you say that, but between us, I appreciate your loyalty."

Brad turned to Amy. "How about you? Would you like to go back to Chicago for a few days?"

"Absolutely not, Brad. I'm not leaving you either." She bit her lip. "It's not that I'm not afraid, because to be honest I am. The shooting yesterday was the most horrible thing I've ever experienced. But I'm with you. I'm not going to let some lunatic scare me away from what we're doing here."

Brad hugged her. "I'm sorry you had to go through that, but I'm glad you're sticking with me."

He stepped away from Amy and looked at Ryan. "That leaves you, bro. What are you going to do?"

Ryan's eyes gleamed. "Are you kidding? This is the biggest story we've had since the campaign started. Don't get me wrong – what happened was horrific, but this sure beats writing about your latest jump in the polls. I was so juiced yesterday; I stayed up all night writing my story."

Ryan laughed. "Nothing like having a gun pointed at your face to get the adrenaline pumping. I didn't mention this before, but I was the one standing right behind you last night. When Tom tackled you, I came face-to-face with that guy. I thought he was going to kill me."

"I'm sorry," Brad said. "I didn't realize. Are you okay?"

Ryan shrugged. "I'm still standing. In fact, I must be in pretty good shape, because if I were going to have a heart attack, it would have happened then. I guess we Newcombs are hard to get rid of. Of course, if I'm going to continue to shadow you, I think I might take some martial arts training so I'm prepared to put down the next would-be assassin." He jumped into a karate position. "Hi ya!"

Brad punched Ryan in the arm. "My little brother – the crusader. Maybe I can get the Secret Service to put you on staff."

"Seems like that's the least you can do if I'm going to take a bullet for you. All kidding aside though, how's Carolyn doing? She was pretty shaken up last night."

"Not good. She's flying back home today and she's made arrangements for the kids to join her for a few days. Personally, I think they'd be better off staying at school and keeping busy. I don't see the point in them all gathering just to stare at each other. But that's what she thinks is best, so I'm not going to stand in her way."

Amy's eyes widened. "That's terrible, Brad. She should be here with you. You're the one who almost got killed. How could she just leave you like that?"

Her hand flew to her mouth. "Oh, God. I shouldn't have said anything. It's not my place. I'm really sorry." She stepped back. "I'm going up to my room for a while. I'll meet you in the lobby when it's time to go." She turned and fled.

Brad watched her go and then looked at Terry and Ryan. "I guess we're all a little on edge. I'm glad I can always count on you guys to have my back."

CHAPTER 22

Carolyn was zipping up her luggage when she heard the door to the hotel suite open. She watched as her husband stepped through the doorway. They faced each other like two boxers sizing up the competition before a match.

Carolyn broke the silence. "My flight leaves in two hours. There's still time for you to change your mind and come with me."

Brad held up his hands. "I don't want to get into another fight. I told you that I'm not going to do anything that can be seen as a sign of weakness. Nobody's going to vote for a commander-in-chief who goes scurrying home at the first sign of trouble."

"First sign of trouble!" Carolyn exclaimed. "Someone tried to kill you yesterday! We both could have died. No one's going to think the worse of you for going home to spend a few days with your family."

She walked over to Brad and took his hands, her eyes pleading. "Please come with me. I need you."

Brad squeezed her hands and then released them, stepping back. "I'm sorry, but I have to stay here."

"If you won't do it for me, do it for the kids."

"The kids are fine. You know I talked to both of them last night and again this morning. They support my decision to stay on the trail."

"They're just telling you what they know you want to hear. Do you really think this hasn't affected them at all? Don't you understand that they need to see you? You need to be with them, to reassure them."

Brad shook his head. "I think the best thing for them would be to stay at school, go to class and get on with their lives. Your flying them home is going to make this a bigger deal than it is."

"It *is* a big deal, Brad. And pretending it's not is not healthy for anybody."

The candidate held up his hand. "Look, I'm not changing my mind."

"Fine. I'll call you when I get home." Carolyn grabbed her suitcase and stormed out of the suite.

* * *

Carolyn was pacing the living room floor, her three corgis following at her heels, when Emily came in. She rushed to hug her daughter. "Oh, sweetie. I'm so glad you're here."

Emily hugged her back. "Me, too. I really needed to see you. I just wish that Dad was here too."

Carolyn took a step back. "I know. I do, too. But he just didn't feel as though he could leave the campaign trail. He thought it would reflect badly on him."

"I know. I understand. I just wish we could all be home together." Emily's eyes filled with tears. "After you called me last night, I turned on the TV and watched the news footage. I know you told me not to, but I couldn't stop myself. And it was so awful. Even though it was all over by then, I felt so scared for you and Dad."

"But you know I'm okay and so is he. And the Secret Service is going to bump up our protection. Nothing's going to happen to us, I promise." Carolyn squeezed her daughter's hand. "Why don't you go upstairs and unpack?"

Emily nodded. "Okay. When does Tyler's plane get in?"

"Not for a few hours still."

"I've got a bunch of homework to do. Why don't you go ride for a while until he gets here? I know how that helps clear your head."

"I think I will. Then when Tyler gets here, we can all spend some time together."

Carolyn's eyes filled with tears as she watched her daughter leave. She was so angry with Brad for not coming home with her. She stood for a few minutes before picking up the phone and calling down to the barn. When the groom answered, she asked him to get her horse tacked up and then, hanging up, she called to her dogs. "Come on, girls, let's go to the barn."

When the dogs heard her words, they raced after her, barking excitedly. A half hour later, dressed in her riding clothes, Carolyn walked up the barn aisle. Alberto handed her the reins and then gave her a leg up. Pressing her legs into her horse's sides, she trotted him to the indoor riding ring.

She began to work her horse, putting him through some warm-up exercises. She tried to focus, but she kept thinking about her fight with Brad. She picked up a canter and steered her horse to a jump. Just before they reached it, the horse ran out to the side. Carolyn flew out of the saddle and landed in the middle of the fence. She felt a horrible pain shoot through her leg and then everything went dark.

CHAPTER 23

It was the middle of the night, and the hospital lights were dimmed when Brad stepped off the elevator. Visiting hours were long past, but when you were the governor, accommodations could always be made.

He stopped at the nurse's station to get the latest report. He had already spoken to the doctors earlier. Carolyn had a broken leg, which would take at least eight weeks to heal – which meant at least eight weeks off the campaign trail. She also had a mild concussion, which was why she was spending a night or two in the hospital for observation.

"Good evening, Governor," the nurse said. "It's such an honor to meet you."

"Thank you, Susan," Brad replied, eyeing her name tag. He gave her his patented two-handed handshake. "How is my wife doing?"

"I just checked on her a few minutes ago. She's sleeping now, although we've been waking her periodically because of the concussion. As long as there are no complications with that, I would guess the doctors will release her tomorrow or the next day."

"That's great. I know she's in good hands here."

The nurse blushed.

"May I go in and see her now?" Brad asked. "I'd like to just sit with her until she wakes up."

"Of course, Governor. That would be fine. She's in room three nineteen, right down that hallway." Susan pointed and then turned back to Brad. "And may I say something? I really hope you get elected president."

"Thank you. It's because of hard-working people like you that I'm in this race. I really appreciate your support." Brad flashed a warm smile, before turning to find his wife's room.

His footsteps echoed eerily in the deserted hallway. When he got to Carolyn's room, he tiptoed in so as not to wake her. He moved silently to her bedside and stood, looking down at her. Other than her broken leg being immobilized, her breathing was even and her face looked peaceful. He lingered for a few minutes, watching her sleep. Then he shook his head, thinking this was not a distraction that he wanted or needed in the middle of the campaign.

With a sigh, he turned and walked toward the guest chair. He moved it closer to Carolyn's bed before sitting down. Taking off his shoes, he propped his feet up gently onto the bed, checking to make sure the jostling didn't wake her. When she didn't move, he sank further into the chair and fell asleep within minutes.

A few hours later, Brad jumped when he felt a hand on his shoulder. Opening his eyes, he saw that the morning light was beginning to filter into the room. He lifted his head and saw the nurse who had been on duty when he arrived.

"I'm sorry to wake you, Governor. I'm here to check on your wife. Has she woken up since you've been here?"

"Not that I know, but I've been lights-out myself."

He watched as the nurse turned to the bed. She reached down and shook her patient's shoulder. Carolyn's eyes flew open, and she stared around her with a look of confusion.

"Ma'am, do you know where you are?"

There was a slight hesitation as Carolyn's eyebrows knitted. Then her features relaxed. "Yes, I'm in the hospital."

She lifted her head and saw Brad. "Oh, honey, you're here." Her eyes filled with tears as she reached her hand out to him.

He jumped up from the chair and came to her side. Taking her hand, he bent over and kissed her forehead. "Of course, I'm here, sweetheart. How are you?"

Carolyn filled him in for a few minutes before the nurse interrupted. "I need to ask you a few more questions, Mrs. Newcomb."

Susan went through a checklist, verifying that Carolyn appeared lucid. Then she took a penlight and checked Carolyn's pupils. When she was finished, she smiled. "Everything looks normal. My shift is over soon, but I'll be back this evening. It was really nice to meet both of you, even if it was under these circumstances."

Brad and Carolyn thanked her and then watched her leave. When she was gone, Brad sat down in the guest chair. "So the doctors tell me that your leg was broken in three different places. They don't think you'll be able to travel for at least eight weeks."

"I know. I can't believe this happened."

"How *did* it happen? You haven't fallen off a horse for years."

"I don't even know. It happened so fast. I was heading for a jump and then suddenly, Dexter ran out. He never does that."

Brad leaned forward in the chair, his hands gripping the armrests. "Did you fall on purpose? To keep both of us off the campaign trail?"

"Brad! I can't believe you would even ask me that." Carolyn's eyes widened with shock. "Of course, I didn't."

"It just seems awfully convenient that just after the shooting, just after we have a huge fight over your wanting to spend some time off the trail, this happens." Brad shook his head. "I'm going to have to stay in town at least until you get out of the hospital, so I don't look like a shitty husband. And you get to stay home for another two months. I can't believe you did this to me."

"I didn't do anything on purpose. It was an accident. Do you really think I'd risk my life just to keep you off the trail for a few days? You're being totally unreasonable."

"All I know, Carolyn, is that you've gotten exactly what you wanted." Brad leapt out of the chair and turned for the door. "I'm going home to spend some time with the kids."

CHAPTER 24

Super Tuesday or, as the political pundits were calling it, Tsunami Tuesday came two weeks after the assassination attempt. Brad had hit the campaign trail the same day Carolyn was released from the hospital, after making sure that there were plenty of photos taken with him accompanying his wife home.

It had been a wild two weeks with the candidate crisscrossing the country, trying to make an appearance in almost every one of the twenty states heading to the voting booths. When he woke up the morning of the primary, it took longer than usual to remember where he was. California. With fifty-five electoral votes on the line, over ten percent of the total, there wasn't a more critical place for him to be.

Brad rolled out of bed and immediately began pacing the hotel room floor. The adrenaline surging through his system was stronger than three pots of Columbian dark roast. He ordered room service and jumped in the shower. When the cart rolled in twenty minutes later, he was fully dressed. He wolfed down his breakfast, his fork in his right hand, the TV remote in his left, as he tried to catch every broadcast and cable networks' take on the day.

They were all in agreement that he was the frontrunner. His polling numbers had skyrocketed after the assassination attempt. He had been interviewed by every major national news organization, as well as the local media in the markets he had travelled to. He couldn't have paid for better publicity. The candidate had been described as strong, courageous, a leader, and best of all, presidential. His own advertising didn't even gush as much as the so-called objective journalists.

The only proverbial fly in the ointment was Carolyn's absence, especially when Brad considered how many more cities they could have covered in the last couple of weeks if she was on the trail. He had made it a point to call her every day, but their conversations were strained. He tried to keep the anger out of his voice, but they both knew it was simmering below the surface.

Brad's thoughts were interrupted by a knock on the hotel room door. Checking his watch, he assumed it was one of his staff. They were scheduled to meet at seven, and it was a few minutes before that. He looked out the peephole, a precaution he took ever since the shooting, and felt his heart skip a beat when he saw it was Amy. He was finding the vow of fidelity he had taken when he had started his presidential run harder and harder to keep.

"Good morning, Amy," he said, flinging open the door. "How do you always manage to look so gorgeous first thing in the morning?"

Amy stepped through the doorway, allowing the door to close behind her. "I had plenty of time to get gorgeous. I was up before five. I just couldn't sleep; I'm so excited about today."

"Me, too. Excited and nervous. Everything rests on today. If I can pull out a big win, I could be close to locking up the nomination."

Amy reached out and squeezed Brad's arm. "I know you're going win – and not just today's primaries, but the party nomination and the general election after that. You're everything the country needs in a president."

Brad covered Amy's hand with his own. "You know as well as anyone how much the presidency means to me. I really feel like I can make a difference if I get elected."

"You will. And I'm just so thankful that you gave me the opportunity to be a part of it all."

Brad cupped her chin in his hand, his eyes riveted on hers. He was tired of being a Boy Scout. "I couldn't have made it this far without you. You've been my right hand from the beginning."

As he leaned in toward her, his mouth inches from hers, there was a knock on the door. Brad and Amy both jumped back, a look of alarm passing between them, as though whoever was at the door could see through it. When he let Terry in a few seconds later, Brad's face was a mask.

* * *

The celebration party lasted well into the night. Brad had taken seventeen out of the twenty states. It was a bigger landslide than anyone had projected. Suddenly the talk wasn't about *if* he was going to win the party nomination, it was *when*. It might have only read March on the calendar, but the results of the Democratic National Convention in August were looking like a foregone conclusion.

For the first time since Brad had started his presidential run, he allowed himself to cut loose. And as he looked around the party, he realized he wasn't the only one. After all the tension leading up to the big day, there was a total feeling of relief now that it was behind them. He watched as someone cranked up the music and started a conga line. As the dancers snaked their way toward him, he felt someone grab him around the waist and push him to the back of the line. Turning around, he grinned when he saw it was Amy.

When the song ended, the dancers cheered and called for more. Brad leaned down and whispered in Amy's ear. "Wait fifteen minutes after I leave the party. Then come to my room."

He heard Amy gasp and saw her eyes open wide. His lips brushed her cheek. "I want you more than anything in the world right now. More than this election. Please, Amy, come to me."

Amy closed her eyes. "I'll be there," she breathed.

CHAPTER 25

April: Seven Months to Go

A month had passed since Super Tuesday. Since the start of the campaign, Brad's staff had grown exponentially, and now included a media consultant, a political strategist, and several aides with expertise and connections in different parts of the country. But Brad's inner circle remained the same -- Terry, Amy and Ryan, with the obvious absence of Carolyn, who was still at home mending her broken leg.

It was this group that was gathered over dinner at an Italian restaurant. Brad had selected a nice bottle of wine – a sign that the dinner was more about a relaxing evening out than a strategy meeting. The waiter brought the bottle to the table and poured a small amount into Brad's glass. The candidate tasted it and nodded his approval.

When the waiter had filled all their glasses, Brad lifted his for a toast. "To you three. I don't thank you enough for all you do. But I know I couldn't be here without you. Cheers."

They clinked glasses and each took a sip. Brad set his glass on the table and cleared his throat. "So I'm just going to say a couple of things about the campaign and then the subject's closed for the evening."

He looked around the table. "We have three months until the convention. Unless something crazy happens, I'm going to get the nomination. Which means we have to start looking down the road. We'll continue to make appearances in the states that have upcoming primaries, but our focus has to be on November now. For the last several elections, the final vote between the Democratic and Republican candidates has been neck and neck. I want to change that. I want to be the candidate the clear majority of the country supports."

He took a sip of wine before continuing. "The Republicans' hands are tied. They're going to nominate the vice-president. And I just don't think he's got the personality to rally the country around him. Which means it's our election to lose. We can do this."

He paused, looking around the table. Terry was nodding his head emphatically. Amy's eyes were lit up like candles, and she wore a wide smile on her face. Brad could see that even Ryan, usually the objective one, was drinking the Kool-Aid.

Brad continued. "I couldn't have gotten this far without each of you. And I'm going to need you even more down the final stretch."

"I'm not going anywhere," Terry said. "Not until I escort you to the White House on inauguration day."

"Me, too," Amy piped in. "I'm here whenever you need me." Underneath the table, Brad felt her bare foot rub up and down his leg, making a brief but emphatic statement at his crotch.

Brad winked at her. "I knew I could count on you." He turned to Ryan. "How about you, bro? Are you going to make it to the end?"

Ryan looked around the table. "You all know this assignment was not something I asked for. And it's been really hard for me to be away from Michelle all these months." He paused, meeting Brad's eyes. "But I can honestly say that I'm glad I'm here. I believe in what you stand for, and I'm proud to be part of the team that's going to get you elected."

Ryan raised his wine glass. "To the next president of the United States."

Brad leaned across the table and clinked his glass with Ryan's. "Thanks, bro. That means a lot to me."

For the rest of the meal, the topics ranged from sports to movies to books – anything and everything except politics. After they finished eating, Brad signaled for the check. "I was thinking about renting a movie in my hotel room tonight. Anyone want to join me?"

Terry shook his head. "I've got work to do tonight."

"Me, too," Ryan said. "I haven't finished my story yet."

Brad looked at Amy. "I guess that leaves you. How about it?"

"I'd love to watch a movie – as long as I get to pick. Nothing with aliens or car chases."

"It's a deal," Brad said. "Your choice, as long as it's not too sappy."

Ryan smiled. "I bet Amy loves a good sappy movie."

Amy shrugged. "I do. I admit it. I'm a sucker for a good love story."

"I thought you might be the romantic type," Ryan said. "In fact, if I didn't know better, I'd think you had a little crush on my big brother here."

Amy's eyes widened.

"That's not funny, Ryan," Brad said, his jaw tightening. "A joke like that could cost me the election."

Ryan raised his hand. "Lighten up. I was just teasing. Everyone knows you'd never cheat on Carolyn." He turned to Amy. "I'm sorry. It must be the wine talking."

"It's okay." Amy stood up. "I'm going to the ladies' room before we leave."

Ryan pushed his chair back. "I'll make a pit stop too."

As they left the table, Brad could hear Ryan apologizing to Amy again.

When they were out of earshot, Terry turned to Brad. "Any truth to that? I see how she looks at you, and I know things aren't so great on the home front."

The last thing Brad wanted was a lecture from Terry about the dangers of an affair. He shook his head. "I don't know if she has a thing for me or not. But I can tell you that even if she did, there's nothing going on between us." He squeezed Terry's shoulder. "You have my word on that."

CHAPTER 26

May: Six Months to Go

It was a glorious North Carolina day, the sun beaming down on the throng of Duke graduates. It was hard to find Emily in the sea of matching caps and gowns.

"I think I've got her," Ryan said, holding his binoculars rigid as Carolyn slid closer to him and peered through the lens.

"I see her!" Carolyn exclaimed. "She looks so happy." She watched her daughter for a few minutes before sitting up straight again. "I can't believe she's graduating. It seems like I was just pushing her in a stroller yesterday. Where did all the years go?"

"God, Mom. You're not going to get all teary-eyed, are you?" Tyler asked.

Carolyn playfully tapped her son's shoulder with her program. "If I can't cry at my daughter's graduation, when can I? Just wait till it's your day – my *baby!*"

Tyler shook his head, blushing. "Dad, make her stop."

"Not me, son," Brad said. "This is a big day for your mother. For all of us. I'm glad we're all here together." He reached over and took his wife's hand.

"I'm just relieved my leg's healed and the doctor has okayed me for traveling," Carolyn said. "There's no way I would have missed being here today."

"Does that mean you're going to join us on the campaign trail again?" Brad asked.

Carolyn pulled her hand out of her husband's grasp and folded her arms. "You're doing so well, it hardly seems like you need me."

Brad's eyes narrowed. "Everybody understands that you've been home recovering from your accident. But you're going to need to make some appearances soon before the media start asking questions."

Carolyn shifted uncomfortably. "Let's not talk about this now. I want to focus on Emily. This is *her* day."

"Well, speaking of Emily, she told me that she's anxious to join me on the trail again. She's going to start writing her blog, and this time she won't have to give it up at the end of the summer. Now that she's graduated, she can work on the campaign until the end."

"I know," Carolyn said. "She told me. And I'm happy for both of you."

"Don't forget about me," Tyler said. "You want me back this summer, don't you, Dad?"

"Of course, son," Brad said.

Tyler picked at some imaginary lint on his khakis. "I've been thinking about taking next semester off so I could stay on through November." He looked up nervously.

"That would be great!" Brad said. "I'd love to have you with me through the election."

Carolyn shook her head. "Let's not get ahead of ourselves, Tyler. Why don't we wait until the convention before we make any decisions? Your dad may not get the nomination and even if he does, I'm not sure I want you to take time off from school."

"I have the electoral votes locked up," Brad said. "You know that. And this is a once in a lifetime opportunity. If Tyler wants to be with me, then he should do it. He'll learn a lot from this experience. As much as if he were sitting in a classroom." Brad paused. "Besides, maybe if the kids were with me, we could lure you back to the trail."

"I said we'd talk about that later," Carolyn said.

"Fine," Brad said, standing up. "I've got to go make a phone call."

"Of course you do," Carolyn sighed. "Just make sure you're back before the ceremony starts."

As Brad made his way past his family, he noticed a look pass between Ryan and Michelle. Great, he thought. Now my brother knows things aren't so rosy between Carolyn and me. I hope that doesn't make its way into one of his columns.

Finding a quiet spot, Brad hit a speed dial on his cell phone. When he heard Amy answer, he closed his eyes. "Hey, baby. I just needed to hear your voice."

CHAPTER 27

Emily sat at the desk in her hotel room, working on her latest blog. Since joining the campaign trail after graduation, her days had been jam-packed as she followed her dad as he went from one event to the next. Whenever they took a break, she would take out her laptop and start blogging. She could understand why her Uncle Ryan loved journalism. She got a thrill out of putting her thoughts into words and watching as her number of followers grew each day.

This evening, her dad had a dinner scheduled, but the rest of the staff was free. Emily planned to finish her blog, order some room service, and curl up with a good book. As she closed her laptop, her cell phone rang.

"Hey, Emily. It's Amy. Do you want to grab some dinner? I hear there's a good Mexican place nearby."

Emily hesitated. "Sure. I was going to eat in my room, but I guess I could go for some Mexican. Did you invite Tyler and Ryan?"

"No. I thought it would be fun to just have a girl's night out. Order some margaritas and let our hair down. If I decide to dance on some tables, I don't want it to make it into your uncle's column tomorrow."

Emily laughed. "How do you know I won't put it into my blog?"

"Because I'm only going to hop up on the table if you join me."

"Yeah, Dad would love that. The candidate's daughter lets loose. See it on YouTube."

"Well, then maybe we better not get too wild and crazy."

"That's probably best." Emily glanced at her watch. "Do you want to meet in the lobby? Say ten minutes?"

A half hour later, the women were settled into a booth, munching on chips and salsa, each a few sips into their margaritas.

"So how do you like being back on the trail?" Amy asked.

"It's great. Last summer, everything was so new. Looking back, I think I felt a little overwhelmed." Emily twisted a strand of hair around her finger, a habit she'd had since she was a little girl. "But this time, I feel like I've settled right into the swing of things."

"Don't you miss your friends?"

"Yes, but everyone scattered after graduation anyway. They took jobs all over the country. So we're staying in touch by phone and email. I probably get three hundred texts a day, so I don't feel too abandoned."

"Any boyfriends?" Amy asked.

"No. I dated a lot in school, but no one serious. Which I guess is good, considering I'm traveling all over the country now. That would be hard if I was in a relationship." Emily reached forward to dunk a chip in the salsa. "Eventually I'd like to find the right guy, but I'm not in a hurry to settle down."

Amy leaned forward. "So what would the right guy be like? What are you looking for?"

"Well, like I said, I'm not really looking too hard right now. But I guess I like guys who have a good sense of humor, you know, who are fun to be around. A lot of the guys at Duke were pretty serious. I mean, they'd go to parties and get kind of wild when they were drunk, but the rest of the time, they were so into their grades and worried about getting a good job."

"And you weren't like that?"

"Not really. I've always done well in school. I didn't need to study very hard to keep my grades up."

"Lucky you," Amy said. "School never came that easily to me."

The waiter arrived with a heaping plate of nachos with chicken for Emily and vegetarian quesadillas for Amy.

"Mmmm. That looks great," Amy said. "I used to be able to eat like that when I was your age. Enjoy it while you can."

The waiter asked if everything looked good. The women assured him that it did and then both ordered a second margarita.

When he left for the bar, Emily turned back to Amy. "So, how about you? Any boyfriends back in Chicago?"

Amy blushed, shifting uncomfortably in her seat. "No. I was married once, but it didn't work out. I'd like to get married again. I'd really love to have kids. But like you said, with all this traveling around, it's hard. It'll be easier once your dad's in the White House, and we're living in D.C."

Emily knitted her brows. "Are you planning to move to Washington if my dad gets elected?"

"Yes, he's promised me a job as his personal secretary." Amy's eyes brightened. "I'd love to work in the Oval Office."

"Yeah, I guess that would be pretty sweet."

"How about you? Do you think you'd want to live in Washington?"

Emily shrugged. "I haven't thought much about it. I had planned to go to law school eventually, but I just sort of thought I'd wait and see how things turned out with Dad before making any plans."

Amy smiled at her. "I know he'd love it if you took a job in his administration. He's told me that he'd find you something if you were interested. He doesn't want to push you into anything, but he'd be thrilled if you worked on his staff somewhere."

"Really?" Emily raised her eyebrows. "He said that?"

Amy nodded. "Sure. He talks about you all the time. He's really happy you and your brother are working on the campaign now. He wants Tyler to take next semester off and then go back to school after he gets elected. And, like I said, he's hoping you'll take a job in the White House."

"I would definitely be interested. I would have asked him about it, but I didn't want him to feel pressured into finding something for me."

Amy laughed. "The two of you need to talk to each other. You didn't want to pressure him, and he didn't want to pressure you."

"I guess I'll bring it up with him now that I know. Do you think he ever reads my blogs?" Emily shrugged, not wanting to seem too eager. "I mean, I know he's busy and all."

"Well, you know how tied up he is during the day. But usually in the evenings, he'll ask me to pull them up so he can read through them. He's really impressed with your writing. He thinks you have a lot to do with his popularity among the under-thirty crowd."

Amy slid out from the booth. "I'm going to run to the rest room. These margaritas are going right through me."

Emily watched her go, wondering when in the evenings Amy was seeing her dad. It had to be after the rest of the staff broke up. In fact, it sure seemed like her dad's personal assistant had a lot of personal information about him. It was as if Amy had taken her mom's place as her dad's confidante. The longer she dwelled on the matter, the more worried she felt. When Amy got back from the bathroom, Emily cut the dinner short, a sickening feeling in her gut.

CHAPTER 28

When they returned to the hotel, Emily said good night to Amy. "I'm going to stop at the front desk. I need to get some more shampoo from housekeeping."

"All right," Amy said. "I had a lot of fun tonight. I'll see you in the morning."

Emily waited until Amy was gone and then walked to the registration desk. "Hi. I'm Emily Newcomb."

The man looked up from his computer and smiled. "Yes, Miss Newcomb. I recognize you. I'm a big fan of your dad's."

"That's great." Emily hesitated.

"Is there something I can help you with?"

Emily leaned her elbow onto the desk and started twirling a strand of hair. "Yeah, actually, there is. I was wondering if I could change rooms. I wanted to be closer to my dad."

"Sure. Let me check on that for you." The man entered some information onto his computer. Looking up, he nodded. "The room right across from your dad's is available. Would that be all right?"

"Perfect," Emily said.

"Do you need help moving your bags?"

"No, I'll be fine."

"Let me give you your new pass card and then after you move, just give us a call so we can send housekeeping up to clean your old room."

"Okay." Emily took a few steps away from the desk before turning back. "Do you know if my dad's here? He had a dinner out earlier this evening."

"I saw him leave, but I haven't seen him return yet. Did you want me to give him a message?"

"No, thank you. That's not necessary."

Twenty minutes later, Emily was settled into her new room. Peering through her peephole, she had a perfect view of her dad's door. She walked over to her bed and took out a book. Normally when she read, she listened to her iPod, but this evening, she didn't want any noise to muffle the sounds from the hallway.

She was about a half hour into her book when she heard the sounds she was waiting for. Leaping from her bed, she ran to the peephole and looked out. She watched as one of the Secret Service agents opened the door and went into her dad's room while her dad and the other agent waited in the hallway. When the first agent came out of the room with the all-clear, her dad said good night and stepped into his room. The agents waited to hear the locks click into place and then moved toward their own rooms on either side of the candidate's.

Emily stood watching for a few more minutes before she went back to sit on her bed. She picked up her book, but found she was too distracted to read. She sat staring off into space, her fingers nervously working her hair. About fifteen minutes later, she heard a light knock. She ran to the peephole just in time to see Amy step into her dad's room. He had his arms open wide and she heard his voice clearly. "Hi, baby. I missed you."

She watched as they started to kiss before the door slammed shut.

For a minute, everything went black. She had always looked up to her dad – he was a hero to her. So how could he be cheating on her mom? Emily's knees buckled, and she slid to the floor. She curled up into a fetal position and lay there, tears streaming down her face. She stayed that way for hours before stumbling to the bed and collapsing. She slept fitfully all night. Each time she woke, her hands would clench the sheets, and she would begin to sob until she cried herself to sleep again.

She woke with a start to her cell phone ringing. She lifted her head and looked at the clock. Eight fifteen. She was supposed to have been down in the lobby fifteen minutes ago. She lay back, letting the phone ring a couple more times before she hoisted herself into a sitting position and answered it.

"Hello," she croaked, her voice raw from crying.

"Hey, sleepyhead," Ryan said. "Did I wake you?"

"Yeah. I don't feel very good. I think I have the flu or something."

When Ryan spoke again, she could hear the concern in his voice. "Can I get you anything? Do you want me to come up there?"

"No. I'll be okay. I'm just going to go back to sleep."

"Are you sure? I don't have to go with your dad today. I can stay here with you."

"No, really, Uncle Ryan. I've got some Advil. I'll take that and I'll be fine."

"Okay. If you're sure. I'll let everyone know. We'll call you later to check in on you."

"Thanks," Emily said, disconnecting the call. She lay back down and closed her eyes, her mind replaying the scene she had watched last night. She waited for the tears, but nothing came. She just felt empty.

She spent the day holed up in her room. She ordered room service and picked at the food. She turned on the TV and flipped from station to station, trying to find something to watch to distract her from her thoughts. Mostly she just slept, her mind and body exhausted.

When the phone rang later in the afternoon, she picked it up reluctantly. When she heard her father's voice on the line, her eyes teared up.

"Are you feeling better, honey?"

"Yeah, a little."

"I'll come up to see you when I get back to the hotel."

"No, Dad. Please. I just want to be left alone."

"Are you sure? I hate the idea of you in that hotel room by yourself."

"Really, Dad. I'll see you guys in the morning. I'm sure I'll feel better by then."

Emily hung up the phone and closed her eyes. Hearing her dad's voice had brought all her emotions to the surface again. She slid down into the sheets and began to sob.

CHAPTER 29

At eight o'clock sharp the next morning, Emily walked into the hotel lobby rolling her suitcase behind her. Her father and the rest of the staff were already gathered.

Brad looked up in surprise. "Where are you going?"

"Home," Emily answered. "I booked a flight this morning. I'm still not feeling well so I decided to go home for a few days."

When Brad stepped forward to hug her, Emily recoiled in disgust and turned her cheek away so his kiss netted him a mouthful of hair. He leaned back, holding her arms gently.

"Are you sure you're okay to travel?" he asked. Maybe you should spend another day in bed before you make the trip."

"I'll be fine," she answered coldly, pulling back from his grip. She could barely stand to look at him.

"I'll call you and your mom tonight," Brad said, turning away from her. "We better get going." He started across the hotel lobby toward the exit.

Ryan lingered behind and when the others were out of earshot, he put his arm around his niece. "Hey, kiddo. Are you sure you're all right?"

Emily turned and put her arms around him. Her eyes filled with tears as he wrapped his arms around her.

When she stepped back from him, Ryan saw her face. "What is it? Is something wrong?"

Emily shook her head. "I'm still not feeling good. I just want to go home."

As Ryan looked down at his niece, he heard Amy's voice from across the lobby. "Come on, Ryan. We're all waiting for you."

He looked up at her. "Go on ahead. I'm going to go to the airport with Emily. I'll catch up with you later."

"You don't have to do that," Emily said.

"Yeah, I do, kiddo."

101

Emily gave him a tight smile. "Thanks," she whispered.

They made their way out of the lobby and got into a cab. Ryan reached across the seat and took his niece's hand, squeezing it until she responded. They sat that way in silence all the way to the airport, Emily staring out the window, not seeing anything.

When they arrived at the airport, Ryan stayed with her up until she got in line to go through security.

Emily gave her uncle a hug. "Thanks for coming with me."

"Sure thing." He took her hand. "Are you sure there's nothing you want to talk about?"

For a minute, Emily thought about telling Ryan what she had seen, but she wasn't sure how he would react. She was afraid he might tell her mom or dad, and she didn't want to have everything out in the open -- at least until she was able to come to terms with her father's behavior herself. Plus, he was a journalist covering her dad's campaign. What if he felt obliged to report the affair? She couldn't allow herself to be the person responsible for ending her father's dreams.

"I'm sure." She gave him a weak smile and turned away.

* * *

Emily set her suitcase down in the foyer. "Mom, are you home?"

"I'm in the family room, honey."

Emily heard the corgis barking before they rounded the corner, a whirling mass of fur. As they jumped up on her, their bodies quivering with joy, she couldn't help but smile. They trailed her to the family room, where Carolyn was sitting, a pile of newspapers spread out in front of her.

Carolyn stood and Emily ran to her arms. After they hugged, Emily dropped into the sofa next to her mother.

Carolyn turned to her daughter. "Is everything okay, honey? Your uncle Ryan called me this morning. He was worried about you."

Emily leaned back into the cushions. "I'm fine. I think I had the flu yesterday and now I'm just tired."

They sat quietly for a few minutes until Emily leaned forward. "Mom, I think you need to join Dad on the campaign trail. I mean, your leg's all healed, right?"

Carolyn sighed. "Yes, the doctor's cleared me for traveling. I guess I've just been trying to avoid it."

Emily wrinkled her brow. "Why?"

Carolyn shrugged. "I just don't like the whole campaign scene. It's all so fake." She shook her head. "I shouldn't say that. I know your dad would make a great president. And he's really sincere about his vision for the country. But the hoops we have to jump through to get to the election. It's just so tiresome."

"What do you mean?"

"You know. You've seen it. All the pretense. Putting on the big smiles and making all the empty promises. I just hate the whole scene."

"But, Mom, you knew what we were getting into when he decided to run. You promised to support him. All the other candidates' wives are out there campaigning."

"I know, I know." Carolyn drew a deep breath. "Before the accident, I was forcing myself to do it. But I guess once I was home recovering, I realized how much I hated it. I was just trying to stretch my convalescence out for as long as possible."

"But it's not like you haven't done this before."

"It was different when the elections were in Illinois. I could make all the campaign appearances I needed to, but still be at home. I wasn't living out of a suitcase."

"Well, I think you've avoided campaigning as long as you should. Dad needs you with him."

"Has he said anything to you?"

Emily shifted uncomfortably, her finger reaching for a strand of hair. "No, but I know how important it is for you to be there."

They sat in silence, while Emily fought back her tears. She waited to speak until she had composed herself. "Please, Mom. You really need to do this."

CHAPTER 30

Emily paced around her hotel room like a caged lion. She had spent a week at home with Carolyn before returning to the campaign trail, not leaving until she had her mother's word that she would join them the following week.

Since she had been back, Emily had kept a close eye on her dad and Amy. Now that she knew about the affair, it seemed as though the tell-tale signs were obvious. For example, how virtually every time they were together for a meal, they sat next to each other. How if someone said something funny, they always glanced at each other like they were sharing a secret joke. How whenever her dad was talking, Amy gazed at him like a star struck teenager.

As obvious as their affair was to her, though, nobody else seemed to notice. Even her uncle, a trained journalist, appeared oblivious. When she had hinted to him about the illicit relationship, he had laughed it off as a mere harmless crush Amy had. Emily had thought about telling him what she had seen that night at the hotel, but couldn't bring herself to do it.

The only other person she thought about confiding in was Tyler, but she couldn't put her younger brother through the same misery she was feeling. He loved her parents as much as she did, and she didn't want to turn him against their father.

She thought about confronting her dad about his affair with Amy, but every time she came close to saying something, she backed off. Instead, she waited and hoped that when her mother joined them, her dad would realize what a terrible thing he was doing. But as each day went by during which she kept her secret, she could feel herself getting angrier.

When she couldn't stand the feeling of being cooped up any longer, she grabbed her purse and took the elevator down to the hotel lobby. She walked into the hotel bar and sat down, ordering a martini.

"Can I see some ID please?"

"No problem," Emily said, pulling out her wallet.

The bartender looked at her driver's license and did a double take. "You're Emily Newcomb. The candidate's daughter, right?"

Emily nodded.

"This first one's on me then. I've been reading your blog. Your dad sounds like a really cool guy. You even got me to send in a campaign contribution. I've never done that before."

As the bartender turned around to make Emily's drink, another man who was sitting a couple stools down moved closer. He introduced himself and asked if he could join her.

Emily shrugged. "Sure."

"I couldn't help but overhear. You're Brad Newcomb's daughter, huh?"

They talked for a while about her dad and the campaign and as soon as her glass was empty, he bought her another drink. When it came, she asked if they could change the subject. Over the next hour and two more drinks, they talked about everything except politics.

When it was closing time, the bartender asked if they wanted a last drink.

"No thanks," Emily said, slurring her words slightly.

As she stood up, she felt wobbly. Her bar companion put his arm around her. "It's a shame the bar's closing. I've really enjoyed talking to you. How about if we go up to my room?"

"I'd like that," Emily said, wanting the night to continue so she could block out the pain she was feeling.

* * *

The next morning when her alarm went off, Emily lay in bed thinking about the night before. It was her fifth one-night stand in as many nights. *Maybe I should start putting notches on my belt,* she thought. *I'm certainly turning into my dad's daughter.* She pushed the sheets off and sat up slowly, her stomach feeling the effects from the drinks she'd consumed the night before. She couldn't even remember how many she'd had. She just knew there had been enough of them for her to forget about her dad and Amy.

She slid off the bed and padded to the bathroom, her head pounding with every footstep. She looked at herself in the mirror. Her smudged mascara framing her bloodshot eyes made her look like a raccoon. She stepped into the shower and began to scrub the night's grime away.

She was dressed and picking at her breakfast when she heard a knock on her hotel room door. Frowning, she looked at her watch. Nobody should be there to hassle her for being late; she wasn't due in the lobby for another half hour. She got up and walked to the door, checking through the peephole before opening it.

"Hey, Uncle Ryan. I'm not late, am I?"

"No, kiddo. I just wanted to talk to you before we met up with the rest of the group. May I come in?"

"I guess." Emily walked back to her desk and sat down. "I was just finishing my breakfast. Do you want some coffee?"

"No, I'm fine," Ryan said, taking a seat on the bed.

Emily nibbled at her bagel. "So what do you want to talk about?"

"I was hoping you'd tell me. What's going on, Emily?"

"I don't know what you're talking about."

"Come on. You've been acting strange ever since you came back from home. And for that matter, before you left. That day I dropped you off at the airport, you just weren't yourself. Why don't you tell me what's going on?"

Emily took a big bite of her bagel and chewed it slowly, using the time to think about how she wanted to respond. Deciding that she still didn't want to reveal what she knew, she swallowed. "I don't know. Maybe I'm just getting sick of the campaign. It's like my mom said, campaigning is just all pretense."

"What do you mean?"

Emily shrugged. "It's like Dad's only putting up this big front. I don't even recognize him anymore. He's just a big fake."

Ryan raised his eyebrows. "Wow. I wasn't expecting that."

"Don't you think he's changed?"

"I think your dad is just doing what he has to do to get elected. You've seen what it's like. Every step he takes, people are hounding him, watching his every move."

Emily put her bagel down and crossed her arms. "Maybe they're not watching him closely enough. Nobody's seeing who he really is. Not even you, Uncle Ryan."

"What do you mean? What am I missing?"

Emily fingered her knife, tapping it on the breakfast tray. She thought again about telling her uncle about the affair. It would be such a relief to share the burden. "I don't know. He's just acting like a jerk."

"Honestly, I'm not seeing it. But if you are, unfortunately that's what politics is all about. He's no different from the other candidates. Everyone's trying to put his best foot forward."

"So it's okay for him to pretend he's someone he's not."

"I guess it is. You know the saying -- the end justifies the means. Once the election's over, things will get back to normal."

"Yeah, right. When he's president, everything will be normal again, huh?"

Ryan laughed. "Well, maybe not exactly normal."

Emily pushed her tray away and looked at her watch. "We should probably get going."

"There's one more thing I wanted to talk to you about." Ryan shifted uncomfortably. "I've heard you've been hitting the bars at night -- hooking up with strangers."

Emily was shocked. She didn't think anyone from the campaign staff knew about her recent behavior. "Who told you that?"

"A couple of the staffers have seen you."

Her shock turned to anger. "Well, it's none of anyone's business – including yours."

"Come on, Emily. This is me you're talking to. Whether you like it or not, I care about you. I know you're an adult and you can drink and sleep with whoever you want, but…"

Emily jumped to her feet. "But, nothing, Uncle Ryan. I'm over twenty-one, I'm single. I can do what I want."

"All that's true, but I want you to stop and think about the danger in what you're doing. I'm sure you know all about safe sex and how important it is to use a condom. But I also know that when people drink too much, they don't always take precautions. And so there's the risk of pregnancy or getting an STD. But the even bigger risk is that one of these guys that you meet up with is some kind of psycho – a rapist, a murderer. You're not at Duke anymore. The guys you're meeting in bars could be anybody."

Emily's eyes welled up with tears. "So what? So what if something bad happens to me? Who cares anyway?"

"I do, and I know your Aunt Michelle does too. Look, I understand that you're having some issues with your parents right now, but first of all you have to know that they both love you very much. And they're not the only ones. Michelle and I love you and your brother as if you were our own kids. Maybe you think I'm interfering, but I couldn't live with myself if something happened to you and I hadn't tried to talk to you."

Ryan stood and put his arm around his niece. "Will you please talk to Michelle about whatever it is you're going through? You know she's a trained therapist; she counsels people for a living. I really think she could help you."

"You're not going to tell my mom and dad about this, are you?"

"I'll make you a deal. If you talk to Michelle, I promise you I won't say anything to your parents. Okay?"

Emily nodded. "Okay."

Ryan squeezed her hand before letting go. "I'd better let you finish getting ready. I'll see you downstairs."

"All right. And, Uncle Ryan -- thanks."

Emily waited for her uncle to leave before she sat down on the bed, wiping away a tear. *What a total mess this thing is,* she thought.

CHAPTER 31

Brad sat in his hotel suite, having a drink with Terry. The day's activities were over and he had a rare evening off. He listened as his campaign manager finished taking him through his schedule for the following day.

"Anything else?" Brad asked.

"That about covers it." Terry stood to leave and then sat down again. "I guess there's one more thing we should talk about."

Brad raised his hand. "If it's about Carolyn, I just talked to her earlier today. She's planning on joining us next week and staying on the trail through the convention. God, I can't believe we're only a month away and I've already got the electoral votes locked up."

"That's great about Carolyn. She's a real asset for us. But that's not what I wanted to talk about."

"So what is it?"

"It's Emily. I'm not exactly sure how to tell you this."

Brad leaned forward. "Is she okay?"

Terry hesitated and Brad could see he was struggling to find the words. "It's just that people have started talking about her. Apparently, she's been seen hanging out in the bars at night and…" Terry blushed, shifting in his seat.

"And what?"

"Well, I guess she's been picking up men. Or letting men pick her up. Whatever."

"*What?*" Brad jumped up from his chair. "How long has this been going on?"

"I just heard about it yesterday, but I guess it's been going on for the last couple of weeks."

"So what exactly are we talking about? How often has this been happening?"

Terry shrugged. "From what I hear, it's been just about every night since she came back on the trail."

Brad began pacing around the room. "Shit, like I need this now. What if the media picks up on this? This is just the kind of thing the *Enquirer* would love to put on their front page."

"I know. That's why I think you should talk to her. The last thing we need right now is any whiff of scandal. Usually the media stays away from the candidates' kids, but with Emily having such a visible role because of her blog, they might think she's fair game."

"Do you think we could wait till Carolyn gets here? She's better with dealing with these kinds of things."

Terry shook his head. "It's too risky to wait."

"You're right." Brad poured himself another drink and took a big gulp. "God damn it, how could she do this to me? She knows how the media's watching our every move. What's she thinking?"

"I don't know, Gov. She's just a kid. She's probably not thinking at all. She's just having some fun."

"Yeah, well, that's not the kind of fun that a presidential candidate's daughter can have. You'd think she would know better."

"I'm sure once you talk to her, she'll stop doing what she's doing. She'll probably be really embarrassed that you even heard about it."

Brad slammed his empty glass on the table. "She damn well better be embarrassed. And then she damn well better stop this shit."

When Terry left the room, Brad called Emily and asked her to come see him. While he was waiting for her, he seethed. To be this close to wrapping up the Democratic nomination and to have his daughter do anything to jeopardize that was totally unacceptable. When she knocked, he flung the door open.

"What's wrong, Dad? You sounded upset on the phone."

"I'm more than upset, Emily. I'm livid. What's this crap I'm hearing about you getting drunk and having one-night stands?"

Emily's eyes filled with tears. "Who told you that?"

"Terry. He said everyone on the staff is talking about you."

Emily wiped away her tears, her voice growing angry. "I'm over twenty-one. I'm not doing anything illegal. It's nobody's damn business what I do with my life – including you!"

As she turned away from him, Brad grabbed her arm. "It most certainly is. In case you forgot, I'm running for president. And as my daughter, everything you do is a reflection on me. Your behavior is totally unacceptable."

"You've got to be kidding." Emily's hands clenched into fists. "You're going to stand there and tell me *my* behavior is unacceptable. What about *your* behavior?"

"What are you talking about?"

"You know exactly what I'm talking about. You and that slut, Amy."

CHAPTER 32

Brad's mouth dropped open, a jolt of fear replacing his anger. "I don't know what you mean."

"That's bullshit, Dad. I know you're having an affair."

"I don't know who told you that, but you're wrong. I know Amy has a little thing for me, but there's nothing going on between us."

"Stop lying to me, Dad. I saw her go into your room. I saw you two kissing."

As the words hung in the air between them, Brad sank into the sofa and put his head in his hands. He couldn't believe his daughter knew. How was he going to get out of this one? Finally, he spoke. "Emily, honey, I'm so sorry. It just happened. With your mom not here, I guess I just got lonely. I know that's not an excuse."

"Don't blame this on Mom."

Brad held up his hands. "No, you're right. It's all my fault. I didn't mean for anyone to find out, especially not you."

"Well, you're too late."

"Have you told anyone – your mom, Tyler?"

Emily shook her head. "No."

"Please tell me you won't," Brad said, his voice pleading. "I swear I'll break it off right away. Amy means nothing to me. You've got to believe that."

Emily stared at him.

"Really, Emily. I love your mom. Our family means everything to me."

"Then why did you do it?"

"I don't know. I swear I've never done anything like this before. It's just the stress of the campaign. And then with all these women throwing themselves at me."

Emily sat down next to her dad, her shoulders sagging. "I know. I've seen the way they grab at you. I've seen them slip their phone numbers into your pocket."

Hearing the compassion in her voice, Brad felt a glimmer of hope. "Exactly. And I've thrown those numbers away. But with Amy, it's different. She really cares about me and the campaign. And I know you don't want to hear this, but it's been really hard on me not having your mom here."

Emily nodded. "I know. I hate that you've done this, but I realize Mom's at fault too. I even tried to talk to her and tell her she needed to be here with you."

Brad put his arm around Emily. "Please forgive me, honey. I promise I'll break it off immediately. Just please don't tell anyone. It would devastate your mom. I know you don't want to hurt her."

Emily sat quietly for a minute, nervously twirling a strand of hair. "All right, Dad. If you swear – I mean, really swear – that you won't have anything to do with that slut again."

Brad felt relief flood through his body as he struggled to sound earnest. "You have my word. It will never happen again."

"Oh, Dad. I was so scared you were going to leave Mom." Emily started to cry.

"Never, honey. I love your mother. You guys mean everything to me."

Brad held Emily for a long time, until her tears finally dried up. When she left, he called Terry and asked him to come back to his room. As he waited for him, he thought about his affair. It hit him that he had been as careless as Emily. It would have been bad enough for the media to find out about Emily's one-night stands; he probably could have weathered that storm. But if they had found out about him and Amy, it would have been the end of him.

God, he had been stupid. Maybe Emily finding out was the best thing that could have happened. It woke him up to what he could have lost. He wanted to be president more than anything in the world. He'd be an idiot to let an affair that meant nothing to him get in his way.

When Terry arrived, Brad showed him in and sat down. "You were right about Emily. But there's more to it. She's been acting out because of me." Brad paused. "I don't know how to tell you this."

Terry shook his head. "It's Amy, isn't it? You've been sleeping with her."

"I'm sorry, Terry. It was stupid. I know it was." Brad held up his hand. "I swear to you she's been the only one since we started the race. And I'm going to put an end to it right away. But I need your help."

"Anything."

"We've got to find her a different job. She can't be my personal assistant anymore. We need to put some distance between us."

Terry nodded. "I agree."

"Come up with something for her – maybe a marketing related job. Whatever, I don't care. Just give her a promotion and a big raise, so she won't fight it. And then I need you to find me a new assistant."

"Done. And this time it's going to be a man."

Brad held up his hands in surrender. "Fine. No argument from me. I know how close I came to blowing it. All I care about is getting elected. I'm not going to let some slut ruin my chances."

CHAPTER 33

Brad checked his watch – ten minutes to go. Amy was supposed to come to his suite at eleven. He had told the Secret Service that he was in for the evening. He wasn't sure if they had ever seen Amy coming or going, but he trusted them completely. They had a long history of guarding the secret lives of presidents.

He picked up the phone and called Amy. "Change of plans. I'm coming to your room tonight." The last thing he wanted was a big scene and having to throw her out of his suite. This way he could leave after he broke the news.

He opened his door and peeked out into the hallway. Amy had been reserving their rooms so that she was always just a few doors down. As his personal assistant, this didn't raise any red flags, but it made it a lot easier for her to sneak to his suite without being seen. The hallway was empty as he made his way down to her room. When she let him in, he made sure the door was closed behind them before kissing her.

She was wearing a flimsy negligee and for a moment, he wavered. *God, she has a gorgeous body,* he thought. *What would one last roll in the hay hurt?* But then he caught himself. It was going to be hard enough to break it off without screwing her one last time. He didn't want to risk pissing her off by waiting to tell her until after they had sex.

She had her arms around his neck and he gently pulled them away. Holding her hands, he looked deeply into her eyes. "Baby, we have to talk." He watched as her eyes grew wide. The last words any woman wanted to hear.

He put his arm around her and drew her into the room. When he got to the bed, he pushed her shoulders gently. "Why don't you sit down? I'm going to make us both a drink."

"I don't want anything."

Brad shrugged and sat down next to her. He took her hand in his. "Amy, what we've had has been so special. You've been my rock over the last few months."

She pulled her hand away. "Oh, my God, Brad. Don't do this."

"I have to, Amy. The convention's next month. We have the votes. I'm going to get the nomination unless someone finds out about us. We've come too far to risk losing it all."

"But Brad, I love you."

"I know you do. And that's why I know you'll do the right thing. I know you believe in me. I know you want me to be the next president. You don't want me to give that up, do you?"

"Of course not. But we don't have to end it. We've been discreet. No one knows and I swear, no one will find out. I'd never betray you."

Brad put his arm around her. "I know you wouldn't. I trust you completely. But someone did find out – Emily."

Amy's eyes widened. "You're kidding? Emily knows about us. How?"

"She saw us together. She saw us kissing. Thank God she didn't tell anyone and she's not going to."

"Oh Brad, I'm sorry. I've been so careful."

"I'm not blaming you. But it just goes to show you. It could have been anybody. It could have been the media."

"Baby, I'll be more careful. I swear, no one else will find out."

Brad shook his head. "Wait, there's more. You know Carolyn's coming back on the trail next week. We're not going to be able to spend our nights together anymore."

"I don't need to spend the whole night with you. We'll steal time together whenever we can. Just please, don't end it."

"We have to. It's the best thing for both of us. You had to know our affair couldn't go on forever. It's been hard enough sneaking around the last few months. Once I'm elected, it's going to be impossible. I'm never going to be alone."

Amy dropped to her knees in front of Brad. She grabbed his hands. "Please, baby, don't do this. I love you so much. I can't live without you."

"I love you too. But we can't do this anymore."

Amy looked up at him, tears streaming down her face. "But, Brad, you can't leave me. I'm pregnant."

CHAPTER 34

Brad leapt up from the bed, pushing Amy aside. "You're *what?*"

Amy rocked back on her knees, crossing her arms. "Please, don't be mad at me."

"You told me you were on the pill."

"I am. I don't know how this happened. I must have missed one or something. I swear, it was an accident."

Brad raised his hand, and it took every ounce of willpower he had not to slap her. Instead he picked up a pillow and threw it against the wall. "God, Amy, how could you have let this happen? Don't you realize what this would do to me if it got out?"

"It won't, I swear."

"Damn right it won't. You're getting an abortion."

Amy's eyes widened. "I can't." She clutched her stomach. "This is my baby. I would never kill an unborn child."

"You can't be serious. You can't really believe that you can have this baby."

Amy stood up, her hands clenched into fists. "I'm going to have our child, Brad. No one's going to stop me."

The candidate collapsed onto the bed, putting his head in his hands. "How could you do this to me?"

Amy sat down and put her arm around him. "I love you so much, Brad. And I love this baby – *our* baby. I understand you can't leave your wife right now, so I'll go back to Chicago. I'll have the baby there. No one will know he's yours until the time is right. After you're in office, you can leave Carolyn. We can be together."

Brad looked at Amy. Could she really be so naïve? Could she really think her little fairy-tale ending could ever happen? He took her hand. "Amy, I'm sorry for how I reacted. This just really threw me. But we're going to work it out. I just need a little time to get my head around it."

Amy threw her arms around him. "Oh, Brad, I knew you'd come around. I know this is bad timing, but God must have a plan for us. Sending us this baby is a sign that we're meant to be together."

"You're right," Brad said, choking on the words. "Just give me a few days to think this all through so we can come up with a plan."

He got up. "I should get back to my room."

Amy stood and put her arms around him. "Don't leave. I need you to stay with me tonight."

Brad looked down at her, repelled. He couldn't believe that this woman who meant nothing to him had the power to destroy everything he had worked for. He lifted her chin and kissed her. Using his anger as an aphrodisiac, he pushed her roughly onto the bed.

When they lay spent, Amy put her head on his chest. "Oh baby, I can't wait until we can be together as a family. I'm going to make you so happy."

Chapter 35

Ryan paced in the airport waiting area. Michelle's plane had landed only ten minutes ago, but it seemed like an hour. When he saw her come through the security gates, his face broke into a wide grin. He watched as she scanned the crowd, searching for him. When she found him, he opened his arms wide and she ran to him, leaping into his arms.

"God, it's good to see you," Ryan said.

"I know. I've missed you so much."

"Let's get out of here." Ryan grabbed her carry-on and put his arm around his wife.

They had taken a few steps when Michelle turned to him. "You know, that suitcase has wheels. You don't have to carry it."

"That's okay. With you here, I feel like Superman. It's faster if I carry it. And right now, speed is of the essence."

"And where exactly are we speeding to?"

"To the hotel so I can make mad, passionate love to my wife."

Michelle grinned. "Okay Superman, sounds good to me."

* * *

Ryan lay in bed, relishing the warmth of Michelle's body against his. She had her head on his chest and his fingertips gently stroked her face and hair.

"So how has everything been going with the campaign?" she asked.

"As well as it can be, I guess. Brad's got the electoral votes to lock up the nomination, so everyone's pretty psyched about the convention. I can't believe it's just a couple weeks away. After all the hard work over the last year and a half, we're going to have four straight days of celebrating."

"I'm sorry I'm going to miss it. I just couldn't get out of that conference."

"That's okay. It's going to be crazy anyway. I'll be spending twenty-hour days chasing Brad around while he sucks up to all his supporters. It's much better having you here now so we can have some time alone together."

"Yeah, it's nice that you can take a couple of days off. So what do you have planned for me, or are we just staying in bed till I have to leave?"

Ryan tilted her head up and kissed her. "Now that sounds tempting, but I guess we have to spend a little time out in the real world. I actually invited Emily and Tyler to have dinner with us tonight. Is that all right?"

"Of course. I'd love to see the kids. How's Emily doing? You were pretty concerned about her there for a while."

"She seems to be doing better. I think the party-girl thing was just a phase she snapped out of."

Michelle laid her head back on her husband's chest. "Do you still want me to talk to her?"

"It wouldn't hurt for you to spend some one-on-one time with her just to make sure everything's okay. But I've been keeping an eye out, and I'm pretty sure her bar crawls have ended. I think it helped to have Carolyn back on the trail with us. Since she got here, everyone's been more relaxed."

"Even Brad? I didn't think your brother ever relaxed."

Ryan laughed. "You're right. I meant Emily and Tyler and the rest of the staff. But Brad's another story. He's actually been *more* on edge lately. But I'm sure that's not because of Carolyn. I think he's just anxious with the convention around the corner."

"Why would he be anxious if he's got the nomination locked up?"

"You're the therapist. You tell me. Isn't it human nature to get a little wound up before a big event?"

"You're right. When people are really excited about something, it's a common reaction to be afraid that something will snatch it away from them. The fear can be totally irrational or there can be something behind it." Michelle raised her head, looking into Ryan's eyes. "Like maybe there are some skeletons in your brother's closet after all."

CHAPTER 36

July: Four Months to Go

It was day three of the Democratic National Convention – the single most important day in Brad's life. Of course, he couldn't have said that to Carolyn. She would have put their wedding or when their kids were born before this one. But in Brad's heart, he knew nothing could top the high he was going to feel today when the Convention nominated him as their presidential candidate.

He looked at his alarm clock. Five-fifteen. Knowing he couldn't go back to sleep, he tried to get up slowly so he wouldn't wake his wife. He had taken a few steps when he heard her groggy voice.

"What time is it?"

"It's only five-fifteen. Go back to sleep."

"No. If you're getting up, I will too."

Carolyn pushed the covers back and stretched. She opened her eyes and smiled. "I have a better idea. Why don't you come back to bed?"

Brad looked at his beautiful wife; she didn't have to ask twice. He slid in beside her for a pre-nomination celebration.

When they were finished making love, Carolyn flopped back on the pillows. "That was a great way to start the day, Mr. President."

Brad raised his eyebrows in mock horror. "You're not going to jinx this thing at the last minute, are you?"

Carolyn smiled. "Not a chance. The only thing you have to worry about at this point is what suit to wear for your acceptance speech tomorrow."

"It's not only picked out, it's pressed and ready to go."

"And you did that all by yourself?" Carolyn teased.

"Not the ironing part, just the selection."

"Impressive, none the less. Didn't you want my input? Now that Amy's not your assistant anymore. How's the new guy working out anyway?"

Brad felt his throat tighten. "Fine. I don't miss Amy at all."

"It's nice that you were able to promote her."

"She deserved it. Terry tells me she's doing a great job with her new responsibilities."

Wanting to put an end to the conversation, Brad got out of bed and stretched before pulling on a robe and going to the door. He looked out the peephole and then opened the door, leaving the chain on. Satisfied that no one was there, he took the chain off and opened the door all the way. He picked up the newspapers and then shut the door, using the double lock and chain again. Ever since the assassination attempt, he was a lot more security conscious.

Turning back to the living area, he saw that Carolyn had gotten up and was seated at the desk.

"Do you want me to order breakfast?" she asked.

"Yeah, my usual. Do you mind if I hop in the shower?"

"No, it's all yours. Even after dragging you back to bed, I've got plenty of time to get beautiful. No one looks at the first lady anyway."

Brad laughed. "Yeah, right. I'm half expecting to read what brand pantyhose you wear in today's paper. Speaking of which, you *are* wearing American designers, aren't you?"

"Don't worry. That's all I've brought with me on this trip."

"I shouldn't have even asked. You haven't made a wrong move yet on this campaign."

"I'm doing my best," Carolyn said.

Brad scooted a chair next to hers and sat down. He took both her hands in his. "So are you really on board with this, or are you just doing it for me?"

"I'm not going to lie to you. I'm not dying to be the First Lady of the United States, unlike being the First Lady of Illinois, which has been a pretty good gig. I've been able to do my own thing and even when I have made an appearance with you, it's not been a big deal. This, on the other hand, is something totally different."

"I know it is. I wasn't that far off with my earlier pantyhose comment."

"No, and I know it's only going to get more intense here on out. But having said that, the simple fact is that I love you. And I know this is your dream. And so I want it as badly as you do, because I want you to be happy. Because that will make me happy."

Brad reached out and cupped her cheek. "I couldn't ask for a better wife."

"You know if I didn't genuinely believe that you would make a wonderful president, my attitude might be different. But I know you are the best person for the job. I would never take this opportunity away from you."

"I'm so lucky to have you. Because even if being the first lady isn't your dream, you're going to make a spectacular one."

Brad leaned over and kissed his wife. "And now I'd better go take that shower."

* * *

Brad was meeting with one of his top supporters later that afternoon when Terry rushed into the room, breathless. "Routhe just called for the suspension of roll call to nominate by acclamation. This is it, Gov. You need to get in there."

Brad felt a surge of excitement as he shook his supporter's hand. "I'm sorry to interrupt our conversation, but it looks like destiny's calling."

On the walk to the convention center auditorium, Brad turned to Terry. "Have you located Carolyn and the kids?"

"Yes, sir. I called them, and they're going to meet you inside."

A few minutes later, Terry pulled the door open and Brad stepped through. Carolyn, Emily and Tyler were gathered in a circle waiting for him.

The candidate kissed his wife, and with his arm around her and their children following closely behind, he made his way up the aisle to the stage. Senator Jerry Routhe, Brad's closest rival in the primary, had announced his support of Brad and released his delegates to vote for him. When Brad walked onto the stage, Routhe stepped up to the microphone. "All those in favor of nominating Brad Newcomb, the respected governor of Illinois, as our Democratic candidate for President of these great United States, please say aye."

The convention center erupted with cheers and whistles. Brad stepped forward, his arms outstretched to the audience, relishing the moment he had worked so hard for.

"All those opposed, please say no," Routhe said.

The center was almost silent, with just a few dissenting no's called out.

"I hereby announce Brad Newcomb as our presidential candidate," Routhe called out.

Brad stepped to the microphone, adrenaline pumping through his body. He shook Routhe's hand and then turned to address the crowd. "Thank you all for your support." He turned back to his family and stood with his arms around Carolyn and Emily. He would make his formal acceptance speech tomorrow. Today he could simply bask in the attention of the five thousand delegates, fifteen thousand media representatives, and an additional thirty thousand supporters gathered to pay him homage.

As he looked out into the sea of faces, he saw a group of his campaign staffers clustered near the stage. Amy was standing in the center of the group, and when he caught her eye, she blew him a kiss. A shudder of fear slithered through his body, eclipsing his previous elation.

CHAPTER 37

Later that evening, Amy lay sprawled on her hotel bed watching CNN. She and Brad had agreed not to have any contact during the national convention; the candidate was being too closely monitored to risk it.

CNN was running a recap of the highlights of the day, culminating in Brad's nomination by acclamation. Amy recalled the excitement she had felt when his name was called out and the delegates voted him in. She felt as proud as any first lady. She already considered herself his wife – it was only a matter of time until the title would be official. Her hand reached down to her belly and began to rub it softly. All her dreams were coming true. Once Brad was in the White House, he had promised her that he would divorce Carolyn, marry her, and then they could raise their baby together.

She thought about what her pet projects would be as first lady -- something with kids, maybe literacy. That was a safe enough platform. But mostly, she would be Brad's partner. She would travel everywhere with him, acting as his sounding board. By the time the next election rolled around, everyone would have accepted her as though she had been his wife from the start.

She knew she would have to lie low as soon as she started showing. She and Brad had agreed that she would head back to Chicago and have the baby there. She would tell people that the father was a man she had met on the trail, but they had split up, and he would not be involved in the child's life. She would never acknowledge the baby as Brad's until he was out of office.

Amy had managed to keep her affair secret even from her closest friends. Now that she was pregnant, she had sown the seeds of their story so that no one would be surprised when she returned home. The hardest part would be going through the pregnancy and birth without Brad, but he had promised he would see her whenever he could. That was part of why they had decided that she would return to Chicago.

He would have a good excuse to return to his home state on a relatively frequent basis.

It wasn't an ideal situation, but the love she felt for Brad and their baby made it all worthwhile. And she couldn't wait to be the first lady. To think that someone from her middle class background would make it onto the national stage. Her dad had been an accountant and her mother a school teacher. She was their only child, and they'd had her late in life after they had already given up trying to conceive. They had both passed away when she was a young adult. At the time, she resented being left alone with no parents or siblings, but now she realized that maybe it was for the best. It would have been difficult to deceive them about the affair and baby.

Amy reached for a glass of water from the nightstand when the CNN coverage switched from the convention highlights to a story on Carolyn. She watched as the reporter talked about how beautiful and gracious Brad's wife was. She sat mesmerized as they showed segments from Carolyn campaigning, always looking meticulous in her expensive clothes.

When the water splashed onto her hand, Amy realized how tightly she was gripping the glass. She took a drink and set it down on the table next to her, turning her attention back to the TV. The reporter was wrapping up the story, a picture of Brad standing with his arm around Carolyn in the background.

Amy hated the idea that people thought Brad had the perfect marriage with the perfect wife. They didn't know how Carolyn had avoided the campaign trail, preferring to stay home with her dogs and horses rather than support her husband. *Everyone thinks Carolyn walks on water,* Amy thought, *but I know the real story. Brad and the rest of the world will see what a real wife is when I'm married to him.*

CHAPTER 38

Terry opened the drapes in his hotel room to let the morning sun in. It was the fourth and final day of the Democratic National Convention, and he had been up for a couple of hours already. Everything had gone as smoothly as he could have hoped.

Carolyn had given a touching speech about hope on the first day that had the audience members in tears; she could work the heartstrings like nobody else. Their vice-presidential choice, Senator Kerry Wilkens, had been nominated and given his acceptance speech yesterday. Terry thought the man was a brilliant choice. He had been in the Senate for twenty years and had strong foreign policy experience, the one area in which Brad lacked expertise.

They had used their free time for Brad to meet with all his key supporters. Between the money they already had in their coffers and the new pledges they had received, the campaign was in excellent financial shape as they headed into the last four months before the general election.

The Republican National Convention was scheduled for next month, and it was clear that Bob Ellington, the current vice-president, would get the nod. Terry couldn't have asked for a better rival. The man had no charisma whatsoever. Obviously he would pull the votes of the staunch Republicans, but Terry thought the Independents would flock to Brad.

Terry walked to the bathroom and splashed some cold water on his face. He looked into the mirror and saw a shadow of his former self. The long hours, lack of sleep, and stress of the campaign had taken its toll. His hair was almost fully gray, there were dark pouches under his eyes, and his skin looked like dry parchment paper. His body looked even worse. He had given up his regular workout routine and had lost twenty pounds – all of it muscle.

It doesn't matter, he thought. After Brad was elected, he would take a long vacation and get his body back into shape before they moved into the White House. For now, there was no time for anything except the campaign. He knew he had become obsessed, but there was no way he was going to back off until Brad was voted into office.

Terry dried his face and walked to his hotel room desk where he sat down and picked up Brad's acceptance speech. He had pored over it several times already, going back and forth with the speechwriters. He knew the staff complained about him behind his back, how he was too involved in the minutia of the campaign, but whatever he was doing had worked so far. If people didn't like it, they could leave. There were plenty of others he could hire in their place.

He was scribbling a couple of notes on the speech when he heard a knock on his door. Opening it, he was surprised to see Brad standing there, flanked by two Secret Service agents.

"Good morning, Terry. I thought we could go over my schedule for today."

"Sure." Terry checked his watch. "I thought we were meeting in your room at eight-thirty."

"I didn't want to disturb Carolyn. She's still asleep. We had a late night, and I want her to be rested for today."

Brad waited in the doorway as one of the agents took a quick look around Terry's room before giving the candidate the okay to enter. Brad thanked him and shut the door behind him, leaving the agents in the hallway.

The men sat down by Terry's desk and went through Brad's schedule. Everything was winding down, with the only major event left being Brad's acceptance speech; they reviewed that until both men were satisfied.

Terry leaned back in his chair. "I think that about covers it, Gov. Is there anything else you can think of?"

Brad got up and walked to the window, looking down at the hotel parking lot. Keeping his back to Terry, he began to speak. "We need to talk about Amy."

"I thought that was taken care of."

Brad turned to face his long-time friend. "Not entirely. There's been a new development." He took a deep breath. "She's gotten herself pregnant."

Terry jumped up from his chair. He could taste the bile rise in his throat. He swallowed hard before replying. "She's *what?*"

Brad held up his hands. "You heard me. And I don't want a lecture from you. She told me she was on birth control. Then when I tried to dump her, she sprang this on me."

Terry pounded his fist on the desk. "God damn it! Everything we've worked for to get you to this point, and that little bitch is going to bring us down? There's no fucking way."

"Trust me. I am *not* going to let her come between me and the presidency."

"Is she getting an abortion? I can help you arrange it."

Brad began to pace back and forth in front of the windows. "No, she's refusing to get rid of it."

Terry sank into his chair. "Shit. You realize that if one whiff of this gets out, you're through. How are we going to hide this?"

"I've agreed to let her stay on the campaign for another month or so – until she starts showing. Then she's going to move back to Chicago. She's going to tell everyone she got knocked up by some guy she met. No one's going to know I'm the father."

"What about Emily? She knows about the affair."

"I'll handle Emily. If she asks me, I'll deny the baby's mine. And even if she suspects, what's she going to do? She's my daughter. She's not going to rat me out."

"Do you really think Amy's going to keep quiet? Can we trust her to keep this secret?"

Brad stopped pacing and sat down. "She knows what's at stake. She wants me to be president."

"So she's willing to just walk away? She doesn't want anything from you?"

Brad picked up a pen and began to nervously tap it on the desktop. "Not exactly. She wants me to divorce Carolyn when I'm in the White House. And then when some time passes, she thinks we can start dating and then get married."

Terry's jaw dropped open. "You're not seriously considering that?"

Brad gave him a withering look. "I'm not an idiot. I'll just keep stringing her along. Telling her the time's not right. Maybe I'll get lucky and she'll meet some other guy."

"And what if she doesn't? What if she keeps pushing you?"

"I swear to you that I'm not going to let her ruin my life. I'll do whatever it takes to make sure she doesn't."

CHAPTER 39

Ryan sat listening as Brad gave his acceptance speech, not bothering with notes since he had a full transcript in his hotel room. He would refer to the text when he wrote his article this evening. For now, he wanted to just absorb the atmosphere in the convention center.

Ryan noted that his brother had managed to bring his "A" game today. He sounded intelligent, sincere, energetic – everything a presidential candidate should be. The crowd was hanging on his every word, injecting the speech with wild applause and cheers every few minutes. It was as though each statement Brad made was new and original, when really it was mostly a rehash of every other Democratic candidate's platform for the last thirty years.

The only fresh issue was gun control. Although a few prior candidates had paid some lip service to the matter, no one had ever made it their campaign's focal point. The stars had aligned this year, in that at long last the issue seemed to resonate with the voters. Some states had recently enacted laws that had given people the right to carry concealed weapons without a permit. In direct correlation, there had been a number of incidents during which people lost their tempers and whipped out their guns, fatally shooting someone. Some shooting crimes were road-rage cases; others occurred in shopping malls and restaurants. The media was starting to report that relaxed gun laws were leading to more crime, particularly among people who had no prior criminal history.

The assassination attempt on Brad's life had played right into his campaign message, giving even more attention to the issue than the candidate could have expected. Over the last few months, it had become routine at each campaign stop that there would be a crowd of people on either side of the gun debate and the clashes between the two further fueled the media coverage. This week, as expected with the national convention as a stage, there was a huge turnout of both gun control supporters and protesters marching on the streets surrounding the center.

Ryan had already written a number of articles on the topic and wasn't sure there was much more he could milk from it. In fact he wondered how many more stories he could write, period – he thought it was time to end the series. But whenever he broached the subject with the *Tribune* management, they insisted that he continue. The syndication market for his articles had remained strong, even growing as his brother became the front runner. Now that Brad was officially the Democratic candidate, the *Tribune* thought interest would be even greater.

At least at this point, Ryan knew there was an end in sight. Only four months until the general election, and he would finally have his life back. He couldn't wait to return to his wife and their home. He hoped that he and Michelle never had to live through another long term separation like this one. He could understand how difficult it was for Carolyn to leave her home for the campaign trail, and yet he knew how much her family needed her.

When Brad finished his speech, Ryan watched as Carolyn, Emily and Tyler joined the candidate at the front of the stage. The smiles on their faces seemed genuine. Ryan knew that Carolyn wasn't all that excited about becoming the first lady, but he could tell she believed in her husband and wanted to support him. Lately, she had been joining them on the campaign trail more frequently, and her influence seemed to have a positive effect on everyone. Even Emily was back to her old self. Ryan had been keeping a close eye on her and had been relieved when she seemed to have given up the excessive drinking and sleeping around phase she had gone through recently. Watching his brother's family on the stage, Ryan couldn't help but think they made the perfect first family.

When the applause began dying out, Ryan joined the delegates as they began to stand up and make their way to the exits. As he walked up the aisle, he felt a tap on his shoulder. He turned and saw Amy. "Hey, stranger," he said, giving her a big hug. "I've missed you."

Amy hugged him back, a smile on her face. "I've missed you too. It's hard not being part of the inner circle anymore. But I love my new marketing position. I'm working with a great group of people. Everyone's so smart and creative. And I've never had a job with so much responsibility."

"I'm glad you're enjoying it. I know you liked working directly with Brad, but you have to admit, there are only so many dry cleaning runs you can make. You're too smart to be spending your days fetching coffee."

Amy nodded. "I think you're right. I like using more of my brain cells. And I know the work I'm doing now is even more important to the campaign. Having the right marketing effort is critical to his election."

They continued talking until they reached the lobby. "I guess I'd better head to my hotel room and start working on my story," Ryan said. "It was good to see you again. I'll tell Brad that you're doing well."

Amy laughed. "That's all right. You don't have to be the messenger boy. I still see Brad pretty often."

Ryan wrinkled his brow. "Oh, I didn't realize that."

Amy smiled and Ryan thought he saw the hint of a blush on her face. "I'm glad I ran into you, Ryan." She reached up and gave him a kiss on the cheek.

Ryan watched as she turned and walked away. He thought it was odd that Amy had said she saw Brad regularly. Given that he himself spent virtually his entire day shadowing his brother and never saw him with her, Ryan wondered when the two met. About the only time Ryan wasn't with Brad was at night. He stood, lost in thought, an island in the middle of a swirling sea of delegates flowing out of the convention center.

CHAPTER 40

When Ryan got to his hotel room, he flopped down on his bed, pulled out his cell phone and called his wife.

"I was just watching your brother," Michelle said. "I thought he gave a great speech. Even I was inspired, and you know what a skeptic I am."

"That's good to know. I'm surrounded by all these rabid Democrats here, so it's hard to tell whether they're the only ones fired up, or whether Brad's engaging the rest of the country."

"Based on my own observation, I think people are pretty excited about him. Of course, everyone who knows I'm related to him makes a point of telling me what a big fan they are. But I've overheard a lot of strangers talking about him -- like in Starbucks or on the El. I think back to some recent campaigns where no one seemed to care who won. This time, people seem energized."

"Brad's always been Mr. Charisma. On the campaign trail, other than the gun control protesters, most of the people I see are big supporters. Anyone who pays money to meet him at a fundraiser, or even anyone who shows up to hear him speak, is usually already a backer. I'm so isolated from the rest of the world, though, I wasn't sure how much he was catching on with mainstream America. There's only so much you can tell from polls – although, God knows, his campaign does enough of them."

"Well, like I said, there seems to be a lot of buzz about him. Although I guess since he's from Illinois, more people here are interested in his candidacy. Maybe you could convince the *Tribune* to send you to a nice beach town in Florida to see what they think of him *there*. I'd be happy to fly out and help you with your research."

Ryan smiled. "Right. Based on your last trip to see me, we'd spend the whole time in our hotel room."

"Sounds good to me. That and a few walks on the beach would be perfect."

"I'm not sure the *Trib* would buy the research idea, but they might go for me taking a few days off."

"That would be great." Michelle paused. "I knew when you accepted this assignment, it was going to be hard on us. I just didn't realize how hard."

"I know, but at least we're getting close to the end."

"I guess I can survive without you for a few more months. Although I may keep you tied to the bed for the first week you're back here."

Ryan closed his eyes, envisioning his wife's fantasy. "You keep talking like that, and I'm going to have to take a cold shower before I start my article."

Michelle laughed. "So what's your subject going to be?"

"Today's an easy one – the acceptance speech. Actually things have been pretty straightforward the last few days. It's when the convention's over that I'm going to be struggling for ideas again."

"You'll come up with something. You always do." Michelle paused. "So I thought Carolyn and the kids looked great. As far as the TV cameras go, they're the perfect Stepford family."

"Yeah, when Brad hired a man to be his new personal assistant, I wasn't sure he'd look as sharp, but he looks as perfect as ever."

"That's right. I forgot Amy is doing something else now. What is it again?"

"She's working with his marketing committee. In fact, I just ran into her today."

"How's she doing?"

"Good. She seems to be enjoying her new job." Ryan hesitated, struggling to put his fears into words. "She said something that kind of threw me though."

"What's that?"

"I told her that I'd say hi to Brad from her or something like that, and she told me not to bother. That she still sees Brad regularly."

"And that's odd?"

"When Brad meets with his marketing people, it's usually just one or two of the senior people on the committee. I've been in those meetings, and Amy's never been there."

"Well, I'm sure they got to be friends when she was his assistant. It makes sense to me that they'd meet for the occasional cup of coffee."

Ryan got up from his bed and began to pace around the room. "I guess. It's just that he's on such a tight schedule, and I'm with him most of the day. About the only time we're not together is at night."

"And you're thinking that's when they see each other?"

"Maybe."

"And you're thinking their meetings are not for a cup of coffee?"

Ryan cringed, hearing Michelle say the words he couldn't. "I don't know what I'm thinking. It just struck me as odd. Maybe it was the way she said it. Almost like she was gloating."

"You know, I wouldn't be shocked to find out Brad was having an affair. I've always thought he was a little too smooth with the ladies."

"So you've said. But I still can't see it. I mean, to risk what he's got with Carolyn and the kids. Not to mention what he's got on the line now."

"He certainly wouldn't be the first politician to go down that road. It must have something to do with the egos of the men who run for office."

Ryan stopped at his hotel window and looked down at the street below. "And Brad certainly has an ego, but still…"

"Well, you were looking for a new subject to write about," Michelle teased. "Here you go."

Ryan laughed. "God, can you imagine *me* blowing the whistle on an affair?"

"You'd probably win the Pulitzer for it."

"At the same time my family permanently disowned me."

Michelle's tone turned serious. "So really, what would you do if you found out there was something going on?"

"God, I don't even want to think about it. What a nightmare."

"You realize if someone else broke the story and you've been following him around this whole time, it would reflect on your credibility. People would think you knew and were covering up to protect Brad. Your whole career would be undermined."

Ryan began pacing again. "Yeah, but could I destroy Brad's career to save my own?"

"And, as you said before, it's about more than just careers. Your family would never forgive you."

"I don't even know why we're talking about this. It's all hypothetical. I have no proof of an affair. This whole conversation is based on one meaningless comment Amy made."

"Except that you're a trained journalist. Something about that comment hit a nerve. And that's not something you can just ignore."

Ryan sat down, putting his head in his hand as the magnitude of his fears washed over him. "Maybe not. But do I really want to go down that road?"

CHAPTER 41

Ryan tossed and turned all night, images of Brad and Amy flashing through his head. Had he really missed the obvious? He had known for months that Amy had a crush on Brad, but it had never occurred to him that Brad might return her feelings. Sure, there had been some casual flirtation, but that was just Brad. He treated all the women he came across that way. It was his style. Even Carolyn teased him about his way with women.

When he woke for good, Ryan made some coffee and decided to go for a run to clear his head. But instead of helping, with each stride, he felt his emotions grow stronger – anger, dread, betrayal.

When he got back to the hotel, he took a quick shower. With the Democratic Convention wrapped up, Brad had given his staff the day off. They would be traveling this evening to their next campaign stop, but until then, they were free. Ryan had invited Brad for a late breakfast in his room and his brother had accepted; he would be there at ten.

Ryan was still debating whether to confront Brad about Amy. A part of him just wanted to stick his head in the sand, but he knew the possibility of an affair between Brad and Amy would just eat at him if he tried to ignore it. The journalist in him wanted to uncover the truth, although he still wasn't sure what he would do with it. If Brad was having an affair, Ryan couldn't see himself outing him. He loved his brother and would protect him, even if doing so damaged his own career.

When he heard the knock on his door, the adrenaline kicked in. He raced across the room and threw the door open.

Brad greeted him with a wide grin. "Hey, bro." He stepped through the doorway and gave Ryan a big hug. "I'm glad you suggested breakfast. Things have been so crazy lately."

Ryan stepped aside so Brad could enter the room. His brother took a couple of long strides over to the hotel room desk and grabbed the room service menu.

"Let's order," Brad said. "I'm starving."

For the next half hour, while they waited for their meals, Ryan listened with half an ear to his brother's recap of the convention and the upcoming road to election day. When their food arrived, the candidate dug into his breakfast, while Ryan picked at his.

When Brad finished eating, he leaned back in his chair. "You're awfully quiet this morning."

"Got a lot on my mind."

Brad raised his eyebrows and waited.

Taking a deep breath, Ryan looked at his brother. "Are you and Amy having an affair?"

Brad exploded from his chair. "What the hell are you talking about?" he yelled, his hands clenched into fists.

Ryan stood up, going toe to toe with his brother. "You heard me."

Brad's face turned three shades of red before he choked out any answer. "No! I'm not having an affair with Amy. And where the hell did you get that idea?"

"From Amy."

"*What?* What did she say to you?"

Ryan took a step back. "Well, it wasn't exactly what she said."

"Then what was it? What the hell are you talking about?"

Ryan held up his hands. "Look, I'm sorry. Maybe I jumped to the wrong conclusion. It was just something she said about seeing you, and how she said it and…"

"Jesus Christ, Ryan. I can't believe you would even think I'd do that."

"I'm sorry. I… God, I'm just glad it's not true." Ryan sank back into his chair, his whole body flooding with relief.

Brad sat down across from him. "Why don't you tell me what brought this on?"

Ryan took a long drink of water, collecting his thoughts. "It's no big secret that Amy has a thing for you – the way she looks at you, the way she's always touching your arm. But I never thought much of it. Until I ran into her yesterday at the acceptance speech."

"What happened?"

"We talked for a few minutes about her new job. And then I said something about telling you that she was doing well. And she jumped in to say that it wasn't necessary -- that you and she still got together. And it was just the way she said it. Like you two were sneaking off together. And then when I thought about it, it was like, when do you have time to see her? Except maybe at night when I'm not around."

Brad shook his head, and his voice dripped with sarcasm. "And based on that, you jumped to the conclusion that I was screwing her? Are you serious?"

"You're right -- I'm sorry. It was stupid. I was totally out of line."

Brad raised his hand. "Hey, it's okay. I shouldn't have jumped down your throat. It's not the first time a reporter asked me a dumb question. I just didn't expect that one from my own brother. I mean, you know me. You know I love Carolyn. I'd never cheat on her. And especially not now, with the election around the corner."

"Trust me, I didn't want to believe it."

"And what would you have done if your supposition was true?"

"First I would have told you what a complete idiot you were. Then I would have told you to end it." Ryan shrugged. "And then after I finished beating up on you, I'd do everything in my power to make sure no one else ever knew."

Brad reached across the table and put his hand on his brother's shoulder. "Thanks, Ryan. I couldn't ask for a better brother. Right now, when there are so many people around me who have their own hidden agendas, I can't tell you what it means to have someone I can totally trust. Someone who I know has my back, no matter what."

"Well, I guess that's true. Because no matter how pissed off I would have been with you, I know I couldn't have betrayed you."

"Luckily you don't have to deal with that." Brad locked eyes with his brother. "I swear to you on my kids' lives that there's nothing going on between me and Amy."

CHAPTER 42

Brad left Ryan's room and went directly to Terry's, his heart racing with every step. When Terry greeted him, Brad leapt through the doorway, slamming the door behind him.

"Why don't you pour me a drink?" Brad asked.

Terry's eyes widened. He glanced at his watch. "It's eleven o'clock in the morning."

"So make it a fucking bloody Mary if that makes you feel better."

Brad glared at his friend until Terry shrugged and walked over to the mini bar.

Handing the drink over, Terry waited until Brad took a couple of gulps. "You want to tell me what's going on?"

Brad tossed back the rest of the drink and slammed the glass on the desk. He sank into the chair and put his head in his hands. "I just had breakfast with Ryan. He asked me if I was having an affair with Amy."

"Shit. How did he find out?"

Brad raised his hands. "First of all, he doesn't know anything. He was just following up on a hunch. He ran into Amy yesterday, and somehow that little bitch managed to give him the impression that there was something going on between the two of us."

"So what did you tell him?"

"I denied it, of course. Even if he is my brother, he's still a reporter. I can't take a chance that this thing might get out."

Terry sat down and moved his chair close to Brad's. "You realize that if Ryan figured it out, it's only going to be a matter of time before someone else puts it together. Especially once she starts showing."

Brad gripped his armrests and leaned forward. "I am *not* going to let that happen to me. Not when I'm this close to my goal."

"The problem is that you can't be hundred percent sure you can control Amy. If she's dropping hints to your own brother about your affair, think about what she's telling her close friends. What if she confides in someone who goes to the media? All it takes is one wrong person to know, and this whole thing could blow up."

"I know. I can't even sleep anymore. I keep waking up in a cold sweat."

"You and me both. I'm in as deep as you are." Terry shook his head. "And let's not forget about Emily. You've already admitted the affair to her. Even though she's keeping it to herself for now, what's she going to do when she finds out Amy's pregnant? Do you really think she's not going to tell someone – Carolyn or Ryan?"

Brad leaned back and closed his eyes. "So what do we do?"

"The only thing we can do." Terry's voice was like steel. "We eliminate the problem."

Brad's eyes flew open. "What do you mean?"

"We get rid of her. You know there's no other way to make sure the truth never gets out."

Brad felt his stomach turn. "I don't know if I can."

Terry pointed his finger at his friend. "*You* don't have to. I'll take care of it."

"You'd do that for me?"

"When I was in the army, I killed people for the good of my country. To me, this is no different." Terry's eyes burned with intensity. "I know you're the right man for president. With you in power, we can turn this country around. This is what we've been planning for the last forty years of our lives. And I'm not going to let some slut who let herself get knocked up stand in our way."

Brad thought about the idea of losing everything he had fought for, and knew he couldn't do it. He had spent his whole life focused on this one goal. Being president was his destiny. "You're right. There's no other way. But how would you do it?"

"I don't know. I'm going to need a few days to come up with a plan."

The men stood and walked toward the door. Brad put his arm around Terry's shoulder. "I will *never* forget your loyalty. Which is why I'm going to make you my chief-of-staff when we get to the White House."

"You know I'd do this even if you didn't give me that position."

"I know you would. That's why you're a true friend."

When Brad made it back to his hotel room, Carolyn was in bed reading the newspaper.

"How was your breakfast?"

"It was great. Ryan and I had a good talk. And then I stopped by to see Terry."

"Everyone's breathing a little easier today after the nomination?"

Brad smiled, a feeling of relief washing over him now that he had a solution to his biggest problem -- Amy. "I'm breathing a *lot* easier." He hopped into bed next to his wife. He grabbed the newspaper, tossing it aside as he leaned down to kiss her.

CHAPTER 43

A few days passed, and Brad found himself back in Terry's room, planning Amy's murder. Both men had come to the conclusion that there was no other way – now it was just a matter of how and when to do it. Terry had suggested killing her in her hotel room and staging it to look like a robbery.

"I have another idea," Brad said, his voice rising with excitement. "What if we made it look like another assassination attempt? Remember how my poll numbers shot up after the first one? Not only do we get rid of Amy, but we give my campaign a boost right as we're headed into the homestretch."

"How would we do it?"

"I was thinking it could be when I was giving a speech – sometime when I'm up on an outdoor stage. I'd have her standing next to me. Then we'd position you somewhere so you could take the shot and make a clean get-away."

Terry thought about it. "I guess that could work."

"Are your sniper skills still as good as they used to be?" Brad asked, knowing that Terry had been a trained marksman when he was in Special Forces.

"I still get to the firing range once or twice a month. It's a great way to blow off some stream." His eyes met Brad's. "You can count on me to make the shot. I have to. There's no one else that I would trust to bring into this thing. We have to keep it between you and me. We can't afford any loose ends."

Brad reached out and grasped Terry's shoulder. "I know you can do it."

"Have you thought about when and where?" Terry asked.

"We're going to be in Dallas next week. I'm scheduled to lay a wreath and give a speech at the Kennedy Memorial there. Wouldn't that be perfect? To be in the same city where Kennedy was shot? For anyone who was old enough to remember that day, it would stir up all those old memories. Link me with the great man himself."

Terry's eyes flashed with excitement. "You're right. That was such an intense time. I can see the media coverage now – interspersing footage from both shootings. It's brilliant."

"I know. If that doesn't sweep me into the White House, I don't know what could."

"You'll be a shoo-in. People will flock to the polls."

"I'm going to need you to plan the details. I know the timing is tight. Can you pull it off?"

Terry nodded. "I'll fly out this week to meet with the event organizers. I can scope out the location and the surrounding buildings. I'll even be able to suggest where and how the stage is set up to give me the optimal shot."

"Perfect. And we'll have access to the Secret Service plans, so that we can make sure you're in a position to get away fast."

"All right. I'll handle the logistics of the shooting itself. Can you take care of Amy?"

"I've already been running through some ideas. First I'm going to suggest to Carolyn that she go home for a few days. It'll be perfect timing. With everything she's done leading into the convention, she's pretty beat."

"Yeah, it would be better if she wasn't around."

"I agree. I don't want her near me when this happens. She was so worked up after the attempt in Wisconsin. She wanted me to quit the race." Brad shook his head, remembering how angry his wife had been that he wouldn't abandon the campaign, even for a few days. "Anyway, it won't take much to convince her. She'll be happy to get back to her animals."

"So that takes care of Carolyn. What about Amy?"

"I think I'm going to tell her that I want her on the stage with me as a thank you for all her hard work on the campaign. I can have a few other staff people there too, so she's not singled out."

"Good. That should work."

"It won't take much to convince her either. She'll love the idea. Carolyn won't be around, and she can pretend she's the first lady. It's exactly what she wants."

Terry looked thoughtful. "Do you think there will be an autopsy?"

"I'm hoping not. I know where you're going. An autopsy would reveal her pregnancy."

Terry nodded. "That would be a messy loose end."

"I know. I mean the cause of death would be obvious, so it doesn't seem like an autopsy would be necessary. And Amy doesn't have any parents or siblings – no one to insist on anything."

"Well, I guess even if they did one and they found out she was pregnant, there's still no link to you."

"Exactly. Nobody would ever think I was behind an apparent attempt on my own life. I mean, who could come up with something that crazy, right?"

Terry smiled. "I think it could be the perfect murder."

CHAPTER 44

When Terry stepped into the gun shop, the man behind the counter gave him a broad smile.

"Good morning, Terry. Good to see you home again. The governor give you a day off?"

"Yeah, I flew in yesterday. Thought I'd kill a few hours at the range."

The two men had become friends over the several years Terry had frequented the store. It was one of the only gun shops in the area that had an outdoor range to accommodate long-distance rifle shooting. The men chatted for a while, first about Terry's life on the campaign trail and then about the latest gun news. After picking out some new ammunition, Terry stepped around the counter and opened the door to the range.

It was a weekday morning, and the range was deserted. Terry chose a station and began his pre-practice routine. First he reached into his gun case and lifted out his rifle as carefully as if it were a newborn baby. He caressed the cool, smooth metal that was so familiar to him. Opening the box of cartridges, he loaded the gun and put on his ear protectors. Next he set up his rifle stand and gently positioned his gun in place.

Stepping back, he faced his target – an outline of a man's head and torso set back one hundred yards. *A piece of cake,* he thought. Positioning himself at his stand, he sighted his target and then ever so gently squeezed the trigger. He leaned back slightly as the gun jumped in recoil; then he lined up his next shot.

After reeling off ten shots, he took a break and checked his results. There were ten perfectly placed holes through the target's brain. He re-sighted his rifle for the target set back two hundred yards. Another ten shots, another set of perfectly placed holes. He methodically worked back in one hundred yard increments up to five hundred yards. The farther back the target, the more his concentration intensified. He took longer to set up his shots; he breathed more slowly; his finger on the trigger was even gentler.

When he was satisfied with his shooting at five hundred yards, he changed stations and practiced some additional shooting at two and three hundred yards. Based on his preliminary research into the Dallas set-up, he thought he would probably take his shot from somewhere in the two hundred yard range.

When he felt himself starting to lose his focus, Terry called it quits. He stretched and did some neck and shoulder rolls before packing up his gear. He went back into the gun shop, purchased some ammunition, and spent a few more minutes talking to his friend before he drove home.

When he got there, Terry oiled his gun and then packed it along with his other equipment into a shipping container. He addressed it to himself at the hotel he would be staying at in Dallas. Then he dropped the package off at a local UPS shipping center.

That afternoon, Terry boarded a plane from O'Hare to Dallas. When he arrived at the Dallas hotel, he let the hotel staff know he was expecting a package to be delivered the next day. The young woman working at the front desk assured him that they would deliver it as soon as it arrived.

Terry went up to his room and unpacked. After a quick dinner, he took a cab to the Kennedy Memorial and walked around, scoping out possible locations to set up his shot. He found a few different buildings that allowed him access to an open rooftop well within his shooting range. As he looked down at the Memorial from these locations, he determined the optimal placement for the speaker's platform. Satisfied with his research, he returned to his hotel and went to bed early.

The next morning, he met with the team coordinating Brad's visit to Dallas. There were representatives from both the local campaign office and the City of Dallas. When the group assembled at the Kennedy Memorial, Terry was able to manipulate the placement of the stage exactly where he wanted it. He spent the rest of the meeting making sure that every other aspect of Brad's appearance would maximize the impact of the event.

After all the details were ironed out, the group walked over to the nearby West End and had lunch at a steakhouse. Afterwards, they broke up and Terry told the others he was going to do some sightseeing. After spending a short time walking around, Terry went back to the buildings he had scouted the prior evening. He wanted to check out his shooting position for the exact time that Brad's speech was scheduled so that he could take into account the position of the sun and shadows. Feeling ever more confident of his selections, he decided to call it a day.

Back at the hotel, he checked with the front desk about his package. The woman working there told him that UPS had delivered it an hour ago and that they had taken it up to his room as he had directed. Terry thanked her and rode the elevator up to his floor. When he got to his room, he unpacked the gun and ammunition, making sure everything had arrived safely.

His final task for the trip was to find a temperature-controlled storage center convenient to the city. After searching the internet and making a few calls, he found one he thought was suitable. He checked out of the hotel, rented a car and drove to the facility. Paying the manager in cash, he rented the smallest unit for the shortest period of time – a month. After he stored his equipment, he drove back to the airport and booked a flight to rejoin the campaign staff.

Sitting in the airplane, Terry leaned his head back and closed his eyes. For a moment, a vision of Amy squeezing his arm and laughing at a joke he had told flashed through his mind. He felt a twinge of guilt about what he was planning to do, but then quickly dismissed it. She was the one who had gotten them into this mess. She had brought this on herself. She deserved to die. She was just collateral damage -- no different from a civilian casualty in a war. Her death was an acceptable cost to ensure that Brad made it to the White House.

CHAPTER 45

A few days later, Brad and his entourage arrived in Dallas. Now that he was the Democratic nominee, everyone wanted a piece of him. He had a packed schedule, culminating in the open-air speech he would give at the Kennedy Memorial. He had invited Amy and several other staffers to join him on stage as a thank you for all their hard work.

About a half hour before the event, the group gathered at the venue. Brad had just finished chatting with the mayor when Amy slipped up next to him.

"I'm so excited to be here," she said.

Brad smiled down at her. "And I can't begin to tell you how happy I am that you're here. When we go up on stage, I want you standing right next to me."

"That's exactly where I want to be. Standing next to you – for the rest of my life."

"Until death do us part, baby," Brad whispered, as he leaned down and kissed her on the cheek.

* * *

Terry stood on the rooftop adjusting his scope. Brad had just begun his speech to the enthusiastic crowd. Terry noted that Amy was in the perfect position – next to Brad, but not too close. And the weather was cooperating; it was a clear day with almost no wind. He was expecting to make a clean head shot.

As he leaned in and looked through his scope, he saw Amy smile up at Brad – a look of complete devotion on her face. Terry felt his breath catch, and then a bead of sweat trickled down onto his forehead. He pulled back from his rifle, shocked by his reaction. When he had been a sniper in the military, he had never been rattled; his nerves and trigger finger were always steady. Now his whole body was shaking. For the first time since he had agreed to kill Amy, he realized this killing would be different. He wasn't executing an enemy; he was murdering a friend.

He slammed his eyes shut and balled his fists, struggling to pull himself together. *I have to go through with this,* he thought. *I have to eliminate the threat. It's the only way to guarantee that we'll make it to the White House.* Taking deep breaths, he began to calm down. Slowly, he unfurled his hands. He rolled his shoulders back and tilted his head from one side to the other until he felt his neck muscles relax. He opened his eyes and looked down at his hands. They were steady.

He leaned back into his rifle and repositioned his shot. He took one more deep breath, letting a wave of stillness wash over him. He felt his mind and body focus on his task. Amy ceased to be his friend and became an anonymous target. At that moment, his finger gently squeezed the trigger. For a second, he saw the hole between Amy's eyes, and then her head whipped back as she dropped to the ground.

* * *

Brad saw Amy go down out of the corner of his eye. His head snapped around and with one glance, he knew she was dead. Before he could react, he was engulfed by the strong arms of a Secret Service agent and dragged away. There was total pandemonium as the group on-stage realized what had just happened and began to scream and run. Then the entire crowd began to scatter. People were pushed and pulled and trampled as the frenzy swept through the audience.

The Secret Service hustled Brad into his SUV, and with police sirens blaring to clear the way, the driver sped off.

"Are you okay, sir?" the agent asked.

"I'm fine," Brad said. "But who was hit? Was it Amy? I think she was standing next to me."

"Yes, sir. It was Ms. Hewlett."

"Is she…" Brad let his words taper off.

"I'm afraid she's dead, sir. There's no way she could have survived that shot." The agent paused. "I'm sorry, sir."

"This is terrible. I can't believe someone was killed because of me."

"It's not your fault, sir."

"No, it was those crazy right-wing gun nuts who have had it in for me from day one. Well, they're not going to scare me off. The first thing I'm going to do when I get in office is to do everything in my power to change the gun laws in this country. Amy will not have lost her life in vain."

"You realize, sir, that from this point forward, we can't allow you anymore open-air venues. You've clearly hit a nerve with the radicals and we can't give them another shot at you. We're going to have to really limit your exposure."

"I understand totally. As long as I can still get my message out there, I'll trust you to protect me as you see fit." Brad pulled out his cell phone. "I need to call my wife before she hears about this some other way."

He was too late. Carolyn had already heard the news when he reached her.

"Oh, my God, Brad. I can't believe this happened again. Are you sure you're all right?"

"I promise you I'm fine, sweetheart. And before you even ask, I'm staying in the race. No one is going to stop me. I *will* be the next president."

CHAPTER 46

The local Dallas office of the FBI had been activated to provide additional protection for Brad's speech, so when the shooting took place, they already had agents on-site. When they determined a murder had taken place, they took immediate control of the investigation. There were no arguments from the Secret Service, whose primary mission was to protect, not run criminal inquiries.

So it was the FBI that organized the initial search for the shooter, sending their own agents, the Secret Service agents who weren't protecting Brad, and the local Dallas cops to comb the area. Special Agent Christine Walker stayed at the scene for hours coordinating the hunt, making sure that every building in the vicinity was scoured, every car was stopped and searched, every person who raised the slightest suspicion was hauled in for questioning.

It was one of the Dallas uniforms who located Terry's rifle and stand, which he'd abandoned on the rooftop of a building overlooking the Memorial. The scene was cordoned off and the FBI's Crime Scene Unit went into overdrive, bagging and tagging every item they found that wasn't nailed down. Unfortunately, there wasn't much, and what little they did find they knew probably didn't come from the shooter, although they would test it just in case. A cursory look at the rifle told them that the serial number had been filed off and that it had been wiped clean of any fingerprints. But there too, they would make sure the lab examined every nook and cranny.

The fact that the shooter had left his equipment made it nearly impossible for the authorities to find the man. They wouldn't be looking for someone carrying a gun, which meant he could disappear into the swarming crowd, just one more anonymous face in a sea of anonymous faces. After an intensive five-hour search, the SAC called it off. She instructed her team to test for gunshot residue on anyone they picked up for questioning and inform her of any positive results. Given that they were in the gun-crazy state of Texas, she knew that even gunshot residue wouldn't be enough to charge someone. Then she hauled herself off to the W Hotel where the candidate was staying.

When she got there, Christine met with the Secret Service agent in charge and asked for his permission to question Brad and his staff. She had already met the man briefly when they were coordinating their respective agents' security coverage for the speech. Although she didn't technically need the agent's consent, she wanted to establish a cooperative liaison between the departments. She knew there would be plenty of finger-pointing to come out of the incident, and she hoped for a mutually supportive relationship. In other words, she wouldn't point a finger at his agents unless he pointed one at hers.

The agent accompanied her up to Brad's suite, where the candidate and his closest staff members were assembled. When Christine walked into the room, Brad leapt to his feet and rushed to the door, his arm extended.

"I'm Brad Newcomb," he said, his handshake firm. "What can you tell me? Did you find the shooter?"

"I'm Special Agent Christine Walker. I'm running the investigation task force." Christine's handshake was every bit as firm as Brad's. She hadn't made it to her level in the FBI food chain without being as tough as any man.

"Unfortunately, sir, we have not apprehended the shooter at this time. We put the whole area on lockdown after the incident, but it appears that he managed to escape. We did pick up a few men for questioning, but at this point, we don't think we have the shooter in custody."

"So what happens next?" Brad asked.

"We'll use every available resource we have in our investigation. Unless he's truly a lone wolf, he's told somebody about his plan. We just have to find a weak link who's willing to talk."

"What do you mean by a lone wolf?"

Christine pursed her lips. "You know, like the Unabomber, Ted Kaczynski. Someone who lives in the middle of nowhere and has virtually no human contact. A person like that can fly under the radar for a long time. But most people don't live that way. Even the nut jobs have their buddies. And all it takes is for the unsub to tell one friend who tells his wife who tells her best friend. This shooting is too big to keep under wraps. Anyone who isn't directly involved but hears about someone who is will talk about it."

"It's probably one of these gun rights supporters," Brad said. "I've been getting a lot of hate mail and threats since I've been campaigning for more gun control."

"That's one of the first places we'll start looking. I've already talked to the Secret Service about releasing those letters to us. We also have our own list of people in the area who are active in that movement. We think there's a pretty good chance that the shooter could be local. We'll start shaking people down and see if we can get someone to talk."

"What about Amy – the woman who was shot? She was my personal assistant for several months. All of us in this room got to know her quite well." Brad turned and gestured to the others. "I know she doesn't have any immediate family. I'd like to make the burial arrangements for her."

"If no family member steps up, we'll be happy to release the body to you when our medical examiner is finished with it. We'll schedule the autopsy for as soon as possible."

"Is an autopsy really necessary?" Brad asked. "It seems like the cause of death is pretty obvious. That poor woman has already been killed. I hate for her body to be defiled any further."

"I know that a lot of people find an autopsy distasteful, but it's standard operating procedure in any murder investigation. I can vouch for our M.E. and assure you that the body will be treated with the utmost respect."

"I appreciate that, Special Agent. Is there anything we can do to assist with your investigation?"

"Actually, there is. We'd like to interview all of you, as well as the rest of your staff who were at the speech. It may seem like a long shot, but one of you might have seen something that will help us."

"Absolutely. I can speak for everyone on my staff and promise you our full cooperation."

"Thank you, sir. And if it's alright, I'd like to start with you."

CHAPTER 47

After moving a table and chairs into the suite's adjoining bedroom, Christine began her interviews with the staff members who were assembled in the candidate's suite. Brad was first on deck. Then she would talk to Ryan, Emily, and Terry. She would plan to track down the other relevant staff members who were intimately involved in the event planning. She wanted to know who had determined the set-up for Brad's speech and who had access to the information. Clearly, the unsub must have had prior knowledge in order to set up his shot.

After waiting for Brad to get comfortable, the agent asked him a number of questions about the venue for the speech. Many times he referred her to others on his staff, claiming he had little involvement in planning the details for any of his appearances.

"It's fairly common," Brad explained, "for me to be handed a schedule for my day's activities in the morning. Often, that's the first time I find out about a specific location. For example, today I knew I was giving a speech outdoors at the Kennedy Memorial, but that was about it. I trust my staff to handle the logistics so I can concentrate on keeping up on all the issues and getting my message out to the voters."

When Christine asked about Amy, Brad described her responsibilities while she served as his personal assistant. "She did a tremendous job for me, which was why we promoted her to work on the marketing task force. We decided she was too talented to be spending her days fetching my coffee."

"Who else was involved in her promotion?"

"Terry, my campaign manager. He runs the nuts and bolts of the campaign and handles personnel issues."

"So how was she doing with her new job?" Christine asked.

"From what I heard, she was doing great. But, of course, that's just from talking to others. I've really had very minimal contact with her over the last few months. It's ironic that we just happened to choose today's event as a way to thank several of my staff members. I was going to acknowledge the people on-stage at the close of my speech."

Brad grimaced. "It's a terrible burden to realize that had we not invited her to be recognized today, she would still be alive. It's such a waste – a promising young life cut short because of someone's political agenda. It just makes me more determined than ever to change the gun laws in this country. I will *not* be intimidated by these radicals."

As she continued her questioning, Christine got the impression that Brad was saddened by the young woman's death, but stoic. Everything a president was supposed to be – strong and resolute in the face of adversity. The longer she talked with him, the more certain she was that she would be voting for him come November. When she shook his hand at the conclusion of her interview, she felt a small thrill at knowing that she might very well be in the presence of the next president.

Next on her list was Ryan. After a few minutes spent speaking with him, she realized that he had even less knowledge than the candidate in terms of what went into setting up the event and publicizing it. She asked him a few questions about Amy for background, although as far as Christine was concerned, in this case the victim was really just incidental to the crime. Obviously she wasn't the target – just someone who was in the wrong place at the wrong time.

Unlike his brother, Ryan was visibly distraught by the woman's death. "She was really a terrific person. Smart, funny, a real joy to be around. No one deserves to die like that, especially not her. I hope you catch the guy who did it," Ryan said, wiping a tear from his eye.

Christine's next interview was with the candidate's daughter. The agent wasn't expecting much new information from her, but felt obliged to speak with each of the staff members who had accompanied Brad to Dallas. With an investigation this important, she wasn't going to leave any stone unturned. As she anticipated, Emily offered little information, but the agent was still surprised by the girl's reaction to the crime. Although she seemed shaken up by another near-miss assassination attempt on her father's life, she was strangely unaffected by Amy's death.

"I'm just really thankful it wasn't my dad. And if anyone deserved to die, it was..." Emily looked up in horror. "I didn't mean that. It's just that, well, I didn't really like Amy. I mean, I know you're not supposed to speak ill of the dead and all, but... well, she was a real bitch."

The agent tried not to show any reaction. After all, when people work closely together, there's bound to be some tension between some of them. God knew she certainly didn't like everyone in her office, but still, the girl's reaction struck Christine as odd.

CHAPTER 48

Terry stepped into the makeshift interview room with a sense of dread. He walked over to the table and sat across from the agent. With his feet planted on the ground, his spine ramrod straight, and his hands gripping the armrests, he felt like a death row inmate strapped into an electric chair.

"Please relax, Mr. Brinson. I know this is difficult for everyone." The agent smiled warmly at him.

"Yes, ma'am." Terry nodded, but didn't return her smile.

For the next twenty minutes, the agent peppered him with questions, to which he replied with minimal responses. When she asked where he was at the time of the shooting, Terry was ready.

"I was standing out in the crowd. Typically that's what I do. I mingle with the audience and try to pick up on their reactions to the speech. That way I can report back to Brad on how his message is being received."

"So then you wouldn't have been looking in the direction of the shooter."

"No, ma'am. I was facing the stage."

With the agent prodding him, Terry elaborated on what he thought he would have seen and heard had he been standing in the crowd – the noise from the rifle shot, Amy hitting the ground, the agents dragging Brad off the stage, the pandemonium around him.

When Christine asked him about Amy, Terry felt his body go cold. "She was a good person. It was a shame that she had to die."

"Excuse me for saying this, but you seem almost..." Christine hesitated, "detached. I wonder if you might be in shock. You might want to have a doctor --"

Terry held up his hand. "No, ma'am, I'm fine. I apologize if my reaction is not typical. I used to be in the military. I've witnessed a lot of death – a lot of collateral damage."

Christine nodded. "Of course. I didn't mean to embarrass you. In my job, I'm often interviewing the family or close friends of a victim. Sometimes, I'm even the one to notify them of the death. Bottom line is I've seen just about every reaction from fainting to throwing up to shutting down. I guess it's become my habit to ask if I can call a doctor."

Terry didn't know what to say. Did his reaction seem abnormal? Should he seem more upset? He was afraid to try to fake a false emotion. He remained silent, barely aware of his fingers twitching against the armrest before he gripped his hands together to keep them still.

Christine finished up her interview with Terry promising to provide her with a list of staff members who were involved in planning the event. Knowing that his involvement in the planning process would probably come out, he volunteered the information. When she asked whether that was typically a responsibility of his, he lied and told her yes. He doubted that she would find out that he normally assigned that role to others.

Later that night, as he lay in bed, Terry replayed the interview over and over in his head, searching for mistakes he might have made. Tossing and turning, he finally drifted off into a restless sleep. Sometime in the middle of the night, he woke with his fists clenching the bed sheets, a silent scream in his throat, his body drenched in sweat.

CHAPTER 49

Ryan woke up in the middle of the night and sat on the edge of his bed. His whole body ached as though he had been pummeled in a boxing ring. He got up slowly and walked to his computer. As he waited for it to power up, he wiped the moisture from his eyes. He took a deep breath, squared his shoulders, and placed his hands on the keyboard.

"A Life Cut Short," by Ryan Newcomb

I first met Amy when I joined my brother's campaign two years ago. I remember her enthusiasm and, cynic that I am, I remember thinking that it wouldn't last. Just give her a couple of months on the trail to wipe that out of her system. But I was wrong, because Amy kept her energy and enthusiasm and bright smile up until the end. Up until the day that her life was cut short by a madman's bullet.

As I sit here, there are so many memories flooding my mind. Amy working feverishly to get a coffee stain off my brother's jacket before a meeting. Amy reaching across a table and giving my arm a supportive squeeze when she knew I was down. Amy bringing us coffee as we all struggled to stay awake during a late-night brainstorming session. Brad stepping down from a stage after an important speech and Amy being the first to give him a hug.

It was all the little things that she did for my brother and the rest of us that made her so special. As Brad's personal assistant, it was her job to try to make his life run smoothly. Or at least, as smoothly as could be expected. And she did that in spades. But she didn't stop there. She took care of all of us. If we were hungry, she fed us. If we were tired, she sent us to bed. But her ministrations went beyond the physical. She handled our emotional needs as well. When we were angry, she calmed us. When we were down, she encouraged us. When we were frustrated, she energized us.

And why? What did she get out of this? Not much money. Living out of a suitcase. Leaving her friends back in Chicago. Putting her life on hold so that a man could chase his dream. Not a recipe for happiness, and yet Amy was one of the most joyful people I've ever known.

Partly because she believed in Brad. She thought he should be our next president, and she was willing to do everything she could to help him get elected. And so her job became her passion. And that passion inspired all of us. To do a little more. To push a little harder.

And now that shining light is gone. And the world is a little darker. And we grieve. And we grieve more because there was no reason, no justification, no greater good. Just a life cut short.

* * *

Ryan hit the save key and then sent the article to his editor. It would get there in time to make the morning edition. It wasn't his best work, but for now, he was just too drained to write anymore. He dragged himself to bed and pulled the covers over his head.

CHAPTER 50

Brad jumped out of bed and threw open the drapes. As he watched the sun rise, he sensed his own resurrection. Over the last couple of months, he had felt like a dead man walking, paralyzed with fear that someone would find out about his affair and Amy's pregnancy. But with that behind him, he was a new man. He stretched and felt the sun's rays beaming down on him. The road to the White House was clear and his for the taking.

Turning from the window, he strode across the hotel room and yanked open his door. With his renewed sense of infallibility, he didn't bother with the peephole and there was no need to anyway. With the assumed attempt on his life yesterday, the Secret Service had bumped up his protection; there was an agent sitting outside his door. Brad greeted the man and scooped up the stack of newspapers. He was anxious to read about the prior day's events.

He wasn't disappointed. He was the front page headline in every paper. As he had hoped, the stories drew comparisons between Kennedy's assassination and the attempt on his own life. Then they went further to compare the two men -- everything from their youth, their good looks, and their passion for their causes. Brad smiled to himself, thinking that causes were not the only passion the men shared.

As his eyes raced across the pages, Brad felt the excitement course through his veins. The coverage he would get over the next few days was worth millions of advertising dollars. The assassination attempt would serve as the perfect platform to further push his gun control policy. Looking at Amy's photo, he realized he couldn't have asked for a better victim -- a young, pretty face to melt the reader's hearts. When he got to Ryan's story, he nodded with satisfaction. *That should tug on a few heartstrings,* he thought.

When he had absorbed every last word on the subject, Brad leaned back in his chair and closed his eyes. Everything was coming together perfectly.

A knock on the door interrupted his reverie. When Terry stepped into the room, Brad's first reaction was revulsion. His friend was unshaven and disheveled. "God, Terry, you look like shit."

When Terry glanced up at him with bloodshot eyes, Brad caught himself. "Hey, man. I'm sorry. I know it was a rough day."

The candidate put his arm around his friend and drew him into the room. "Why don't you sit down? I'll pour you some coffee."

When the cups were filled, Brad sat next to Terry, leaning in close. "You and I know this had to be done. We didn't have any other choice. Amy brought this on herself."

Terry shook his head. "Right. It was all *her* fault. *You* didn't have anything to do with it."

Brad sat back, stunned. He opened his mouth to respond and then thought better of it. Realizing he was going to have to tread softly, he lowered his voice. "You're right, Terry. I have to accept responsibility for my actions. I should never have gotten involved with her. I made a terrible mistake. One that I'm not going to repeat."

A strangled laugh came from Terry's throat. "You've made that promise before."

"I know I have, but you were there, Terry. You know that Carolyn and I went through a rough patch. And you saw how Amy threw herself at me. But still, I should have resisted."

Terry gripped the table top. "This can *not* happen again. I won't stand for it. I don't care how many women you screw once you're in the White House, but until then, you need to knock it off."

Brad bit his lip and stared at Terry. *Who the hell does he think he is? I'm going to be the next president of the United States and this hack is talking to me like this.* Brad's hand curled into a fist and it took every bit of control he could muster not to smash it into Terry's face.

The candidate counted to three and took a deep breath. "I'm sorry, Terry. I'm sorry for what I did and that you had to get involved. But we have to put this behind us and move on."

Terry sagged into his chair like a popped balloon. "You're right. I was out of line. I'm sorry."

Brad smiled, relieved. "We have to think about the good that came from the shooting. Amy and her bastard child are out of my life. The media is setting me up as the second coming of Kennedy. I'm going to be a shoo-in come November. All we have to do is focus on that."

Terry nodded.

Brad reached over and put his hand on his friend's shoulder. "So we're good, right?"

"We're good," Terry mumbled.

CHAPTER 51

When Christine opened the door to the morgue, all her senses went into overload. Her ears rang with the sound of Rolling Stones music, cranked up loud, pulsating through the room. Her nose twitched at the smell of harsh chemicals that almost but didn't quite cover up the stench of the dead bodies. Her arms popped with goose bumps in the refrigerator-temperature cold, forty degrees colder than the sweltering outdoor summer heat.

She gave her body a few seconds to adjust before walking across the room to where the medical examiner was huddled over the examination table. With the music drowning out the other sounds and engrossed in his work, Dr. Irving was oblivious to her approach. When the agent stepped into his field of vision, the doctor jumped back, his surgical tools clanging onto the table.

"Sorry, Doc," Christine said. "I didn't mean to startle you."

"No problem. It's not like I can nick an artery. There's no more damage I could do to this poor girl."

Their eyes met, and Christine could see the compassion in the doctor's gaze. "So what have you found so far, or is it too soon to say?"

"I'm actually just about finished and what I found is what you'd expect. Cause of death is a gunshot to her head. I've already sent the bullet to ballistics. Other than that, she was a young, healthy female. It's a real shame."

"All murders are tragic, but this one feels worse because we know she wasn't even the intended target."

"There's one other thing that makes it even more terrible."

"What's that?"

The doctor shook his head. "She wasn't the only casualty. She was pregnant – about three months along."

Christine rubbed her hands along her arms, feeling a chill from more than just the cold. "What's ironic is that most of these gun nuts

165

are way right on everything, including being pro-life. And yet not only does the unsub kill an innocent victim, he kills an unborn child."

"Makes no sense, does it? But he's probably out there celebrating anyway. Figures he's made his point. And maybe he has -- maybe Newcomb will back off from his gun control agenda."

The agent reached down and stroked the victim's hair. "Not according to him. He told me this woman's death has just made him more determined to push the issue."

The doctor raised his eyebrows. "You've got to give the guy credit. After two assassination attempts, no one would fault him for putting gun control on the back burner. I hope at least he stops giving outdoor speeches."

"From what I've heard, the Secret Service is going to be all over him from now on."

The doctor moved to a sink, stripped off his gloves, and began to wash his hands. "So are you going to be able to catch this guy?"

"I sure hope so. He didn't leave us with a lot to work with, but we're tracking down every lead. Hopefully, it's just a matter of time."

The doctor gestured to his assistants. "I'm through here. You can take her."

Christine watched as they moved the body to one of the morgue drawers. She turned to the doctor. "As soon as I sign off on your report, you can release the remains."

"No one from her family has contacted me yet."

Christine shook her head. "No, apparently there is no family. Newcomb told me that he would take care of the arrangements."

"I guess it's the least he can do. The poor guy must feel pretty awful knowing the bullet was meant for him."

"I'm sure he does. It seems like this hit everyone on his staff pretty hard." Christine turned to leave. "Thanks, Doc. I guess I better go chase down the bad guy."

When she got to the door, she turned back. "You know what? Before you release the body, let's pull a DNA sample from the fetus."

The doctor looked puzzled. "What for? Does it matter who the father is?"

"Probably not. She wasn't married, and nobody I've talked to has mentioned a boyfriend. It's possible that whoever the father was didn't even know about the baby." Christine shrugged. "I know it doesn't have anything to do with the case, but let's do it anyway. This way if someone does surface, we can give him some closure. It seems like the right thing to do."

CHAPTER 52

Christine pushed her way through the throng of reporters jostling for a good camera position outside the church at Amy's funeral. The Secret Service and the Chicago Police Department were keeping a tight rein on who was allowed inside the building. It was supposed to be a private service, but the location had been leaked, and the media had turned out in force.

She flashed her credentials to one of the cops at the church door, and when he waved her through, she entered the vestibule. A few people still milled around, but most had already taken their seats. She stepped into the sanctuary and sat down in the back pew on the far left side, giving herself a good view of the room.

There were two elderly women seated in the first pew, who Christine guessed were Amy's great-aunts. That was it as far as relatives went. Brad Newcomb sat with his wife and son in the second pew. Christine noted that the candidate's daughter was absent -- not surprising, given how the girl had bad-mouthed the victim, the only one who had done so in all the interviews. Christine wondered what had happened between the two that had caused such animosity.

As the agent looked around the room, she recognized a number of other people she had interviewed, including Terry Brinson, the candidate's campaign manager, and Ryan Newcomb, his brother. She guessed that most of the other attendees were people Amy had worked with in Chicago.

The minister stepped onto the altar and held up his arms for everyone to rise. He gave a short blessing and then moved to the podium, inviting them to sit. He said a few prayers and then began to speak about the young woman who had joined his congregation when she moved to the city ten years earlier. Christine looked around the room and saw that most people sat quietly, their expressions sad, but composed. She noticed only one woman who was sobbing, her shoulders heaving, her face mottled.

When the minister finished speaking, he invited anyone who wanted to say a few words to step up to the podium. When Brad Newcomb stood, there was an expectant rustle throughout the crowd. The candidate walked to the front of the church and looked out over the mourners. He paused before speaking, and Christine sensed that he was milking the audience, although when he began to talk, he sounded sincere.

"Amy's death at such a young age would have been a tragedy under any circumstance. But that her death came about because of someone trying to make a statement about my views on gun control only makes it even more tragic. It's a terrible loss of life. Amy was a sweet, kind, vibrant woman who brought joy to all of us who knew her. She didn't deserve to have her life cut short by a fanatic."

As Brad continued, Christine couldn't help but think that his eulogy sounded like a campaign speech. Maybe that was to be expected. *You just can't take the politics out of the politician,* she thought.

When he was finished, there were four others who took turns addressing the mourners. They each spoke of Amy's kindness and sweet nature. One of the speakers was the victim's ex-husband, which surprised Christine. There weren't very many people who were able to maintain a good relationship after a divorce. As Christine listened, she was touched by the memories the speakers shared. This was the hardest part of her job – hearing what a good person the victim was and watching the grief-stricken mourners left behind. Many of her fellow agents wouldn't bother with attending a funeral, but Christine felt a responsibility to honor the victim.

As the service continued, Christine's mind began to wander. Something had been bothering her about the shooting. It had been niggling at the edge of her consciousness, but she hadn't been able to pinpoint it. She closed her eyes and flashed back to the autopsy. Standing over Amy's body, stroking her hair, it had struck the agent how the bullet hole was positioned so perfectly in the center of the victim's forehead. What were the odds of a missed shot landing in the perfect kill zone? If the unsub was not a very skilled marksman, or if his shot was interrupted, wouldn't it be more likely that the bullet would either have missed everyone or struck someone in an arm or leg or torso? What was the likelihood of such a perfectly placed headshot?

Christine's eyes flew open, and she looked at Brad Newcomb. Could the unsub have wanted to miss hitting the candidate? Could he have just wanted to scare the man? But then surely he wouldn't have wanted to kill an innocent bystander. And then she was back to the question of that perfect kill shot. Could the unsub have actually been trying to kill Amy?

Christine looked around the church. All these people here mourning the young woman, even her ex-husband. Could Amy have had such an enemy – a truly ruthless killer? And even if she did, what was the likelihood of him choosing such a bizarre way of killing her? The odds of that were probably higher than the precision of the missed shot.

The minister raised his arms for everyone to stand and Christine did, still lost in her thoughts. Unless the unsub wanted everyone to think that the candidate was the target to throw the investigation off track. That would make sense. In fact, that's exactly what happened. The FBI was focused on finding a fanatic gun rights supporter. They weren't even considering the possibility that Amy was the intended victim.

Christine surveyed the crowd again, this time looking for a killer. Could someone in this room have wanted to murder Amy? Her eyes landed on the one woman she had seen sobbing before. Given that she was clearly the most distraught person at the service, she must be a close friend of Amy's. That woman was someone she needed to talk to. Maybe she could provide some background on the victim.

Her eyes shifted to the candidate. It occurred to her that there was one other person she needed to speak with again – Newcomb's daughter. Not that Emily was a likely suspect, unless Christine found out she was a trained marksman. But there had to be some reason for her intense dislike of the victim. And if she hated Amy that much, maybe someone else did as well.

As the service ended, Christine stayed in her pew, watching the mourners file out. In any other murder investigation, she would have been all over the victim's life, but in this case, she and the rest of her team had just assumed that Newcomb was the target. Maybe it was time to rethink that strategy. She needed to start digging into who Amy really was and who might have wanted to kill her.

CHAPTER 53

The next morning, Christine boarded a flight to Washington. She was scheduled to meet with her boss that afternoon to bring him up to date on her team's progress. As the plane took off, she looked out the window, watching Chicago gradually disappear. When all she saw was clouds, she closed the blind and leaned her head back, hoping to catch a few hours of sleep. She had been up most of the night, working on her new theory.

The thought of sharing it with her supervisor, Frank Elliot, made her nervous. What if Frank thought she was wrong? Best case, he'd tell her to drop it. Worst case, he'd pull her off the investigation. And there was no way she could let that happen. This was a once in a lifetime, career-making assignment. She wasn't about to give it up. She was going to have to tread carefully.

When she got to FBI headquarters, Christine took an elevator up to her boss's floor, assuming they were meeting in his office. Instead, Frank's secretary sent her to a conference room down the hall -- her first clue that she might be meeting with more than merely her supervisor. Still, she was taken by surprise when she opened the door and found a whole swarm of people crammed into the room. Looking around, she recognized her boss, her boss's boss, and even his boss, along with a medley of assistants.

Christine tried to ignore the sudden panic she felt as she reached out to shake hands with the upper echelon of the bureau. After asking about her plane flight and the cab ride over, Frank asked her to begin the briefing. It was clear that no one in the room had time for small talk.

Christine had prepared a memo outlining the investigation in detail. Not expecting a crowd this size, she had made only a few copies. She handed one to an assistant and asked that he make additional copies. Giving the ones she had to the head honchos, she began her presentation. She took them step-by-step through the shooting, the evidence her team had gathered, and the interviews they had conducted.

She felt her throat tighten when she began, her voice sounding two octaves too high. But as she got further into the details of the investigation, she became engrossed in her presentation, and her nervousness was replaced by confidence. The other agents fired question after question at her, and she fielded them all with ready answers. She and her team were doing everything within their power to track down every lead they had, concentrating on the most vocal opponents to Newcomb's gun control platform.

When she was finished telling them everything she knew they wanted to hear, she brought up her new theory that potentially the victim was in fact the intended target. The reaction was immediate. Whereas minutes before, heads had been nodding and agents had been taking notes, suddenly everything turned. Pens were dropped, expressions turned to disbelief.

Frank was the first to speak. "You're not really suggesting that this victim, who was basically a nobody, had some crazed person in her life who decided to murder her by shooting her in front of thousands of potential witnesses at an event swarming with cops. Are you serious?"

Christine felt her face grow hot, and she knew she was blushing as red as the tie her boss was wearing. "I'm not saying it's a likely possibility. But I don't want to leave any stone unturned in this investigation. If this were any other murder, it would be standard operating procedure to look at the victim's enemies."

"But clearly, this was *not* a typical murder," Frank said. "No one in his right mind would go through so much trouble to kill someone. I mean really. We have thousands of murders on file, and I can't think of a single one where someone plotted out a scenario like this one."

Christine took a deep breath, trying to regain her composure. "I merely brought this up as a theory to let you know we were exploring all possibilities. Given how perfectly placed the bullet was for a head shot if she was the intended victim, I believe we have to at least consider the option."

"You can proceed under the assumption that this option has been considered and dismissed," Frank said. "We can't afford to waste any of our resources on a wild goose chase. Unless there's anyone else in this room who thinks that Newcomb wasn't the intended target?"

Although his question was posed to everyone, Christine noticed that he only looked at his superiors. And based on their vigorous head shaking, apparently they thought her theory was as crazy as he did. Looking at the underlings in the room, she knew there wouldn't be anyone else committing career suicide by supporting her.

As she looked around the room and saw the incredulous faces staring back at her, Christine made a quick decision – the only decision she could make if she wanted to keep her assignment. "As I said before, I just wanted to throw the idea out there. However, since the most obvious scenario is that Newcomb was the target, I have assigned my team with that in mind. It is not my intention at this time to divert any of our resources to an alternative theory."

Christine could see the relief on everyone's faces. Apparently, they had decided that she wasn't a nut job after all.

"I appreciate your thoroughness, Christine," Frank said. "Let's plan to reconvene next week for another update."

He stood up, and after a brief nod in her direction, he turned away from her, huddling with his superiors. Christine gathered up her notes and stuffed them into her briefcase. She left the conference room and started walking briskly to the elevators, anxious to leave the meeting behind her.

That was a close call, she thought. *For a minute there, I think they were ready to replace me. I won't make the mistake of assigning any of my team to my alternative theory, but I'm not willing to dismiss it myself. If I have to do all the legwork on my own, then that's the way it's going to be. I've vowed to find Amy's killer, and I'm going to look everywhere until I do.*

CHAPTER 54

At the end of Amy's funeral service, Christine had approached the woman she had seen sobbing and taken down her name and address. They had agreed to meet after the agent returned from her trip to D.C., so Christine found herself standing in front of the woman's brownstone in Chicago's Lincoln Park neighborhood.

She rang the doorbell and looked down the bustling street as she waited. A few minutes later the door opened, and Amy's friend, Tina, invited her in. They shook hands and Christine thanked the woman for seeing her.

"I'm happy to do whatever I can to help you find the man who killed Amy. She was my best friend."

Tina began to cry, lifting a Kleenex to her face. She turned and started walking into her living room, Christine on her heels. They sat, and the agent waited for Tina to compose herself.

"I'm so sorry," Tina said. "I've been like this ever since I heard. I'm supposed to go back to work tomorrow, but I don't know how I'm going to do it."

"That's okay, just take your time. I'm in no rush."

Tina sat up tall and took a deep breath. "I'm ready. What would you like to know about Amy?"

"Why don't we start with how you met Amy and the two of you became friends?" Christine asked, hoping the topic would help Tina relax.

Her strategy had the desired effect and before long, Tina was talking freely about how she and Amy had met while both were working for the state and had quickly become friends, eating lunch together most days.

"In some ways, we were so different, but in spite of that, we just clicked. Take marriage -- I've been happily married for years. Amy was divorced, but hoping to find a new husband and start a family."

Christine jumped in, taking advantage of the subject. "Was Amy dating anyone?"

"Not recently. She had been seeing someone. It was a guy she had met on the campaign trail. But they had broken up a couple months ago."

"Do you know his name?"

"No. In fact, she was really secretive about him. Even with me. She told me there were 'complications.' " Tina wiggled her fingers like quotation marks.

"What do you suppose those complications were? Do you think he might have been married?"

Tina's eyes widened. "Not a chance." She shook her head vehemently. "Amy would *not* have been dating a married man. Not only was she really against that morally, but she also wanted a husband and kids. She was smart enough to know that most married guys never leave their wives, no matter what they say."

"Smart girl," Christine said. "So then, what do you think the complications were?"

"I just assumed it was that she and the guy were both on the campaign staff. Amy had always resisted dating anyone she worked with." Tina gave a sad smile. "She had a whole bunch of dating rules."

"That's not a bad one," Christine said. "So did she tell you why they broke up?"

"No. In fact, it was kind of weird. One day he was Mr. Perfect. And then the next time she called, they had broken up and she told me she didn't want to talk about it."

"How often did you talk to each other?"

"When she was first on the campaign trail, it was every few days. But then, over time, our contacts became less and less frequent. Lately, we probably only talked about once a month." Tina shrugged. "She was so busy and she always worked really late. She just didn't have much time for herself."

Christine hesitated, unsure if she wanted to share the information she had, but then decided to go for it. "Did you know that Amy was pregnant?"

"Yes," Tina said, her eyes welling up with tears. She began to cry again and then jumped up from the sofa. "Would you excuse me, please?"

Christine watched her leave the room and then stood up, walking to the fireplace and picking up a photograph from the mantel. Tina and Amy had their arms around each other, beaming into the camera. When Tina returned, the agent set the photo back down.

"That's the last picture I have of Amy. She was here at my house for a party."

Tina walked to the sofa and sat down, placing a glass of water on the cocktail table in front of her. "I'm sorry. I should have asked you before. Would you like something to drink?"

"No, thanks. I'm fine." Christine sat down across from her. "So can you tell me about the baby? Do you know who the father was?"

Tina hesitated, clearly struggling with sharing something she had been told in confidence. She finally spoke, her head lowered. "It was just a guy she had a one-night stand with. He didn't even know about the baby." She raised her head and held up her hands. "That was so unlike her. You have to understand, Amy was really pretty. She could have had any guy, and she knew it. She was a big flirt, but she never just jumped into bed with anyone. She always waited until she was in a committed relationship."

"But not this time?"

Tina lowered her hands to her lap and began to pick at a fingernail. "She said she was on the rebound. You know, after breaking up with the guy she had been dating. She felt really embarrassed about it."

Tina looked up and leaned forward. "But she had decided to keep the baby anyway. She was planning on quitting her job and moving back here to have it. She knew it wasn't the ideal situation. You know, without having the father involved. But she really wanted the baby. It was a dream come true for her."

Tina sagged back into the sofa, weeping softly. "I just can't believe she's gone. That someone killed her and an innocent baby. It's just so awful."

Christine stood and moved around the table. Sitting down next to Tina, she put her arm around the woman. "I'm really sorry for your loss. I promise you I will do everything in my power to find whoever killed her."

CHAPTER 55

The next morning, Christine flew back to Dallas. She had spent the rest of the previous day interviewing a few more of Amy's friends in Chicago. Other than Tina, the victim had not kept up with anyone else other than through the occasional email. No one else the agent talked to knew Amy was dating someone. Since that was a dead end, Christine had kept the pregnancy to herself.

When she got to her office, Christine assembled her team in one of the conference rooms. She had organized them into groups following up on different leads. Her senior investigator, in charge of the group assigned to the gun rights fanatics, was the first to give her a progress report. "We're running down every lead we have, but it's pretty dry out there. Either no one knew what this guy was up to, or no one's talking."

"It's unusual that nobody has stepped forward to take credit," Christine said. "Usually these types of groups like the notoriety associated with an incident like this."

"Not this time. There's some chatter on their web sites. But it's just the usual stuff – support for what happened, but nothing indicating who's behind the crime."

"Maybe they're embarrassed that they missed Newcomb," Christine said. "That they killed an innocent woman by mistake."

"Maybe. I don't know. But we'll keep digging."

Christine turned to another agent who was working as a liaison with the Chicago field office, handling threats to Newcomb stemming from his responsibilities as Illinois governor. "Have you had any better luck?"

The agent shook his head. "Not yet. But we've got a ton of material to go through. I wouldn't say Newcomb was any more of a target than most governors, but there are still plenty of people with a grudge against the guy. You already know about the gun rights supporters who were opposed to the new laws he pushed there. Plus, there were incidents with some local transportation and construction companies, some of which may have ties to the mob."

"Like what?" Christine asked.

"There were contracts in place for highway work that were very lucrative. When Newcomb got into office, he didn't like the price the state was paying. He managed to find some loopholes to get out of the contracts and hire new companies for a lower fee. That pissed off some people."

"Sounds promising, except for the fact that it's kind of ancient history."

"Well, some of these folks carry grudges for a long time. Maybe they were just waiting for the right time and place. Planning a hit far away from Illinois takes them off the radar screen."

"It's certainly a lead worth pursuing," Christine said.

"Yeah, and like I said, we've just barely skimmed the surface. There are a lot more leads to follow up on there."

"Is the Chicago field office cooperating?" Christine asked.

"They've been great. They're happy to have some extra eyes on their cases."

"Okay, keep searching then." Christine turned to the next agent, who was working with the authorities in Wisconsin, where the previous assassination attempt had taken place.

The agent cleared his voice before speaking. "We've interviewed the perp. He's in jail awaiting trial. As you would expect, he was delighted that someone else took a shot at Newcomb. He told us that he hopes the third time is the charm. Other than that, he hasn't given us much. We have his computer from the initial search warrant, and we're still following up with his known associates, but so far, we haven't found anything concrete."

The last agent to speak was in charge of all the miscellaneous leads. "We've found plenty of crackpots with various political agendas, but no red flags yet. Unfortunately, we may be dealing with some whack job who has no prior history or political affiliation. Let's not forget the Reagan attempt. All John Hinckley wanted was to get Jodie Foster to notice him. With someone like that, there's no logical way to track him down if he doesn't come forward."

"It's certainly a lot easier when they get caught in the act," Christine said. "Like Hinckley and the shooter in Wisconsin. With our unsub on the loose, he could be anywhere, and unfortunately, he may turn up again."

"I bet the Secret Service is having fits."

Christine nodded. "From what I've heard, they're not letting Newcomb go to the bathroom without sixteen agents surrounding him."

"If that's the case, maybe we'll get lucky and this guy will try again and get caught this time."

"I think I'd prefer that we catch him before he makes another attempt," Christine said, dryly.

"Well, sure, I didn't really mean I wanted someone taking another shot at Newcomb," the agent said, blushing.

Christine laughed. "Don't worry about it. I won't put you on our watch list for making a death threat against the candidate." She looked around the room. "So does anyone else have anything more they'd like to share?"

A few agents jumped in with ideas, and they all spent the next half hour hashing out additional strategies. When they were finished, Christine made sure everyone had their marching orders before she dismissed them. After the team had cleared out of the conference room, Christine headed to her office. She had a stack of messages and non-urgent emails that had piled up while she was traveling, and she spent the next couple hours sorting through them.

It wasn't until her stomach started growling that she realized it was well past her usual lunchtime break. She pulled her purse out of her drawer and stood up. She was halfway out of her office before she turned back. *One more thing,* she thought, as she sat back down at her desk.

Picking up the phone, she called a technician at the FBI lab who was assigned to her investigation. She asked whether he had received the DNA that the medical examiner had taken from Amy's fetus. When he confirmed he had it, Christine asked him to run it through their data bases.

"How long will that take?" she asked.

"I should have the results in a few days. As you know, this case is top priority. We're processing everything we get immediately."

"Great. Call me when you have them. I'd like to know who that baby's father is."

CHAPTER 56

Brad drummed his fingers impatiently. He was seated at a table in his hotel suite, surrounded by a group of staff members, his wife, and his brother. They were all waiting for Terry, who was late again. Ever since Amy's death, his campaign manager's behavior had been erratic, and Brad was getting tired of it. When Terry finally walked into the room a few minutes later, Brad couldn't hold his tongue. "Nice of you to join us."

Terry shuffled to the table, not bothering with a response. The others watched him approach and then looked at each other, expressions of disbelief on their faces. Terry looked like he had rolled out of bed and not bothered with a shower. His clothes were wrinkled, his hair uncombed, even the way he carried himself was different. Instead of his usual military bearing, his shoulders were slumped, his head lowered. He pulled out a chair and sagged into it.

Brad clenched his jaw, trying not to let his impatience show. After a minute of silence, he spoke. "Well, Terry, this is your meeting."

Terry raised his eyes, his pupils unfocused, and took a deep breath, pushing his shoulders back. "Right, let's get started. I've got the day's schedule here."

He handed out copies and began to take everyone through Brad's agenda. There was the usual smattering of meetings and appearances in the morning, and then most of the afternoon was blocked out for a rehearsal for an upcoming debate between the candidate and his Republican counterpart, Bob Ellington.

Brad looked at the staff member who was going to play Ellington's role in the rehearsal. "So are you ready to take me on, Tom?"

Tom held up his hands, waving his fingers in a come to me signal. "Bring it on, Governor."

The other staff members laughed, breaking the tension in the room -- except for Terry, who didn't even crack a smile.

"Just wait till I zing you with my pro-life platform," Tom said. "You know how some of the debates have gone in the past. With the Republican trying to get the Democrat to admit he wouldn't want his wife or daughter to get an abortion. And the Democrat trying to get the Republican to admit that in some cases, he would."

"That's right," Carolyn said. "Who was it who asked one of the Republican candidates, 'Would you want your wife to get an abortion if she was raped?' God, these things can get so ugly."

"Well, I've got my answer for that one," Brad said. "I would want my wife to have the right to make her own choice on the matter, and then I would support whatever choice she made." He looked around the table. "I think that's what most of my supporters want to hear, which is fine with me. I don't consider a fetus to be a human being."

Terry's face went white and he pushed himself out of his chair. "I think we're finished here," he mumbled on his way out of the room.

The others sat in silence until he left; then Ryan chimed in. "Is he okay?" he asked, looking at his brother. "I mean, I know we're all dealing with Amy's death. It's been hard on everyone, but he seems to be really struggling."

"Ryan's right," Carolyn said. "I've never seen Terry like this. I think maybe you need to suggest he take some time off."

Brad shook his head. "Obviously he's taking it really hard, but he needs to keep his focus on the election." He looked at his staff. "I appreciate the rest of you doing your best to move forward. We all miss Amy, but we have a campaign to run. We can't let whoever killed that poor woman win by taking our eye off the ball."

"Not everyone has your fortitude, Brad," Ryan said, a hint of sarcasm in his voice. "For me personally, work helps me deal with what happened. But we all grieve differently. I agree with Carolyn that you need to give Terry some time off."

"Fine," Brad said, not wanting to continue debating the issue. "I'll talk to him about it. I don't think it's what's best for him, but if that's what he wants to do, we'll just need to adjust."

The candidate dismissed his staff and summoned Terry for a private meeting. As he waited for his friend to join him, Brad weighed his options. Watching Terry disintegrate under the stress he was feeling was making the candidate nervous. Sending Terry away for a few days would eliminate the risk of him breaking down and telling someone what they had done. On the other hand, Brad was concerned about not having Terry nearby where he could keep an eye on him.

When Terry arrived, Brad decided to confront him. "Listen man, you have to pull yourself together. Everyone is talking about you. The way you're acting could make someone suspicious."

"Come on, Brad. No one suspects what we did." Terry gave a strangled laugh. "After all, we planned the perfect murder, didn't we?"

Brad's face turned red. "God damn it, Terry. You need to get over this. I don't know why the hell you're acting this way. You've killed people before. As far as I'm concerned, Amy was an enemy of the state. She was going to bring me down. I don't have any regrets about what we did and you shouldn't either."

"Don't tell me how I should feel," Terry shouted. "You weren't the one who pulled the trigger."

Brad raised his hand. "All right, just settle down." He gripped Terry's shoulder. "I appreciate what you did for me. And whatever you need me to do now, just tell me. If you need some time off, take it. Just tell me what you want."

Terry shook his head. "No. The last thing I need is to sit in my apartment and stare at the walls. I'll be fine. Like you said, I've killed people before. I'll get over it."

Brad watched his friend go, anger simmering below the surface of his calm demeanor. *I should be home free with Amy gone,* he thought. *Not dealing with Terry's bullshit remorse.*

CHAPTER 57

Christine sat at her desk, poring over the latest reports from her investigative team, when the phone rang. She answered and heard the voice of the FBI lab technician.

"I have your DNA results," he said, not bothering with any small talk.

"Great. What do we have?" Christine asked.

"Nothing. A big goose egg. No matches found."

"So that means the baby's father is not a convicted criminal, and he isn't in law enforcement or the military."

"Right. Which leaves you with the remaining eighty percent of the males in this country."

Christine laughed. "Really narrows it down, doesn't it? In fact, we don't even know that he's an American citizen. So that leaves about ninety-seven percent of the males in the world. So much for the wonders of modern technology."

"Sorry I couldn't help you."

"I knew it was a long shot," Christine said. "I appreciate the fast turnaround."

"No problem. Like I told you before, this case is top priority for all of us."

"Tell me about it." Christine hung up, thinking about all the people in the FBI and beyond who were pressuring her to wrap up the case. With no great leads, she knew it was going to take a lot of old-fashioned legwork, mixed with some luck, to break it.

She pondered her next move and then picked up her phone. If she wasn't going to get the answer from DNA testing, she was going to have to find someone who knew who the baby's father was. She called her secretary and told her to find out where Newcomb and his staff were going to be tomorrow and then book her a flight there this afternoon. It would be easy to cover her trip with her superiors. They wouldn't have to know that she was still working on her theory that

Amy was the intended victim. She would just tell them that she was conducting follow-up interviews with the eyewitnesses to the assassination attempt.

When her secretary called back with her travel itinerary, Christine was happy to hear she was heading to San Francisco; it was one of her favorite cities. She pulled out her notes and located the cell phone number for Terry Brinson, Newcomb's campaign manager. She would ask him to coordinate the interviews.

* * *

The next morning, Christine sat across the table from Terry in a conference room in the hotel where the candidate and his staff were staying. He handed her a piece of paper with a list of names, each corresponding to a half hour time block.

"I've pulled together a list of all the staff members who traveled to Dallas with the governor that day. I've set up a schedule for you to talk to everyone who was there."

"This is great," Christine said. "I really appreciate your help."

"We're all anxious for you to find the person who tried to kill the governor. We're happy to help you any way we can."

"I see that you're first on the list."

Terry nodded. "Yes, ma'am. I'm not sure I have any new information for you, but I'm willing to try."

Christine glanced at her watch and then began her questioning. She pulled as many details about the shooting as she could from Terry before switching gears.

"I have a few questions about the victim," she said.

"You mean the governor?"

Christine frowned, put off by his response. "No. Actually, I meant Amy Hewlett."

"Oh, sorry. I guess I think of the governor as the victim. Seeing as he was the target." Terry rapped his knuckles on the arm of his chair. "So what would you like to know about Amy?"

"Did you know that Ms. Hewlett was pregnant?"

Christine watched as Terry's eyes darted to the side before looking down at his hands. After a brief hesitation, he raised his head and looked at the agent. "No. I wasn't aware of that."

Christine had interviewed a lot of people over the years, and her instincts were screaming that Terry was lying. But why, she wondered, deciding not to press him on it. "We've kept that information out of the media, and I would appreciate your discretion in keeping it to yourself."

Terry nodded.

Christine leaned forward in her chair. "Do you have any idea who the father might be?"

This time, there was no hesitation on his part. "I have absolutely no clue. I worked with Amy, but we weren't close personally. She never talked about her private life with me."

"Do you know anyone on the staff who had been close to her?" Christine pressed. "Anyone who might know who she had been involved with?"

"I really can't help you there. I don't pay attention to that kind of thing. As long as people do their jobs, I couldn't care less about their personal lives."

Christine raised her eyebrows. "I should think, with the way the staff works so closely together, that you would know everything about each other."

"Not really. We're all so focused on the campaign. It's a twenty-four/seven job. Actually, I'm surprised to hear that Amy was pregnant. I don't know how she had the time to meet anyone." Terry paused. "I guess I have heard that a lot of the staff hook up with people they meet in bars. You know, just one night stands. It is kind of lonely being on the road all the time."

"I imagine," Christine said, thinking about the ninety-seven percent of the world's male population she had narrowed it down to. She realized that tracking down the baby's father was not going to be easy. She looked down at her notes. "I think that's all I have for now."

Terry stood up and started to make his way across the room. He was about halfway to the door before he turned back. "I hope you don't take this the wrong way, ma'am, but I am curious how Amy's pregnancy relates to your investigation?"

Christine shrugged. "We're just trying to tie up all the loose ends."

* * *

Terry left the conference room and walked to the elevator bank, stepping into an empty car and punching the button for his floor. When the doors closed, he sagged against the side.

Why was the FBI interested in who knocked Amy up? How could that possibly be relevant? It couldn't be -- unless they suspected that she was the real target. And then, as he was all too painfully aware, her pregnancy was very relevant.

CHAPTER 58

Ryan walked into the conference room and shook hands with Christine. "It's nice to see you again. Have you made any progress on your investigation?"

"Yes, we're making good headway. We have a lot of leads to track down though, so it may take a while."

"In other words, you're not close to finding the shooter."

Christine raised her eyebrows. "That's not what I said at all."

Ryan shrugged. "Sorry – occupational hazard. We reporters always try to read between the lines." He sat down and looked across the table. "But really, from what you're telling me and what I've read in the papers, it doesn't sound like you've got any suspects yet, right?"

"And here I thought I was supposed to be interviewing you, Mr. Newcomb."

Ryan smiled, realizing he had pushed her too far. "As I said, old habits die hard. And please, call me Ryan."

"All right, Ryan. How about if I ask *you* some questions? I'll even make you a deal. When I'm finished, you can ask me whatever you'd like."

"How can I refuse an offer like that?" Ryan leaned back in his chair. "Go ahead. Ask away."

With the agent's prodding, Ryan walked her through everything he could remember about the shooting. "I've thought more about it since you interviewed me the first time, and I haven't come up with anything new. I wish I could. I can't tell you how much I'd like you to find the guy who murdered Amy."

"I'm sure it's been very difficult for you to have been there for two assassination attempts against your brother."

Ryan nodded. "Yes, even though the first guy was caught, it's hard knowing there's still someone else out there who wants to kill Brad. And who knows how many others are just waiting for a chance. He's really touched off a hot button with his gun control platform." Ryan paused. "And it's not just about Brad. It's about Amy, too. She was a really special person. She didn't deserve to die that way."

"Were you close to her?"

"Yes. She was Brad's personal assistant when she first joined the campaign. The two of us traveled everywhere with him. We spent hours every day together for over a year."

"Do you know if she was involved with anyone?"

"Amy -- dating anyone? No way, she didn't have any time for dating." Ryan laughed. "Actually, she kind of had a thing for my brother."

Christine stopped taking notes. She put her pen down and leaned forward. "She had a thing for the governor? Could you elaborate on that?"

As soon as Ryan saw the agent's reaction, he wished he could take back what he had said. He raised his hands defensively. "I shouldn't have said anything. I mean, there was nothing to it. It was just a silly crush."

"Then I take it you didn't know that Ms. Hewlett was pregnant?"

"*Pregnant?*" Ryan felt the blood drain from his face. "That's not possible. Are you sure?"

"Positive. We did an autopsy."

Ryan leaned back, his shoulders sagging, shocked by the news. "I had no idea. So it wasn't just Amy who was killed. The shooter killed her unborn child too."

"Unfortunately, yes," Christine said, picking up her pen and tapping it on the table. "And there's no one you can think of who could be the father?"

Feeling the agent's eyes boring into his, Ryan began to stammer. "I...I really don't know." For Ryan, the rest of the interview passed in a blur.

When it was over, Christine kept her word. "So a deal's a deal. Do you have questions for me?"

Ryan leapt from his chair. "Maybe some other time." He raced across the room, feeling like the walls were closing in on him. When he got to the door, he yanked it open and then slammed it shut behind him. His legs moved like train pistons, powering him down the hall.

His mind was going in a hundred different directions. How could Amy have been pregnant? Who was the father? He thought back to the National Convention when Amy told him she still saw Brad regularly. When he had confronted Brad, his brother had denied an affair. Had he lied? Was Brad the baby's father?

Ryan found himself outside on the sidewalk. He had walked out of the hotel without knowing it, his body propelling him forward on its own accord. He stood, looking across the street, the cars zooming past him. He saw drivers and passengers staring at him, and he realized that his fists were clenched like some lunatic's.

Taking a deep breath, he turned around and walked back into the hotel, finding a chair in the lobby. He sat, rested his head in his hands and tried to wrap his mind around what he had just learned. He kept going back to the same question. Could Brad be the baby's father? Not only had his brother denied the affair, he had sworn on his children's lives. But Ryan knew that Amy wasn't dating anyone openly, and if she was pregnant, then clearly she was involved with someone. Who else could that be, if not Brad?

And if it was his brother, did he know about the baby? Ryan thought back over the last couple of weeks. Since Amy's death, Brad had seemed more pumped than ever about the campaign and his chances for election. Ryan himself felt devastated, knowing that the baby could have been his niece or nephew. Surely if his brother had known about his unborn child being killed, he would feel the same way. He couldn't possibly be so callous as to care more about being president than his own child's life. Could he?

CHAPTER 59

Christine's last interview of the day was with Brad, and she was anxious to speak with him. Once Ryan had revealed Amy's crush on the candidate, the agent had asked others about it. Some expressed surprise, but others had noticed what Ryan had. And no one else had come up with any possibilities for the baby's father. In fact, no one was even aware that Amy had been dating anyone.

When Brad walked into the conference room, Christine flashed him her most disarming smile. "It's nice to see you again, Governor. I really appreciate your taking time from your busy schedule to meet with me."

Brad reached forward and shook her hand. "Of course. I want to do everything I can to help you nail the bastard who killed Amy."

"I'd like to start by reviewing everything you can remember from the day of the shooting. I realize that we covered all this when I first spoke with you, but I know you and the others were probably in a state of shock then. I've often found that people are able to remember more details after some time has passed."

"That makes sense. We were all pretty shaken up that day."

As Brad began to relate his memories of the shooting, Christine interrupted him periodically with questions or to ask him to elaborate on certain points. When the agent was satisfied that she had all the information she could get from him about the shooting, she switched the focus to Amy.

Wanting to broach the subject slowly, Christine reviewed what she had learned about Amy's responsibilities on the campaign, both from Brad when she had first spoken with him, as well as what she had culled from her other interviews. Once that groundwork was laid, she asked about Amy's life outside of work.

"I'm not sure I can help you with that," Brad said. "Amy never shared any details about her personal life with me. I know she had been married and divorced, but that's about it."

"How about more recently? Do you know if she was dating anyone?"

"No. If she was, she never mentioned it."

Christine leaned forward, looking directly into Brad's eyes. "Did you know she was pregnant?"

"Amy -- pregnant? I had no idea." Brad looked genuinely surprised. "That's awful. That means there were two victims in this tragedy. Has the baby's father come forward?"

"No. That's why I asked the question. If I could find out who he is, I'd like to inform him. I think he has a right to know."

"I wish I could help you. I suppose it could have been someone on the staff. But if no names have come up yet, it's possible it was just a fling." Brad turned his palms up. "The travel schedule we keep is hard on everybody. I'm sure some people are resorting to one-night stands."

"Terry Brinson had the same theory. Although most of the others I've talked to didn't think Amy was the type. Unfortunately though, they didn't give me any other alternatives. No one seems to be aware of her being involved with anyone."

Christine shuffled some papers around before continuing. "In fact, the only name that came up was yours."

Brad's eyes widened. "*Mine?* What do you mean?"

"A few people I talked to mentioned that Amy had a crush on you."

Christine noticed the candidate's jaw tighten, but when he spoke, his voice was calm. "That may have been the case. As I'm sure you're aware, some women seem to be attracted to men in office. We get our share of groupies. I don't understand it myself. It's not like we're rock stars."

"So was Amy one of those women?"

Brad shook his head. "I really don't know. If she had any feelings for me, she certainly never made them known to me. Which is not surprising. Amy was well aware that I am very much in love with my wife. She would have known that there was no chance for a relationship between us."

"Has anyone else ever mentioned her feelings for you?"

"Not that I can recall."

"Not even your brother?"

Brad raised his eyebrows. "Ryan? Ryan told you that Amy had feelings for me?"

Christine nodded. "Yes, actually he's the one who first brought it to my attention."

Brad scratched his head, looking puzzled. "I suppose it's possible that he mentioned it to me at some point. I really don't remember. If he did, I'm sure it was just an offhand comment, and I wouldn't have paid any attention to it. As I told you before, that sort of thing comes with the territory. I've gotten used to it over the years, but Ryan's new to the political world. I'm not sure if he's noticed how regularly women throw themselves at me."

"I appreciate your candor." Christine's lips curved in a wry smile.

"Look, I have a beautiful wife whom I'm very much in love with. I would never disrespect her that way. Carolyn and my children mean more to me than anything. I would never jeopardize my marriage in any way."

Christine smiled. "Your wife's a lucky woman."

"I assure you, I'm the lucky one." Brad looked at his watch. "Is there anything else? I have a cocktail reception I need to get to. It's not good form for the guest of honor to be late, you know."

"No problem. We're finished here." Christine stood and extended her hand. "I hope I didn't offend you in any way."

Brad took her hand. "Not at all. I know you're just doing your job."

When he left, Christine jotted down some additional notes. Her impression of the candidate was that he seemed very sincere, but then again, most politicians came across that way. Years in the public eye seemed to leave them all with that smooth veneer. They could look you straight in the eye, and lie through their teeth. Was that the case with Newcomb? *Was everything he had just told me a lie?* she wondered.

CHAPTER 60

After leaving the conference room, Brad marched through the hotel lobby, flanked by two Secret Service agents. They took the elevator up to his suite, where the agents checked his room and then positioned themselves outside the door. As soon as he was alone, Brad picked up the phone and called his brother.

He couldn't hide the anger in his voice. "I need to see you right away. Can you come up to my room?"

"Sure, I'll be right there," Ryan said.

The candidate paced the room, fuming, as he waited for his brother to arrive. When Ryan stepped through the door, Brad pounced on him. "What the hell did you tell that FBI agent? She said you told her Amy had a thing for me? What the hell were you thinking?"

Ryan took a step back. "It just slipped out. She was asking questions about Amy's personal life and --"

Brad closed the gap, his face inches from his brother's. "And you thought you'd mention some phantom crush she had on me? Are you an idiot? The FBI's conducting a murder investigation. They're looking for a killer. And you're telling them about some schoolgirl *crush* – like we're in sixth grade or something. I mean, how could that possibly be relevant?"

There was a flash of anger in Ryan's face. "It's not. As long as that's all it was."

Brad grabbed Ryan's shirt, yanking his brother forward. "What the hell do you mean 'if that's all it was?' Of course that's all it was. You asked me before and I told you there was nothing between Amy and me. Even if she did have a thing for me, you know I would never cheat on Carolyn."

Ryan raised his hands in surrender. "Look, I'm sorry. I shouldn't have said anything to the FBI."

Brad gave his brother a shove back, releasing his shirt. "Damn right, you shouldn't have. Jesus, you're a reporter. Do you not understand the ramifications of something like this getting out? What

193

if the media got wind of it? Do you think they'd care that nothing happened between us? No, they'd just run with their stories about how this poor woman was in love with me. And could we have been having an affair? And could her baby have been mine?"

Brad pointed his finger at Ryan's face. "And before you ask, no, I didn't know she was pregnant until the FBI told me. And I don't know who the kid's father was." He dropped his finger and shook his head. "Either Amy was involved with someone we didn't know about or just hooked up with some guy. It's a damn shame about her and the baby, but outside of feeling very sorry for what happened to them, I'm not part of this."

Ryan's expression went from defensive to angry. "How can you say you're not part of this? Amy and her baby were killed because someone was trying to assassinate you. I understand that's not your fault, but clearly you *are* part of this."

Brad stepped back, trying to put a conciliatory look on his face. "You're right. I misspoke. I do take responsibility for what happened. If I hadn't been so vocal about my gun control platform, that nut wouldn't have taken a shot at me. And not only that, but I was the one who invited Amy to be up on that stage with me."

His let his shoulders sag, trying to evoke pity. "And I have to live with that every day. Knowing that Amy was killed because of me. Can you even imagine how that's tearing me apart?"

Ryan put his arm around his brother. "Hey, bro, it wasn't your fault. You didn't do anything wrong. The gun control issue is an important one and you're right to take a stand on it. Besides, you were only trying to honor Amy and the other campaign workers that day. How could you have known that the day would turn out the way it did?"

Brad pulled away from Ryan, shaking his head. "Logically, I know everything you just said is true. But how can I not feel like shit for what happened? It's been eating at me ever since that day."

"You have to just move on. We all loved Amy, and the best way to honor her is to keep doing what you're doing. Get the guns out of the hands of the crazy people so something like this doesn't happen again. If you get yourself elected and push for stronger gun laws, you could be responsible for saving thousands of lives. Then Amy's death wouldn't have been in vain."

"You're right. That's what I'm trying to do. I have to win this election. I have to be president."

"Listen, I'm sorry about what I told the FBI. It was really stupid of me."

Brad touched his brother's shoulder, faking a forgiveness he didn't feel. "I think we've both beaten ourselves up enough for one day. Let's just agree to move forward, all right?"

"All right. And I'm sorry I ever thought you and Amy were involved. I never should have doubted you."

Brad waited until Ryan left his suite before he pounded his fist on the table. "That idiot! He better not have cost me the election."

CHAPTER 61

October: Four Weeks to Go

It was the evening of the first scheduled debate between the Democratic and Republican presidential nominees. The stage was lit up with what seemed like hundreds of lights. The cameras were not going to miss a thing. Every bead of sweat, every wrinkle, every nervous tic would be magnified and sent across the air waves to the television audience.

Brad strode across the stage and shook hands with Bob Ellington, the Republican nominee. He offered a few pleasantries and then headed back to his podium. As he looked out over the audience, he could sense their excitement and he felt a surge of adrenaline. This was going to be a piece of cake, he thought. He looked over at the sitting vice-president. The man looked like a basset hound on his last legs. He was twenty years Brad's senior, with yellowing gray hair, a pasty white complexion, and a good thirty pounds of extra flab around his waist.

Brad had heard that Ellington's advisors had been harping at the man to lose some weight and go to a tanning salon, but he obviously hadn't listened. In contrast, Brad knew he looked young and vibrant and the television cameras were going to love him.

It wasn't just in their looks that Brad thought he outmatched his competitor. Ellington was an old-time politician who had been in Congress for thirty years before being asked to serve as vice-president. As far as Brad was concerned, the man represented everything that was wrong with the government. While he was the in the House and then the Senate, Ellington always voted along party lines, never sponsored any significant legislation, and was an easy target for any lobbyist who was willing to make a campaign contribution.

His greatest sin of all, though, was that he was just plain boring. Spending the last eight years attending functions that were too unimportant for the president to bother with had only made the man even less relevant than he had been as a congressman.

Brad was sure that he was better prepared this evening than his lazy counterpart. If all went as planned, tonight's debate would be the final nail in his competitor's coffin. Brad was already ahead by a good ten point margin in the polls, an unheard of lead with only four weeks left until the election. After tonight, he expected that number to leapfrog even higher.

He turned his head to look at the moderator, Jaclyn Harmon, as she banged her gavel to silence the audience and begin the debate. She was a retired political reporter who had spent most of her career at the *Washington Post*, shattering glass ceilings and serving as a mentor and role model for the women following in her footsteps. Brad listened as she greeted both candidates and gave a quick synopsis of the debate rules. She would read from a list of prepared questions, first covering foreign policy and then moving into domestic issues. The candidates would take turns going first and they would have five minutes to address each issue. Based on an earlier coin toss, the first question would go to Brad.

Although foreign policy had not been his strong suit at the start of the campaign, Brad had attacked it like the A student he had been in school. He had become well educated in his country's current policies, and he had crafted a number of new strategies that he wanted to implement when he took office. So as he waited for his question, he was completely confident that it was one he had considered and was ready to address.

He knew that usually the first topic in a debate tended to be a softball question so that both candidates could get their footing. No doubt the issue would be the threat of Iran's nuclear program or the on-going difficulties in maintaining peaceful, quasi-Democratic governments in Iraq and Afghanistan. He had a prepared response for either.

The moderator turned to address him. "Governor Newcomb, could you please give us your assessment of the primary causes for the unrest in Turkmenistan and what steps you would take to diffuse that situation?"

Brad looked at the moderator and his brain went blank. *Where the hell was Turkmenistan?* He felt his whole body go clammy, drops of perspiration popping out on his upper lip and forehead. *My God,* he thought, *I'm going to look like Nixon.*

He opened his mouth, trying desperately to try to coax his brain to engage, but nothing happened. A full twenty seconds of silence stretched to infinity. He looked down at the podium as though he might find a cheat sheet there. Raising his eyes, he blinked rapidly and then reached for the glass of water at his fingertips, taking a long draw.

Finally, the answer hit him. He set the glass down and cleared his throat. "I'm sorry. My voice was completely gone there for a moment. I guess I've been doing too much talking lately." He flashed one of his most charming smiles. "Please forgive me. Now to address your question."

Brad began his remarks on the topic, but he had already lost too much time. The moderator interrupted him before he got to the crux of his proposed policy changes. As he listened to Ellington give a coherent, well-prepared response, Brad realized his competitor had just won round one. Trying to shake it off, Brad focused on the second question. With Ellington taking the lead on that one, Brad had plenty of time to formulate his own response and when his turn came around, he rattled off his answer with no hitches.

As he listened to the third question, Brad felt a moment of panic again. Not wanting a repeat performance, he began speaking immediately after the moderator was finished, but he stammered for the first ten seconds while he racked his brain searching for his prepared response. When it came to him, he rushed through the answer, not knowing how much time he had already wasted and afraid that he would get cut off again. When he finished his remarks, he realized he still had a minute left. Trying to fill the time, he repeated an earlier statement almost verbatim. Realizing his mistake, he threw out a final comment in a lame attempt to wrap up his position.

When he finished, he turned to Ellington and saw the man flash him a condescending smile before addressing the audience. "As much as I respect my esteemed colleague, I don't feel he has truly grasped the serious nature of this issue." The vice-president proceeded to give another thoughtful response while Brad seethed with frustration.

As the debate dragged on, it wasn't until the topic switched to domestic policies that Brad finally felt himself grounded again. Although he finished on a high note, he wondered how many viewers had turned off the television before he had recovered. How many people had just witnessed him sounding like a blubbering fool?

He crossed the stage and shook hands with Ellington, noting the self-satisfied gleam in his competitor's eyes. After the men exchanged the standard pleasantries, their families were asked to join them on the stage. When Carolyn leaned forward to kiss him on the cheek, she whispered, "Are you okay, honey?"

"I'm fine. Leave it alone," he hissed back.

After going through the final motions of small talk and photographs, the candidates left the stage to join their respective camps. Brad walked over to where his father and brother were standing.

His father looked at him with disappointment in his face. "I was just telling Ryan he's got his work cut out for him. That was a debacle. I don't know how he's going to manage to spin that debate in your favor." He turned and walked away before Brad could answer.

Ryan put his arm around Brad's shoulders. "Don't let Dad get to you. It wasn't that bad. Everyone has an off night."

Brad looked at him coldly. "With four weeks left, I can't afford an 'off night.' That was a monumental disaster."

CHAPTER 62

Christine sat watching the presidential debate in her apartment. Her living room was cluttered with whiteboards, file folders, crime scene photos, and hundreds of pages of scribbled notes, all relating to the Newcomb case. She kept switching her attention back and forth between the television and the case. She wasn't that into politics, but since the start of her investigation, she had tried to immerse herself in Newcomb's world.

She had already watched the candidate give a number of speeches and had been impressed with how poised he seemed. So tonight's performance was a big surprise. Instead of his usual Teflon-coated act, Newcomb seemed completely ill at ease. He was stumbling through his answers as though he was unprepared and lacked even a basic knowledge on some topics.

As the debate went on, Christine found herself turning her full attention to the spectacle. Whereas she had planned to vote for Newcomb, she was starting to wonder whether he was qualified to be president. It occurred to her that she could articulate a better response to some of the questions than he was giving. Even at the conclusion, she could still see the man's discomfort in the gleam of sweat covering his pinched face.

As she listened to the media pundits tear apart his performance, Christine realized that she wasn't the only one who thought he was off tonight. The talking heads were even questioning whether the two assassination attempts had rattled the candidate to the point that he was uncomfortable speaking in front of a crowd.

When the networks switched back to their regularly scheduled programs, Christine turned off her television. She leaned back on her sofa and closed her eyes, her mind wandering free, recalling snippets of interviews she had conducted during the last few weeks of the investigation. She keyed in on her talk with Amy's best friend, Tina.

Why had Amy been so secretive about the man she was dating? Tina had assumed he was someone on the campaign staff. But she had told the agent that Amy wouldn't even use the man's first name. Could he have been someone that Tina would have known? Someone high profile – maybe even the candidate himself?

Brad Newcomb had dismissed the rumors of Amy's crush on him. He had sworn his loyalty to his wife, but how many politicians had made that same claim and then had their indiscretions revealed. If Amy had been involved with the candidate and then gotten pregnant, wouldn't that be the mother of all motives?

Christine's eyes flew open and she launched herself from the sofa. Her hands scrabbled through the file folders until she located the one she was searching for. It had her notes from her interview with Terry Brinson. When she had questioned the campaign manager about Amy's pregnancy, he had denied knowing about it. And yet, she had made a note to herself that she thought he was lying.

If Brinson did know about the baby, why not admit it? And if he did know, how did he find out? He had said that he wasn't very close to Amy, so it was unlikely that she would have taken him into her confidence. But if Amy didn't tell him, then who did? The baby's father, most likely, which brought her right back to Newcomb – Brinson's best friend.

It made perfect sense that the campaign manager would cover for the candidate. But would he go even further than that? If Brinson knew that Amy was pregnant with Newcomb's child, how far would he go to protect his friend?

As the agent reviewed her notes, she noted that Brinson had been in the military. With growing excitement, she grabbed her cell phone and dialed her go-to analyst at the bureau.

"Do you have access to military records?"

"Depends if they're classified. Tell me what you're looking for and we'll see."

Christine gave Brinson's name to the analyst. There was more than one Terry Brinson in the system, but working with his age and probable dates of service, they were able to pinpoint the right one. There was silence on the phone as the analyst did a quick read-through of the man's file. When he finally spoke, Christine realized she had been holding her breath.

"I'll email you the whole file. Looks like he was in Special Forces. He was a sniper. Is that helpful?"

CHAPTER 63

Christine sat at a table in a conference room of the hotel in New York where Newcomb and his staff were staying. She drummed her fingers on the table, her impatience growing with each minute that went by as she waited for her first meeting. She had struggled with how to proceed with her investigation. She wanted to get Newcomb's DNA to compare to the sample the medical examiner had pulled from Amy's fetus, but she knew that once she opened that door, there would be no going back. It would be career suicide if she accused the candidate of involvement in Amy's murder and then he was proven innocent. She was right in the middle of a political minefield, and she was going to have to tread very softly.

The agent also knew that even if she had proof that Newcomb was the baby's father, it didn't mean he was involved in Amy's murder – if, and it was still a big if, Amy was in fact murdered. It was still possible that she was a random victim of an assassination attempt on the candidate. Or even if she was the intended target, her killer could be someone operating outside of Newcomb's knowledge.

In short, Christine knew she was a long way from gathering enough evidence to indict anyone. She would have to proceed carefully and stay under the radar – both her boss's and the media's – until she had enough proof to go public with her suspicions.

Because of that, she had decided the easier track was to go after Terry Brinson first. If he had been the shooter, whether he was acting alone or with Newcomb's knowledge, and she could nail him, she would solve the murder. And then maybe if Newcomb was involved, she could get Brinson to turn on his friend.

When Terry walked into the conference room, she was still debating on how to best handle the man. As he sat down across from her, she realized she was just going to have to wing it. She started by asking him to review what he had observed before, during, and after the shooting. As she listened carefully to his answers, she became convinced that he wasn't telling her the truth. Although he said he was in the audience and watching the stage, some of what he relayed to her was inconsistent with other witnesses' reports. That in itself wasn't a lot to hang her hat on, but she was definitely starting to feel as though she was on to something. She decided to push a little harder.

She had a whiteboard with a drawing of the stage and the people who were on it at the time of the shooting. She referred to the board now. "When Amy was hit, you said that the Secret Service agents dragged the governor off the stage. Can you show me specifically where they exited the stage?"

Terry reached out and pointed to the chart. "The governor was standing here at the podium. When Amy went down, this agent here grabbed him and pulled him this way." He moved his finger, indicating the path the men took.

Christine wrinkled her brow. "Are you sure? Because the other witnesses said that he exited the stage in this direction." She moved her finger to the opposite side from where Terry had pointed.

Terry bit his lip. "I guess that might be right." He shrugged. "It all happened so fast. It's hard for me to remember now."

"But you said you were looking right at the stage."

"I was at first. But then after the shot, everyone around me started panicking. They were screaming and running. I was being pushed all over the place. I must have stopped looking at the stage and been focused more on the people around me."

Christine watched as Terry yanked at his tie knot, pulling it lower. As he undid the top button of his shirt, Christine could see that his hand was shaking. She leaned back in her chair and crossed her arms, staring at him silently, watching the man fidget under her gaze.

Finally, she leaned forward and grabbed the edge of the table. "Why did you lie when you told me you didn't know who the father of Amy's baby was?"

Terry's eyes grew wide, his mouth started working, but no words came out. Finally he began to stammer. "I didn't know who the father was. I mean, I still don't know." His hands balled into fists. "Do you know who the father was?"

"I can't reveal that information at this time." Christine paused, watching his reaction. She could see the beads of sweat on his forehead. "Since you knew she was pregnant, I find it hard to believe you didn't know who the father was."

She could see the confusion on his face and knew he was struggling to remember what he had told her in their last interview. "But I didn't know she was pregnant."

Christine pretended to look at her earlier notes. "I have it written here that you told me you knew she was pregnant, but not who the father was."

Terry blinked hard. "I don't remember telling you that." He scratched at his face. "Are you sure I said that?"

Christine looked down, pretending to read something that wasn't there. "I have it here in my notes, but let's move on." She looked up, waiting until Terry met her eyes. "Let's talk about your career in the military – specifically your training as a sniper."

Terry leapt from his seat, looking like he was going to flee. Then he sat back down, his body shaking. "How is that relevant?"

"I thought that, as a trained sniper, you might be able to shed some light on the shooter. Maybe you could walk me through how he might have prepared for the shot. Why don't you tell me what *you* would have done?"

This time Terry jumped up and didn't sit back down. He looked at his watch. "I'm late for a meeting. We're going to have to continue this later."

Christine watched as he ran from the room, looking as though he were on the verge of a nervous breakdown. *Forget about playing it safe,* she thought. *I'm going to get to the truth.*

CHAPTER 64

October: Two Weeks to Go

Brad sat in his hotel room, nursing a nightcap. It had been a good day. In spite of his weak performance during the presidential debate, thanks to the low ratings for the event, he had only slipped a couple of points in the latest polls. Election Day was less than two weeks away, and he was still well ahead of Ellington. He felt as relaxed as he had been for a long time. He could hear Carolyn singing in the shower, and he was looking forward to her joining him.

When his cell phone rang and he saw the caller was Terry, he almost ignored the interruption. His friend had been acting more strangely each day. Brad was wondering whether he should have taken Ryan and Carolyn's advice and sent him home for a break, but it was too close to the end of the campaign. He couldn't lose his manager in the home stretch, and he still thought he was better off keeping Terry close by so he could keep an eye on him.

After the election, he planned to ship Terry off to the Caribbean for an extended stay, away from the prying eyes of both the FBI and the media. With luck, once Brad was elected president, Terry would see that killing Amy had been the right thing to do. After all, it was Terry who had said he could kill her for the greater good. Brad couldn't understand why Terry had taken her death so hard. Maybe a couple of months of sun and sand, knowing he was slated to be Brad's chief-of-staff, would help Terry put things back into perspective.

Brad was about to hit the End button to send the call to voicemail, when he sighed and pressed Talk – might as well deal with whatever it is. "Hey, Terry. How are you?"

Terry's words came out in a rush. "Not good. We have to talk."

"All right, why don't you swing by in the morning?"

"No, we have to talk *now.*"

"Shit, Terry. I was just about to go to bed. Can't it wait till tomorrow?"

Terry's voice went up an octave. "No, it can't. That FBI agent was here asking questions again. I think she's on to us."

"*What?*" Brad felt a trickle of dread as he gripped the phone hard, his knuckles turning white. "What did she say? Wait! Don't say anything over the phone."

"I'll come see you."

"No, Carolyn's here. We'll have to meet in your room. I'll be right there."

Brad hung up before Terry could respond. On his way out, he stopped in the bathroom and told Carolyn he had to go see Terry for a few minutes to go over some details about tomorrow's schedule. When he walked out of his room, his two Secret Service agents looked up in surprise.

"We thought you were in for the evening, sir."

"I have to meet Terry in his room. Something's come up, and I don't want to disturb Mrs. Newcomb."

The three men walked down the hall and took the elevator up a floor. The agents stepped out first, looked down the empty hallway, and then motioned for Brad to follow them. When they got to Terry's room, one of the agents went in first to do a quick search while the other waited with Brad at the doorway. After the agents verified that Terry was alone, Brad entered the room and shut the door behind him while the agents stationed themselves outside.

The candidate looked at Terry and held his finger to his lips, then motioned to the far side of the room where there was a desk and chair sitting by the window. He walked over and closed the drapes before turning to his friend who had followed at his heels. "These rooms are pretty soundproof, but we need to keep our voices down just in case." He waited until Terry nodded his acknowledgement. "Now why don't you fill me in?"

"Like I said, I think that FBI agent's on to us," Terry hissed, his eyes wild. "I think she knows you were the one who knocked up Amy."

"That's bullshit. There's no way she could know that. All she has to go on are some rumors. There are no voicemails or emails – nothing that could prove an affair."

"What about DNA? You know how sophisticated they are these days. What if they have DNA linking you to the baby?"

"They don't. My DNA's not in any system, and I'm certainly not going to volunteer to give it to them. And they sure as hell don't have enough evidence to get a warrant for it."

Brad was trying to keep his voice calm, but his attempt was having no effect on Terry. His friend's face was drenched in sweat, and his hands shook.

"Well, they sure as hell have *my* DNA from when I was in the military. I thought I wiped down my rifle good, but what if they found something? That agent was all over me about my sniper training."

"If they had any evidence, they would have charged you." Brad reached out and put his hand on his friend's shoulder. "You need to relax. Maybe get away for a few days."

Terry brushed Brad's hand away, his voice getting louder. "Are you not listening to me? She knows I did it. I can't take this anymore!" He turned and slammed his fist against the wall.

Brad listened to his friend losing control and knew Terry could destroy his chances for election. He panicked – his throat closed up; he couldn't breathe. He had to stop him! He grabbed a paperweight from the desk and smashed it against Terry's skull. There was a moment when everything seemed suspended in time – Brad's arm raised, Terry's head tilting to the side, an eerie silence filling the room, and then Terry fell to the ground with a quiet thud as his body hit the floor. Brad looked down and saw blood oozing from a small gash on the back of Terry's head. His friend lay still. Brad dropped to his knees and felt for a pulse. There was none.

CHAPTER 65

Brad leapt to his feet, his first instinct to flee the scene. Halfway across the room, he froze. He was trapped – a dead body behind him and two Secret Service agents in front of him. He had to come up with a plan. Taking slow, deep breaths, he tried to calm himself.

He realized with a sense of relief that the agents hadn't heard anything, because if they had, they would have barged in to rescue him. Now he just had to figure out a way to get out of there without raising suspicion. When Terry's body was found, the agents would know that Brad had come to see him, so he needed to stage a plausible murder scene to throw the police off his track.

Making it look like a hotel room robbery gone bad was probably his best chance. He would need to take any money Terry had on him. He thought about credit cards and cell phones, but didn't want to have to dispose of anything. Luckily Terry didn't wear any jewelry other than a cheap watch – nothing a robber would want -- so it would just be the cash. He should probably make it look like there was more of a struggle too. With Terry's military training, it would make sense that he would have tried to fight off a robber. Unfortunately, Brad couldn't do anything to the door to make it look like a forced entry, so he hoped the police would assume the robber disguised himself as a hotel employee to gain entry.

He tried to recall what he knew about fingerprints and DNA. He guessed that it wouldn't be unusual for a robber to wear gloves so he wouldn't leave any evidence behind. Brad considered what he had touched and figured that as long as his prints weren't found on anything relating directly to the robbery or murder, he should be okay. He would have to wipe the paperweight off and remove Terry's wallet without leaving any prints. If the police found his prints anywhere else, they could be explained away.

Going into the bathroom to see what he could use, Brad took a clean hand towel from the counter. If the police found his prints on it, he could say that he used the bathroom and washed and dried his hands. Carrying the towel, he walked back into the bedroom, watching where he stepped, and made his way over to the body, avoiding the pool of blood. He lifted the paperweight, wiped it down, and then tried to set it back exactly how it had fallen.

Then he turned to the body and gingerly rolled it over, his face grimacing with disgust. Still using the towel, he reached into Terry's back pocket and tugged until his wallet popped out. Then he gently turned the body back to its original position. He stood up and flipped the wallet open, removing the cash, and then tossed the wallet next to the body.

Looking around the room, he tried to envision a robbery attempt. The body was at the far side of the room, away from the door. If a robber had posed as a hotel repairman, it would make sense that Terry would have opened the door and led him into the room. From the entry, there was a short hall leading to the bathroom, then the bed and then the desk and chair by the window. A robber could have waited until he was by the desk to make his move, so Brad decided to limit the signs of a struggle to that area.

Using the towel, he swept a few items from the desktop to the floor and then pushed the chair over. He made sure nothing landed on or too near the body or paperweight so as not to disturb them. Stepping back, he reviewed the scene, decided it looked real, and nodded with satisfaction as though he were a movie director evaluating his set.

He walked back to the bathroom, hung the towel on a rack, and then washed and dried his hands. He looked into the bathroom mirror, turning his head from side to side, examining his face closely. No blood that he could see, although he would take a shower when he went back to his room just in case. He leaned back from the mirror and looked down at his clothes and shoes. Nothing there either, but as a precaution, he would send his things out to be cleaned that evening.

The last thing he would have to do would be some acting, which shouldn't be too difficult; his whole life these days was a stage play. He went into the hall and then opened the hotel room door. As he stepped through the doorway, he looked back over his shoulder.

"Thanks, Terry," he called out. "I'll see you in the morning."

He closed the door behind him and smiled at the agents. "We can head back to my room now."

When they got to his suite, Brad told the agents he was in for the evening. After they cleared his room, he locked the door and turned his attention to Carolyn.

"I'm going to take a shower and then how about a drink before bed?" he asked.

"Sounds good to me. How did everything go with Terry?"

"Great. We just needed to fine tune some talking points. In fact, I'm glad he called to suggest it. Now that it's done, I feel like a burden has been lifted off my shoulders."

He grabbed his wife and gave her a kiss. "It's clear sailing to the White House, Madam First Lady. Nothing's going to stand in my way now."

CHAPTER 66

The next morning, Brad woke with a smile, feeling as though the weight of the world had been lifted from his shoulders. He lay in bed and thought about the events of the night before. Terry had been a good friend to him for years, but he had let him down in the end. They had managed to commit the perfect murder, getting rid of Amy and getting a pop in the polls after the supposed assassination attempt. They should have been riding their good fortune all the way to Election Day, but instead, Terry had lost his nerve.

Maybe the guilt he had felt for killing Amy had triggered some underlying post-traumatic stress disorder -- that seemed to be the one-size-fits-all diagnosis for veterans these days. All Brad knew was that he couldn't have let Terry blow everything they had worked for over the last twenty years. Now that his co-conspirator was gone, nothing could stand in his way. Even if the FBI was able to prove Terry was Amy's killer, Brad could deny that he knew anything about Terry's plans, insist that Terry must have acted on his own.

He would just have to make it through the next few days, pretending to be grief-stricken over his best friend's death, and then he would be home free and able to focus on wrapping up the campaign. In only a few months, he'd be taking the oath of office for the most important job in the world – President of the United States. He was exactly where he always knew he would be. Feeling energized, Brad hopped out of bed.

Carolyn woke up while he was reading the paper, and they ordered room service. After breakfast, Brad showered and dressed and a few minutes later, his immediate staff began to arrive at his room. They discussed various campaign issues as they waited for Terry to join them. When fifteen minutes had passed, Brad suggested someone call him.

"There's no answer on his room or cell phone, sir," the aide said, after allowing both phones to ring several times.

"He's probably on his way down here," Brad said. "He must just be running late."

The group resumed their discussion for another fifteen minutes before Brad suggested another phone call. When there was still no answer in Terry's room or on his cell, the candidate summoned his Secret Service agents.

"Would you guys go check on Terry? He was supposed to be here a half hour ago. We've tried calling him a couple times, but there's no answer."

After the agents left, Brad checked his watch. "They'd better find him soon. We need to leave for our first meeting in about a half hour."

"He's been having a rough time lately, you know," Ryan said. "Maybe he went out for a walk to clear his head this morning. Lost track of time or something. I still think you ought to send him home for a few days."

"I think you're right," Brad said. "I'll talk to him about it today."

Twenty minutes later, the agents returned, their faces grim.

"I'm sorry to have to tell you this, but Mr. Brinson is dead." The agent looked around the room at the horrified expressions. Brad and Carolyn both jumped out of their chairs.

"What happened?" Brad asked, doing his best to appear distraught.

"When we got to his room, we knocked and there was no answer. We called security and they came and unlocked the door for us. It looks like a robbery gone bad, sir. There were signs of a struggle, and Mr. Brinson's wallet had been picked through. His cash was gone."

"How did he die?" Ryan asked.

"It appears he was struck in the head with a paperweight. We'll have to wait for an autopsy to confirm that."

"Oh, my God," Carolyn cried out, falling into Brad's arms. "First Amy and now Terry."

The candidate held his sobbing wife while the rest of the staff was silent, a sense of shock permeating the room. When Carolyn's tears subsided, Brad led her to a chair, and then he looked around at the others. He instructed one of his aides to cancel his morning meetings and lunch.

"I want to be available to help the police in any way. Once they give us the okay, we'll schedule a press conference – maybe this afternoon."

Brad dismissed his staff, warning them not to tell anyone else about the murder until the police had made it public. When the others had left, he turned to Carolyn and Ryan.

"I can't believe this has happened," Carolyn said. "It's like your campaign is jinxed."

Brad turned to his wife, angry at her outburst. "Carolyn, please. This is a tragedy, but it has nothing to do with some cosmic design. The last thing we need is to have a statement like that get out to the media."

"I'm not an idiot. I'm not giving a public statement. I'm talking to my husband and my brother-in-law." Carolyn covered her face with her hands. "I spend my days like a Stepford wife, trying to be the perfect future First Lady. If I can't even express my real feelings to you, I'll go crazy."

Brad sat down next to her and took her hands, gently moving them from her face to her lap. "I'm sorry. You're right. I guess I'm just in shock. You know Terry was my closest friend. I don't know what I'm going to do without him."

A tear escaped from his eye and Carolyn reached up to wipe it away. "We'll get through this, honey," she said.

Ryan cleared his throat. "I'm going to head back to my room now. I want to tell Michelle before she hears this on the news."

Brad stood up and walked him to the door. "Would you do me a favor? Go talk to Emily and Tyler. Let them know what happened. I don't want to leave Carolyn."

"Of course. I'll do that right away."

"Thanks, Ryan."

When they opened the door, there were two policemen flashing their badges at the Secret Service agents. "Can we come in, Governor? We have some questions for you."

CHAPTER 67

After leaving his brother's room, Ryan went to see Tyler first. When he told Brad's son about Terry, the young man seemed sad, but not too upset. Tyler had always been a bit of a loner, more interested in his computers than people, so Ryan knew his nephew hadn't been very close to Terry. Based on his reaction, Ryan wasn't too concerned about leaving Tyler alone, but before he left, he suggested meeting for lunch later, after his nephew had some time to absorb the information.

Ryan knew the more difficult conversation would be with Emily. With her naturally vivacious personality, she was friends with almost everyone she met. Knowing she would take Terry's death harder than her brother had, Ryan knocked on her door with a feeling of dread. As he waited for her to answer, he thought back to when Emily had gone through her stage of partying and picking up strangers. It seemed that she had stopped her destructive behavior when Carolyn rejoined the campaign, but Ryan was worried that news of Terry's murder might push her over the edge again.

Emily opened the door with a big smile on her face. "Hey, Uncle Ryan. What's up?"

Ryan gave her a small, sad smile in return. "Hi, Emily. Your dad asked me to talk to you about something. May I come in?"

Emily led him into her room and they sat on her bed.

Ryan turned to his niece. "There's no good way of telling you this." He reached down and took her hand. "Terry was killed last night."

Emily's eyes widened. "*What?* Oh, my God. What happened?"

"It looks as if someone tried to rob him in his hotel room. There was a struggle and the robber hit Terry on his head with a paperweight."

"When?" Emily choked out.

"It must have been yesterday evening sometime. Terry was supposed to go to your dad's room this morning for their briefing.

When he didn't show up, we tried calling him, but there was no answer. Your dad asked the Secret Service agents to go check on him and they had hotel security let them into his room. That's when they found him."

"Oh, God. I can't believe this. I loved Terry. He was like another uncle to me." Emily dropped her head and began to sob.

Ryan put his arm around his niece's heaving shoulders, letting her get her grief out of her system. When her cries subsided, he rubbed her arm. "I'm so sorry, Emily. I know how hard this must be for you. First we lost Amy and now Terry. It's a lot to handle."

Emily pulled back from Ryan. "Amy was nothing to me," she said, anger filling her voice. "I'm glad that bitch died."

Ryan stared at his niece, shocked by her reaction.

Emily began to twirl strands of hair around her finger. "Sorry. I shouldn't have said that." She looked up defiantly. "But it's true."

As she began to cry again, Ryan put his arm around her. "What's this about? I thought you guys were friends. What did Amy do to make you feel this way?"

"If I tell you, you have to swear you won't tell my mom."

Ryan leaned forward, afraid of what he was about to hear. "I promise, Emily. What happened?"

"It was her, Amy, and my dad. I still can't even believe it." Emily shook her head, spitting the words out. "They were sleeping together."

Ryan's first reaction was disbelief. She must have seen the same signs he had and assumed the worst. "Are you sure? I know Amy had a thing for your dad, but I asked him about it and he swore there was nothing between them."

Emily tugged at her hair again. "If he told you that, he was lying."

"How can you be sure?"

Emily jumped to her feet and began pacing around the room. "Because I saw them together. I saw her go into my dad's room one night. I saw them kissing."

Ryan felt a shiver go through his body. How could Brad have done something like this to his family? He closed his eyes and felt his body sag into the bed. When he opened his eyes, Emily had stopped pacing and was looking at him.

"He lied to me, too, at first," she said. "He didn't admit the affair until I told him I had seen them together."

"When did all this happen?"

"It was back when Mom broke her leg, and she was at home recuperating. You remember when I was drinking and stuff." She blushed. "That was why. I guess a shrink would say I was acting out."

"What did your dad do when you confronted him?"

"He swore he would end the affair if I didn't tell anyone." Emily shrugged. "I guess he did. That's when Amy got her 'promotion'." She made quotation marks with her fingers. "I didn't see them together after that."

Ryan stood and went to his niece, placing his hands on her shoulders. "I'm really sorry about what your dad did and that you had to deal with it all by yourself. I wish you had come to me."

"I thought about it, but I was afraid you'd tell my mom. You won't, will you?" Emily looked up at him, nervously biting her lip. "You promised."

"No, Emily, I won't tell your mom. You know you can always count on me to keep my word." He gripped her shoulders tightly. "But I am going to have a talk with your dad. What he and Amy did, and then what he put you through – there's just no excuse for his behavior. He may be our next president, but he's still going to answer to me for pulling that shit."

CHAPTER 68

Ryan left Emily's room and took the elevator up to his floor, where he made his way down the hall, his stomach churning as fast as his legs. He opened the door and saw Michelle sitting at the desk, reading the newspaper. She had taken vacation time and was spending the last few weeks of the campaign with him.

"Hi, honey," she said when he walked into room. Her smile faded when she saw his face. "Are you all right? What's wrong?"

For a minute, Ryan had no words. He stood in the middle of the room, feeling as though the blood had been drained from his body.

Michelle jumped to her feet and went to him. "Tell me what happened."

"I don't even know where to begin," he said. Taking a deep breath, he began to relay the events of the morning, starting with Terry's death.

Michelle was shocked by the news, both that of losing Terry, whom she had come to know well over the years, and by the brutality of the crime. She put her arms around her husband and they held each other for a few minutes.

"There's more," Ryan said.

"I think I'd better sit down."

They walked to the bed with their arms around each other for support. When they were seated, Ryan reached for his wife's hand.

"Brad asked me to tell the kids about Terry. Tyler seemed okay, but then I talked to Emily. She took it hard. She and Terry were pretty close."

"That poor girl. Do you want me to go talk to her?"

"Maybe, but first let me finish. She was really upset, crying, exactly what I expected. And then I brought up how we just lost Amy too. She went nuts."

Michelle wrinkled her brow. "What do you mean?"

218

Ryan's hand tightened around his wife's. "She told me that Brad and Amy were having an affair."

Michelle's eyes widened. "Is she sure?"

"Positive. She saw them together, and then she confronted Brad. He denied it at first, just like he did with me. But when she told him what she had seen, he finally admitted it. He told her he'd break it off if she promised not to tell anyone."

Michelle shook her head. "Oh, honey. I wish I could say I'm surprised, but I'm not. It's really horrible. Not only the affair, but then to put such a terrible burden on Emily."

"I guess you were right about my brother after all," Ryan said, the bitterness creeping into his voice. "All my life, I've put him up on a pedestal, even during these last couple of years on the campaign trail. During all the time we've spent together, he's never let his guard down."

"Do you think he was the father of Amy's baby?"

"I think he had to be. The timing fits, and it would explain why Amy kept her pregnancy a secret." Ryan crossed his arms, dropping his head. "And the thing is, if he was sleeping with Amy and that was his baby, you'd think he would have been devastated by their deaths. Instead, he's acted as though she was just another employee. As if she and the baby meant nothing to him."

Michelle put her hand on Ryan's thigh and squeezed. "I'm sorry, honey. I'm sorry he's not the man you thought he was."

"At this point, I don't know what to think of him. I hate what he's done. But he's still my brother and I love him. Is that totally twisted?"

"No, that's totally normal. Almost all the people I treat for addiction have family members who love them no matter what. But like I tell the families, you can love the man, but not condone his behavior. You're going to need to talk to Brad. Tell him you love him, but you can't support what he's done."

"I know, and I plan to do exactly that. I'm not sure if I'm more sad or more angry, but either way, I'm going to let him know what I think of his bullshit."

Michelle nodded. "Good. Are you going to tell Carolyn?"

"No, partly because I promised Emily I wouldn't. With everything she's gone through, I need her to know she can trust me. But I am going to do everything I can to get Brad to tell her the truth. He needs to come clean, no matter how difficult that might be."

"Do you think he confided in anyone?"

Ryan thought about it. "I'm guessing Terry knew. The two of them went back forever and they were really tight. I think Terry was probably the one person who Brad would have trusted with the truth."

The idea struck Ryan with the force of a hammer. "Oh, shit." He leapt to his feet.

"What is it?" Michelle asked.

He turned and faced her. "If Terry knew about the baby and he was afraid it would get out, he might have felt like he had to protect Brad."

Michelle looked up in horror. "You don't think he had anything to do with Amy's death?"

Ryan's hands closed into fists. "He was a trained sniper in the military."

"Oh, God, honey. He couldn't have." Michelle raised her hands to her face.

"I think he could have. I think he wanted the presidency as much as Brad does, and I think he would have done anything to make sure Brad won the election." Ryan shook his head. "And having killed Amy would explain his behavior lately. The remorse he must have been feeling. That's why he's been such a basket case. God, it all makes sense now."

Michelle got to her feet, taking Ryan's hands. "What about Brad? Do you think he knew?"

CHAPTER 69

Christine sat in the hotel café eating a bagel and cream cheese and drinking her second cup of coffee. Her chair was arranged so that she could see anyone entering the restaurant as well as a good portion of the hotel lobby, including the registration desk. Her seat selection wasn't even something she had made a conscious decision about, but after all the years she had spent in the FBI, she instinctively chose positions to maximize awareness of her surroundings.

When she saw the uniformed policemen dash into the lobby, her radar went up. Five minutes later, the hotel was swarming with police activity. She saw detectives with their shields displayed and others wearing jackets identifying them as being with the coroner's office. She glanced at her check, threw some cash on the table, and made a quick exit into the lobby.

Knowing the police didn't always welcome FBI involvement, Christine bypassed them and went to the concierge. Flashing her credentials, she identified herself and asked why the police were there.

In a voice that was so soft it was almost a whisper, the concierge told her about Terry's murder. Christine was stunned. She had just interviewed the man yesterday, and now he was dead. She asked for Terry's room number and then thanked the concierge. With a few quick strides across the lobby, she was at the elevator bank. She punched the call button several times, as though that would speed the car's arrival. When the doors opened, she hopped in and pressed the button for Terry's floor. During the whole ride up, her fingers tapped a staccato rhythm against her thigh.

When she arrived, she flew down the hall, coming to an abrupt halt two doors from Terry's room. She pulled on her jacket to straighten it, drew her shoulders back, and took a deep breath. With a measured pace, she took the final steps to Terry's room and knocked on the door. One of the uniformed cops she had seen before answered, his body blocking her view into the room. She identified herself and asked to speak with the detective in charge.

The uniform hesitated before allowing her through the doorway. "Wait here. I'll go get him."

As she stood watching, she saw heads swivel in her direction. The uniform huddled with the detective a few minutes before returning to her. "He's coming."

She cooled her heels for another five minutes before the detective sauntered over. "FBI, huh? To what do we owe this great pleasure?"

Christine tried to keep the impatience out of her voice. "I'm Special Agent Walker in charge of the investigation into the assassination attempt on Brad Newcomb. Your vic was his campaign manager and a key witness in my investigation."

The detective shrugged. "And?"

This time Christine didn't hide her irritation. "And his murder may be directly tied to my case."

The detective peered distastefully at her through thick glasses, as though she were a bedbug on the hotel sheets. "I don't see how. This looks like a pretty open and shut case of robbery. Happens more often than these fancy hotels like to let on. Guy shows up at the door, dressed in some kind of uniform. Says he's with the hotel to check on something. Vic lets him in. Next thing, the guy pulls a gun and robs him."

"And how often do these robberies end in murder?" Christine asked.

For the first time, the detective looked a little uneasy. "They don't usually. But this guy must have tried to fight back. It may be unusual, but it's not unheard of."

"And if that's how it went down, then the case is all yours. But there's a chance that this is a murder set up to look like a robbery. And if it is, then it's most likely tied to my investigation, in which case, the FBI will take jurisdiction." She paused, letting her words sink in. "So for now, I suggest we work together until we figure out exactly what happened."

The detective stared at her for a minute, before shrugging. "Whatever. I sure wouldn't want to interfere with an F-B-I investigation," he said, drawing out the bureau initials sarcastically.

"Glad to hear we've got your full cooperation," Christine said, adding her own touch of sarcasm. "So why don't you fill me in on what you've found so far?"

She followed him into the room, where the rest of his team was gathered over the crime scene. She listened as he went through his theory again, pointing out the signs of a struggle and the likely murder weapon.

When he was finished, she crouched beside the body, making a visual examination while being careful not to touch anything. "Before you move the body, I'd like to bring in our forensics team."

The detective crossed his arms over his chest and she could see his resistance. Then he surrendered, dropping his arms by his side. "Fine with me."

Christine nodded before turning away. She went out in the hall, took out her cell phone, and made a couple of calls, first to her boss, then to the local FBI office. When she was finished, she went back into the room to inform the detective that the forensics team was on their way. Then she asked to speak to the first responders. After he directed her to the hotel security guard and the uniforms, she spent the next several minutes getting their full reports.

"So it was Brad Newcomb's Secret Service agents who contacted you?" she asked.

"Yes, ma'am," the hotel security guard responded.

"And where are they now?"

This time the uniform answered. "They left after we arrived and secured the scene. They told me they would be with the governor if we needed to talk to them again. I have his room number if you need it."

"Yes, thanks. I'll wait here until my crime scene unit is finished. Then I'm going to need to talk to them."

Christine found an unobtrusive spot to wait for the forensics unit to arrive. Her mind was going a mile a minute. She didn't buy the whole robbery gone bad scene. Another death in the Newcomb campaign camp was just too coincidental. And this death was especially suspect because she thought Terry had been involved in Amy's murder and that she was close to getting him to admit it. *Someone is trying to tie up loose ends,* she thought, *and the one person who has the best motive is the candidate himself.*

CHAPTER 70

One Week to Go

Christine parked her rental car in the parking lot at FBI headquarters in Quantico. She glanced at her watch and saw that she had about fifteen minutes before her scheduled meeting time with her boss, Frank Elliot. She had filled Frank in on Terry Brinson's murder last week and then made an appointment for today to go over her findings in more detail. This time, she had his assurance that the meeting would be between only the two of them, not the dog and pony show she had walked into the last time she came in for a briefing.

She sat for another five minutes, collecting her thoughts and preparing herself for the grilling that she knew she would face. Then she stepped out of her car and began to walk to the entrance of the building. She shivered, partly due to the fall chill in the air, and partly due to the tension running through her body. After showing her identification to multiple security personnel, she arrived at her supervisor's office and faced the last sentry, his secretary.

In spite of having met Christine at least a dozen times, the secretary still eyed the agent suspiciously. "Mr. Elliot has you scheduled for thirty minutes, but he's very busy today. He's already running about twenty minutes late."

Christine nodded and took a seat in his waiting area. She opened her file and began to review her notes. She had spent hours putting together a cohesive presentation pointing to Terry Brinson as the man responsible for killing Amy and implicating Brad Newcomb in the plot. Now it looked as though she was only going to have about ten minutes to sell her boss on her theory.

She watched as Frank's door opened and a group of people she didn't recognize exited. A couple of minutes later, Frank came out looking as frazzled as she felt. He greeted Christine and then asked his secretary to bring them some coffee before he led the agent into his office and had her join him at a small round worktable.

"So there have been some new developments?"

"Yes, sir."

"Well, let's see what you've got."

Christine began to present her findings as methodically as if she were in a courtroom. When their coffee arrived and Frank told his secretary to push back his next two meetings, she knew she had him hooked.

For the next hour, she took him through all the evidence she had linking Brinson to Amy's murder. She led off with background on his close relationship with the candidate, going back to when they were in school together and progressing to when Brinson started working for Newcomb. Next she provided him with Brinson's military records, including his training as a sniper. Having laid the groundwork for Brinson's loyalty to Newcomb as a motive, and his military training as an opportunity, Christine began to delve into the logistics of the crime.

She had hotel receipts for when Brinson was in Dallas the week prior to the shooting, when she believed he planned the fake assassination attempt. She had statements from witnesses who were on the Dallas task force that worked with Brinson setting up the logistics for the candidate's speech. They'd all agreed that he was instrumental in determining exactly where the stage and podium were to be set up.

She had a record of Brinson's flight to Chicago and a receipt from a shooting range near his home, showing that he had been practicing that same week before the Dallas speech. The owner of the range and gun shop also provided a statement verifying that Brinson owned the type of rifle used in the shooting, and that he sold him bullets matching those found in the victim.

Christine also explained to Frank how a thorough search of Brinson's Chicago apartment had failed to turn up the rifle, which she believed was in the custody of the FBI. Unfortunately, with the serial number filed off and no fingerprints or DNA evidence, they would probably never be able to prove definitively that the rifle had belonged to Brinson.

Next Christine pulled out a copy of a UPS tracking slip indicating that Brinson had shipped a box large enough to accommodate a rifle from Chicago to his hotel in Dallas. She had yet to determine where he had hidden the rifle before the murder, but she had her team canvassing storage unit facilities in the hopes that someone would recognize Brinson's picture.

Although Frank hadn't said much up to that point, Christine could feel that he was moving from skeptic to believer as she laid out her case. With her confidence growing, the agent began to review the highlights of her interviews with the suspect.

"When I first met with Brinson right after the shooting, he referred to the victim's death as collateral damage. It was such an inappropriate comment. I think that was when the first seed was planted in my mind that this so-called assassination attempt might not really be one."

Christine reminded her supervisor how her suspicions were further raised when the autopsy revealed a perfect head shot, which she thought was too coincidental to be a miss.

"And I remember telling you to dismiss that theory," Frank said.

"In fairness, sir, I did devote all of my team resources to investigating the case as if it were an assassination attempt against Newcomb. I did most of the legwork on this myself up until Brinson was murdered."

Frank raised his eyebrows, but chose not to comment. "What about motive? I buy into his loyalty to Newcomb, but why kill the woman?"

"That's the final piece of the puzzle, sir." Christine drew a deep breath. "I believe the victim was pregnant with the candidate's baby."

Christine watched as her boss gripped the edge of the table and brought his face within inches of hers. "You've got to be kidding me!" he bellowed.

Christine had to smother a smile. This was the first time she had ever seen her ice cold supervisor lose his composure.

"Do you have any proof of that?" he asked.

"That's what I need your help with, sir." Christine began to tick off her points with her fingers. "First, I have proof of the pregnancy based on the autopsy. Second, I have witnesses to a possible affair between the candidate and the victim. Third, I have DNA for the fetus."

She lowered her hand, her eyes boring into Frank's. "Now I just need to get a warrant for Newcomb's DNA so that I can match it to the fetus."

"Holy shit. Do you realize what you're asking for? This man is probably going to be elected president in…" Her boss looked up at a calendar over his desk, a serene picture of snow-capped mountains over the block of dates. "Jesus, a week from today."

"Yes, sir. That's why we have to move on this now."

Frank shook his head. "Even if you can prove that Newcomb was this baby's father, how do you know that he was involved in the plot to murder his lover?"

"Because someone killed Terry Brinson. I was about to break this guy, and he turned up dead the next morning. That's too big of a coincidence for his murder to be a hotel robbery gone bad. Someone was tying up loose ends."

"Yeah, but Brad Newcomb?"

"Did I mention that he was the last known person to see Brinson alive?"

Frank put his head in his hands. "And the hits just keep on coming." He looked up. "I need some time to absorb this."

"Sir, we don't have --"

He held up his hands. "Not another word. The political ramifications of this thing are huge, and I'm not willing to throw myself in front of a train if the whole case derails." He stood up, indicating the meeting was over. "I'll give you an answer tomorrow."

CHAPTER 71

Christine sat hunched over her computer in her Dallas office. She was trying desperately to distract herself as she waited for her boss's decision, but every time the phone rang she felt her heart leap to her throat. When she hadn't heard from Frank by lunchtime, she decided to go to the gym and work off some nervous energy.

When she got there, she started with a five mile run around the indoor track, clocking in at eight minutes even. Then she went to the weight room and did a circuit through the machines, working her legs, arms, and abdominals. When she had pushed herself to her limit, she took a quick shower to rinse off the sweat and put on a swim suit. She dove into the pool and swam laps until her muscles screamed for her to stop. On shaky arms, she pushed herself up onto the side of the pool and let her legs dangle in the water while she caught her breath.

As she sat there, she thought about the investigation. Like her boss, she didn't want to see her career go down in flames if she was wrong about Newcomb, but her gut was telling her she was spot on. She was sure the candidate was the father of the vic's baby and that he had authorized her murder. She didn't believe that Brinson would kill his best friend's lover without his consent.

Unfortunately, with Brinson dead, she wasn't sure how she could ever prove Newcomb's complicity in the murder. The man was just too smooth to ever confess to a murder plot. She was sure he would maintain that Brinson had acted on his own, and she was resigned to the idea that if the DNA showed a match and the information was made public, then at least Newcomb would lose any chance of being president. Of course, that assumed the information *would* be made public. She had no idea if someone in the upper echelon of the bureau would decide to bury it.

As cynical as it sounded, she worried that the choice whether or not to reveal the truth would be made based on whether the decision-maker was a Republican or Democrat. If he wanted the Republican candidate elected, he could drop the bombshell. If he wanted Newcomb elected, he could try to keep it under wraps. She could hear the voice in her head, deep and confident, explaining to her that it was in the country's best interest not to taint the election over a private affair.

Christine shook her head to make the imaginary voice go away. With a sigh, the agent drew her legs out of the water and stood up. She felt light-headed from her workout, but at least her nerves had stopped jangling. As far as she was concerned, exercise was a lot healthier alternative than Valium.

She headed to the locker room and took another shower, this time a long and soapy one. Afterwards, she dried off and put her work clothes back on. On the way back to her office, she stopped in the break room and grabbed her lunch out of the refrigerator. A turkey sandwich on whole wheat, light on the mayo, heavy on the lettuce and tomatoes, an apple, and a bag of potato chips, because, after all, one didn't want to be too healthy.

Before she got to her desk, she stopped at her secretary's station and picked up her messages. She thumbed through them anxiously, her shoulders sagging with disappointment when she didn't find the one she was looking for. It wasn't until she had eaten her lunch and spent another few hours working that the much anticipated phone call came through.

"We've made our decision, Christine," Frank said.

Christine wondered who the royal we was, but decided not to ask. "Yes, sir?"

"First of all, let me make it clear that this will be handled with the utmost confidentiality."

Christine's face broke into a wide grin, and she was glad her boss was on the other end of a phone line instead of standing in front of her.

"You have your warrant. I got it signed by a judge here in D.C., whom I trust implicitly. Besides him, there are only a few people here at the bureau who know about this. So I'm warning you now that if there are any leaks to the media, they will be on your head."

"Yes, sir."

"You are authorized to get a sample of Newcomb's DNA, but nothing else. And you are to handle the matter yourself. No one else in your office is to be involved. Am I clear?"

"Crystal clear, sir."

"Good. Furthermore, no one on Newcomb's staff is to be present when you collect the sample. You make sure the DNA collection is done in complete privacy."

"I got it, sir."

"All right. Any questions?"

"Just one, sir. What do we do if we get a match?"

There was a long silence on the other end of the phone line. "I have no idea. That decision's going to be made by someone way above either of our pay grades."

CHAPTER 72

When his wife stepped into their hotel room, Brad rushed to her side, lifting her off the ground and spinning her around in a circle before setting her back down.

"I take it you had a good day," Carolyn laughed.

"It was a great day!" Brad said. "The latest polls came out and we're celebrating. A few days till the election, and I've got a twelve point lead."

"Honey, that's wonderful. You're going to make an amazing president. I'm so proud of you."

Brad took his wife's hand and led her over to where he had arranged a table and a couple of chairs. He had a bottle of champagne chilling along with some strawberries and whipped cream. He seated her and then popped open the bottle. The cork flew out and the bubbles spilled over, drenching his hand. They both laughed as he poured the champagne into their glasses.

"To the most beautiful First Lady to ever grace the White House," Brad said, clinking his glass against Carolyn's.

"And to the best president this country will ever have," Carolyn replied.

Brad pulled his chair close to his wife's and they held hands as they sipped their champagne.

"So, do the kids know?" Carolyn asked.

"Yes. I just saw both of them. They were with me when the numbers came in."

"I bet they were excited."

"They were. I think they've had a great time working on the campaign, but they're ready to move on – especially if we're moving on into the White House."

"Do you think they'll want to live there with us?" Carolyn smiled. "I'd love for us to all be under the same roof again, and I think living there and the traveling they could do would be a once in a lifetime experience for them."

"I'm not sure. I think Tyler will want to be back at Stanford for the spring semester."

"I imagine you're right, and that's probably what he should do. What about Emily?"

Brad shrugged. "I suppose it's possible. I would like her to consider taking a position on my staff. But she may want to get her own place. Live a little more independently. I think she's probably tired of the fishbowl we've been living in."

"So what about you? What are you most looking forward to?"

"The power," Brad blurted out. "Having everyone in the world at my beck and call."

The minute he said the words, he regretted them, especially when he saw how taken aback Carolyn looked. "Just kidding, sweetheart," he said, hoping she'd believe him. "I can't wait to tackle all the issues I've addressed during my campaign. If the polls are right, the Democrats should control the House and Senate, and I should have a real opportunity to push my agenda through. I want to get as much done as I can in my first term in case we lose the upper hand in the mid-terms."

"I'm sure you will. You've always had a talent for inspiring and uniting the people under you."

"Thanks, dear. After all these years, it's nice to know you're still my biggest fan."

Carolyn squeezed his hand. "Always, my love."

There was a knock at the door. "Expecting someone?" Carolyn asked.

"Not me." Brad raised his voice. "Come in," he said, knowing the Secret Service agent had a key.

The man entered, keeping the door ajar behind him. "Sorry to interrupt, sir, but Special Agent Walker is here to see you. Should I send her in?"

Brad was annoyed and didn't bother to hide it. "Fine, but tell her she's got exactly five minutes."

Christine slipped into the room. "That's all I need, Governor."

She waited until the Secret Service agent left, closing the door behind him.

Brad stood, watching her approach. He noticed that she looked at Carolyn, and he saw a moment of indecision cross her face. Then she continued walking forward, reached out, and handed him a piece of paper.

"I have a warrant here for your DNA in connection with the investigation into Amy Hewlett's murder – and the murder of her unborn child." She pulled a test tube and swab out of her pocket. "Would you please open your mouth?"

Brad stared at her dumbfounded. "What the hell? You have no right."

"According to the warrant, I do."

"What's this all about?" Carolyn asked.

Christine kept her eyes locked on Brad's. "Would you like me to explain it to her, sir?"

"Just take your sample and get the hell out of here," Brad said, opening his mouth.

As the FBI agent wiped the inside of his cheek, the candidate knew she was wiping out any chance he had to be elected president. When Christine left the room, Brad collapsed into the chair, devastated, as all of his dreams evaporated into thin air.

CHAPTER 73

Ryan pushed the key to send his article to his editor and then closed his laptop. He got up from his chair and went to the bed where his wife was reading a book.

Michelle looked up when he laid down next to her. "Are you finished with work?"

"Yes, I just sent my article off. It's been a real struggle these last few days for me to write about the campaign. I feel like I'm sitting on the biggest story of my career and there's no way I can write it."

Michelle set her book aside and patted her thighs. "Would some head cuddles help?"

Ryan scooted down and put his head on her lap. "Thanks, hon."

They were silent, Ryan lost in his thoughts until Michelle interrupted them. "So what are you going to do?"

"I don't know. When I first talked to Emily and she told me about the affair, I was so mad. I was going to confront Brad and force him to admit what he'd done. But I couldn't do it."

"What's holding you back?"

"I guess I'm not sure I want to know the truth. All my life I've looked up to Brad and now I know he's not the man I thought he was."

Michelle worked her fingers through Ryan's hair. "I know losing a hero is a lot to deal with, but wouldn't it be better to have everything out in the open?"

"Maybe, but then the other issue is: what do I do with the information? I'm a journalist. Tracking down the truth and then getting it out there is my job. It's who I am. Right now I feel like a fraud, writing these puff pieces instead of fulfilling my responsibility to reveal what I know regardless of what the implications of my knowledge might be."

"I hear what you're saying, and in an ideal world, you'd be right to reveal what you know. But you have to admit that the media has always shaded the truth. You of all people have to admit that a free and open

234

press is a bit of a joke. Fox slants everything to the right; most of the other networks slant everything to the left. We haven't really had an objective news source for years, if we ever did have one."

"So you're saying it's okay for me to sit on this story. I'm just doing what every other media whore does."

Michelle slapped her husband playfully on the back. "That's not exactly how I characterized it. I think that on the whole, journalists try to present the truth, but the fact is that everyone is shaped by their beliefs and values. And those beliefs and values are going to come out in their writing. That's especially true if you're writing about a member of your family. It's totally understandable to value your relationship with your brother more than getting a news story out. I don't think anyone would expect you to be the one to blow the whistle on your brother's love affair."

"I know that. I've thought about the ramifications. Mom and Dad would disown me. Carolyn and the kids would hate me. And everyone else would think I was a cold-hearted prick."

"That about sums it up."

"But isn't it my duty to report what I know? How can I live with myself if I hide the truth and let the American people elect someone who is not who they think he is?"

"In other words, you're between a rock and a hard place."

"Yes, and as the election gets closer, I feel as though both sides are closing in on me. Based on what Emily told me, I believe Brad did have an affair with Amy, which means her baby was probably his. As a journalist, every fiber in my being says that the voters should know that. But he's my brother and I simply can't see being the one to bring him down."

Michelle rested her hand on Ryan's shoulder. "What if there was more to all this than merely an affair? What if Terry did kill Amy, and Brad knew about it?"

Ryan sat up, fear coursing through his body like a jolt of electricity. "That scenario takes everything to a whole different level. How could I just sit back and allow a murderer to be elected president?"

Michelle took her husband's hand. "You know you can't avoid this any longer. You have to talk to him."

Ryan closed his eyes, dread overtaking his fear. "I know -- even if it ends his career and rips my family apart."

CHAPTER 74

Brad sat in the chair, his head in his hands, all his hopes and dreams smashed into tiny pieces.

Carolyn stood hovering over him. "What was that all about? Why did the FBI take your DNA?"

Brad was silent, gathering his thoughts. He knew the FBI was going to match his DNA to that of Amy's child. His affair and her pregnancy were going to be front page news. He couldn't hide the truth any longer. He stood up and put his hands on his wife's shoulders. "I'm sorry, Carolyn, but there's something I have to tell you."

He drew in a deep breath, struggling for the words, some excuse that would allow his wife to forgive him. "Remember how angry you were with me after the assassination attempt in Wisconsin, when I wouldn't leave the campaign to take a few days off with you?"

Carolyn nodded. "Yes."

"And then you flew home to be with the kids and you fell off your horse. And I was mad at you because I thought you were trying to avoid being on the campaign trail with me."

"Of course I remember all that, but what does that have to do with anything?"

"Please, just hear me out. We were both angry with each other. You have to admit it was a low point in our marriage. And then on top of that, with your broken leg, we were separated for a couple of months."

Carolyn put her hands on Brad's arms. "What are you trying to tell me?"

Brad looked deep into her eyes, willing her to understand. "I was alone and miserable without you and there was so much stress with the campaign. And Amy...well, she just kept coming on to me."

Carolyn jumped back, pushing Brad away. "Oh, my God, no. You slept with her?"

Brad stepped forward, trying to close the space between them. "I'm so sorry. It just happened. She meant nothing to me."

Carolyn held up her hands like a shield. "How long did this go on?"

"Only a few months."

"Oh, Brad, how could you? How could you do this to me, to us, to our family?"

"I know it was stupid. It was the biggest mistake of my life. I've never cheated on you before, and I swear to you I never will again."

Carolyn wrinkled her brow, looking puzzled. "I still don't understand what that has to do with the FBI taking your DNA."

Brad looked down, trying to come up with words to soften the blow, but his silver tongue failed him. "Amy got pregnant. I don't know how. She told me she was on birth control, but she must have been lying to me."

He watched his wife's face crumple. "You got her pregnant?"

The candidate's hands curled into fists. "And now I'm sure the FBI is trying to match my DNA with the fetus's. They think Terry had something to do with Amy getting killed, and they're trying to establish a motive. I can't believe they're doing this to me right before the election."

Carolyn gaped at him in disbelief. "You're telling me you had an affair, got this woman pregnant, and Terry might have killed her -- and all you care about is the election?"

"No, of course not. I love you. I don't want to lose you."

Brad reached out for his wife, but she slapped his hand away. "It's too late for that. This marriage is over. And whether the FBI matches your DNA to Amy's baby or not, I will go public with this. I'm not one of those weak political wives who stand by their husbands no matter what they do. I'm not going to condone your behavior."

Brad watched helplessly as Carolyn turned and ran from the room. When the door slammed behind her, he turned to the table where the celebratory champagne stood mocking him. He swept his hand across the table top, sending the bottle and glasses flying.

The hotel room door flew open and both Secret Service agents raced into the room, their guns drawn. "Is everything all right, sir?"

"Everything's fine. Just get the hell out of here."

The agents holstered their weapons, their stoic faces masking their emotions. They left the room, but within minutes, Brad heard a knock on the door. He marched over and flung it open. "What the hell do you want now?"

Ryan stood between the agents, an expression of shock on his face.

"This is not a good time, Ryan."

"I don't care, Brad. We need to talk."

"Fine, then. Come in. I can deal with this shit all at once." The candidate turned and walked back into the room, trailed by his brother. When he reached the now empty table, he spun around. "So what, did you run into Carolyn? Did she fill you in?"

"I passed her in the hall. She was crying, but she wouldn't tell me why. Does she know about you and Amy?"

Brad pounded his fist on the table. "What do you mean? What do *you* know about Amy?"

"Emily told me about your affair. I had to hear about it from your own daughter." Ryan paused. "So does Carolyn know too?"

Brad sank into a chair. "Yes, I couldn't keep it from her any longer. Thanks to that FBI agent."

Ryan stood, looking down at his brother. "What does the FBI have to do with anything?"

"They showed up with a warrant for my DNA today. Right in front of Carolyn." Brad glanced up, seething with anger. "So now everything's out in the open. Is that why you came? You want an exclusive? You can write all about me and my lover and our bastard baby."

"So it's true then?" Ryan asked. "She was pregnant with your child?"

"Yes, and now everything is going to come out. I poured my soul into this campaign, and now it's all over, thanks to that stupid bitch."

Ryan stared at his brother. "So it was all her fault, right? You didn't have anything to do with it?"

Brad narrowed his eyes. "Oh please, spare me your holier than thou routine. I made a mistake. I admit it. I'm not the golden boy that you and Mom and Dad have always tried to make me into."

"Jesus, Brad. Now you're going to blame us?"

"I'm not blaming anyone. If you want to put the whole mess on my shoulders, fine. But it was Amy who seduced me and lied to me."

Ryan sat down next to his brother, drawing his chair in so that their knees were touching. "And is that why she had to die? Did Terry kill her to protect you?"

Brad closed his eyes, gripping the chair's armrests. Whatever he said now was going to have to be his story from this point on. He might have lost the presidency, but he sure as hell was not going to go to prison.

He opened his eyes and looked straight into Ryan's. "I honestly don't know. Apparently that's what the FBI thinks and they may be right. But if they are, I swear to you, I didn't know anything about it. If Terry killed Amy, he did it on his own. I had nothing to do with it."

"I want to believe you, Brad, but you've been lying to me this whole time about your affair. How can I trust you now?"

"Because you're my brother. You know me. I admit I screwed up big time, but do you really think I could have anything to do with murdering an innocent woman?"

CHAPTER 75

Ryan and Michelle sat in their hotel room watching Brad's press conference. All the networks had interrupted their programming to cover it. Having a nominee resign days before the general election was an historical event. The candidate stood alone at his podium, no supportive wife or kids at his side.

Brad apologized to the country, admitting his affair with Amy and to fathering her unborn child. He said that the affair was brief and that he had ended it months ago. He insisted he was still very much in love with his wife, and that he hoped she would forgive him. He did not mention the possibility that Amy had been murdered, or that Terry might have had a role in her death.

He concluded his speech by saying that he still believed he was the strongest candidate for the president, and that he didn't feel his poor judgment on a personal matter should be considered relevant to his ability to run the country. But then he went on to say that he was a realist and that he didn't want to be responsible for the Democratic Party losing the election. When he finished his remarks, the media erupted in frenzy. The journalists jumped to their feet, shouting out questions. Brad held up his hands, thanked them, and turned away from the microphone, making a speedy exit from the stage.

Michelle turned to Ryan in disbelief. "What an ego."

Ryan shrugged. "I guess that's just who he is."

They turned back to the television, listening to the media analysts. It was clear to them that this was unchartered territory; no one knew what was going to happen next. Would the election proceed as planned, pretty much guaranteeing a Republican win? Or would the Democrats try to delay it so they could nominate another candidate and allow him some time to campaign? Nothing was certain except that everyone was going to be busy the next few days poring over election laws.

Ryan stood and walked to his laptop, opening the file containing the story he had written in anticipation of Brad's resignation. He read through it one last time before sending it to his editor. He was relieved that his brother had chosen to take himself out of the race, since he still wasn't sure whether he would have broken the story if Brad hadn't come clean.

As he turned to Michelle, there was a knock on the door. When Ryan went to answer it, a hotel employee handed him a FedEx package, the sender information showing a law firm in Chicago that Ryan had heard of, but didn't have a relationship with. He ripped the package open and pulled out the papers, skimmed the letter and then looked up at Michelle.

"It's from the attorney processing Terry's will. Apparently, Terry left a sealed letter that was to be given to me in the event of his death."

"What's that about?"

"I guess we'll see," Ryan answered, ripping open the envelope as he walked to the desk. He sat down and began to read.

Dear Ryan,

You know that I have always loved Brad as though he were my brother. You and I have that in common. And because of that, I know I can trust you to do the right thing with the information I share with you here.

If you are reading this, then I am dead. My death may have been accidental or it may have been by my own hand. As I write this, I know suicide is a possibility, as I am struggling with the consequences of my actions. I am also not naïve enough not to acknowledge that my death may have come at someone else's hands. For I am a loose end – the one person who could destroy Brad's political career.

I imagine you may already suspect what I am about to confirm. I killed Amy. Whether it was my idea or Brad's, I don't even remember now. I think we both came to the conclusion that she had to be eliminated for the sake of his campaign. We planned her murder to look like an assassination attempt so that it would not only get rid of her, but also push to the forefront Brad's gun control policy.

We viewed Amy as collateral damage, and at the time, I believed it was the right thing to do. I convinced myself that sacrificing her life was necessary for the greater good of the country. In the weeks since her death, I have come to the conclusion that I was horribly wrong. No one's political ambitions should be valued more than an innocent life.

I am truly sorry for my actions. I let my own aspirations cloud my judgment, and I made a terrible choice – one I will never forgive myself for. In light of my actions, I no longer trust myself to make the right decision -- whether to go to the authorities or not. And so I leave that to you. I apologize for putting this burden on you, but there's no one else I trust.

Terry

Ryan felt the blood drain from his face as he handed the letter to Michelle. All he could think of was that he held his brother's life in his hands. It wasn't merely Brad's career anymore. That was over. But Ryan knew that if he handed Terry's letter over to the FBI, Brad would be charged with murder. Could he do that to his own brother?

EPILOGUE

Two Years Later

Ryan parked his car and walked through the parking lot, the drab gray building looming in front of him. He thought about everything that had happened over the last two years. He was back on his old beat, writing stories he was passionate about. He and Michelle were closer than ever; she would always be his rock. In the middle of the night when he couldn't sleep, he would sit at his computer, pounding out a story he had to write even though he wasn't sure he would ever try to publish it – a story about a man who had it all and lost it all – a victim of his own ego.

When he got to the building's entrance, he stopped, his breath catching in his throat. Every time he came here, he felt as if someone had kicked him in the stomach. Pulling himself together, he forced himself to keep going. His brother needed him now more than ever, living in this hellhole they called a prison.

Twenty minutes later, Ryan watched his brother walk into the visitation area.

Brad picked up the phone. "Thanks for coming, bro."

"How are you doing, Brad?"

"As well as can be expected, I guess, given that I'm going to spend the rest of my life in here."

"Any word from Carolyn or the kids?"

Brad's eyes filled with tears. "No. They've abandoned me, just like Mom and Dad. You're the only one who's stuck with me."

Ryan shrugged. "You're my brother."

ABOUT THE AUTHOR

Linda Johnson is the author of two novels, *A Tangled Web* and *Trail of Destruction*, and several award-winning short stories. Originally from Chicago, she now lives in North Carolina with her husband and corgi. Find her online at www.LindaJohnson.us

ALSO BY
LINDA JOHNSON

"A Tangled Web" - a novel - enjoy an excerpt at the end of this book

Divorce is unpleasant and messy. Murder is simple. Cathy Nelson is a young, successful career woman and mother. When her marriage sours, she turns to a time-honored solution: arsenic. Toni Ambrose is a young, but relentless detective, assigned to the murder case. Her instincts tell her that Cathy is guilty and she defies her superiors to doggedly build a case against this black widow disguised as a grieving wife.

Excerpt from **"A Tangled Web"**:

PROLOGUE

Adam Nelson's body writhed in pain, his face covered in sweat, his fists clenching the bed sheets. His mouth opened and a low, rumbling groan filled the room. Cathy leapt from the guest chair and ran to the hospital bed, grabbing the nurse's call button. Her thumb was poised over the button as she watched her husband's body slacken, and heard a soft sigh replace the groan. She checked to make sure he was still asleep. Then she replaced the call button and walked back to her chair. For the past several hours, she had felt like a marionette controlled by a manic puppeteer who yanked her up and down out of her chair, back and forth to her husband's bedside.

Just as Cathy started to doze off, the pre-dawn light crept into the hospital room. The vinyl chair made sucking noises as she pushed herself up onto unsteady legs. Half-asleep, she stumbled to the steel-framed window and peered down at the hospital parking lot.

Even at this early hour, she saw a steady stream of activity: cars looping up and down the rows, as their frustrated drivers searched for vacant parking spaces; hospital personnel marching briskly, eager to face the new day; visitors walking hesitantly, their faces consumed with worry, dreading what they might find waiting for them on the other side of the hospital doors.

Cathy grabbed the pull cord dangling next to the window and yanked it down. As the blinds slammed shut, the pale pink light receded so that the room was plunged into a lifeless gray. She turned from the window and glanced toward the hospital bed, checking to make sure she had not disturbed her husband. But Adam lay still, his eyes closed, his breathing shallow but steady.

The door opened and Dr. Melanie Vreeland strode into the hospital room, her open lab coat fluttering at her sides. Her flaming red hair and blue eyes commanded attention. "Good morning, Cathy," the doctor said. "Have you been here all night?"

"Yes," Cathy whispered. "I didn't want to leave him. My parents drove in yesterday. They're staying at our place with the baby."

Adam began to stir, the voices evidently waking him from his restless sleep. "Hey, Doc," he said weakly. Then he turned to Cathy, forcing a smile as he reached for his wife's hand. "Hi, honey. Are you still here?"

"Of course," Cathy replied. "I was just telling Dr. Vreeland that I didn't want to leave you last night."

"Are you feeling any better?" the doctor asked.

"A little," Adam said. "I'm not sure I could run a marathon, but maybe a 5K if there were enough sick bags at the water stations."

Dr. Vreeland smiled. "Sure. I could have the nurses wheel you down to the parking lot so you could run a few laps."

Adam's smile turned into a wince. "Any luck with the tests you ran yesterday?" he asked.

"Not yet, but we haven't given up," Dr. Vreeland replied. "I'm going to send the nurse in to draw some more blood. And we're going to try you on a liquid diet today. We have to see if you can start keeping things down. If you can, we'll be able to remove the IV."

"That'll make running my 5K a lot easier. I was concerned about dragging around this IV line – it'd probably cost me first place."

The doctor laughed out loud this time. "I can just picture you running in your hospital gown, back flap open, IV in tow. You've made my day, Adam."

"You could make my day if one of these tests could tell me what I've got. You think next time I see you, you'll have an answer?"

"I wish I could promise you that," Dr. Vreeland said. "Most likely you've got some type of viral infection, but so far we haven't been able to nail it down. And if it's not viral, it could be a host of other things. We just have to keep treating your symptoms and running more tests until we figure it out."

"I know there are hospital rules, but is there any way that Cathy could bring our daughter in to see me today?" Adam asked. "Getting a dose of her would be the best medicine you could prescribe."

The doctor shook her head. "I think we'd better hold off on that. Until I can be certain you're not contagious, I don't want to take the chance of exposing your daughter. The immune system of a one-year-old is not very robust."

"How about Cathy then?" Adam asked. "Is it safe for her to be here with me?"

"I'm not going anywhere," Cathy said determinedly, looking at her husband. "You remember those vows we took… in sickness and health. I'm staying right here."

She turned to the doctor. "These new tests you mentioned. What are you testing for?"

"Well, with Adam's symptoms, there are all sorts of possibilities. We've already eliminated a lot of the most common illnesses we've been seeing lately. So now we'll have to start digging deeper. I'm not giving up until I have an answer."

Dr. Vreeland scribbled a couple of notes on Adam's chart and turned to her patient again. "I've got to finish up my rounds now, but I'll be back to check on you later. Let the nurse know if you start vomiting again or if the stomach pain gets any worse."

After the doctor left, Cathy turned to her husband. "I'm going to run down to the cafeteria and get some breakfast. While I'm down there, I'll call Mother and Daddy and see how Abby's doing. She should be up by now. "

"You really should go home, honey. Spend some time with her," Adam said. "I'm probably just going to fall asleep again as soon as the nurses finish poking me."

"I'll run home this afternoon," Cathy promised. "Right now, Abby's in good hands and you need me more than she does."

She stepped into the shoes that she had kicked off during the night. She combed her fingers through her hair and tried her best to smooth the wrinkles from her slept-in clothes. As she passed by the bed, she reached down to stroke Adam's arm. "I'll be back in a few minutes. I love you, honey."

Cathy left Adam's room and took the elevator down to the hospital lobby. As she passed through the hospital doors, she began to search for a secluded spot away from the bustling entrance. She walked to an empty bench nestled into a landscaped area of potted plants, a quiet oasis in the middle of the hustle and bustle. As she sat down, she opened her cell phone, powering it on. She hit a speed dial button and then heard a groggy male voice, thick with sleep, answer.

"It's me." Cathy spoke rapidly, a note of panic creeping into her voice. "He's still alive. And the longer he's here, the riskier it is. The doctor's running all sorts of tests to figure out what he's got." She paused and took a deep breath to regain her composure. When she spoke again, there was steel in her voice. "We need to end this thing."